The Round-Up

BAR 20

BOOKS BY

CLARENCE E. MULFORD

THE ORPHAN
BAR 20
BAR 20 DAYS
THE MAN FROM BAR 20
TEX
BRING ME HIS EARS
JOHNNY NELSON
THE BAR 20 THREE
THE COMING OF CASSIDY— AND THE OTHERS
HOPALONG CASSIDY
BUCK PETERS, RANCHMAN
BLACK BUTTES
RUSTLERS' VALLEY
HOPALONG CASSIDY RETURNS
COTTONWOOD GULCH

HOPALONG CASSIDY'S PROTÉGÉ
THE BAR 20 RIDES AGAIN
CORSON OF THE J.C
MESQUITE JENKINS
ME AN' SHORTY

CLARENCE E. MULFORD

The Round-Up

AEONIAN PRESS, INC.
LEYDEN, MASS.

The Round-Up

CHAPTER I

Bob corson, owner of the JC ranch, and sheriff of
Cactus County, had been over near Bentley, on the Old
California Trail, serving a writ. The task performed,
he slipped his badge into a pocket and headed back
toward town, intending to go home over the regular
wagon road. Reaching the mouth of Lucas Arroyo, he
remembered that he had not been through it and along
the old, abandoned trail, since a boy. He and his
father had followed it, camped for the night at
Packers Gap, and finished the ride the following day.

Curiosity made him hesitate. Knowledge that he
would save a few miles by taking the old trail decided
the matter. He was anxious to get back to the ranch
and on to the JC wagon. Round-up conditions this
spring were different from what they had ever been
before, and he wanted to keep in touch with his outfit.

He found the trail in fair condition and was a little
surprised to see that it was still being used considerably. Two miles below the Gap he struck the first steep
pitch and remembered it well. Close at hand, if his
memory served him fairly, there should be a draw
cutting in from the right. He rode on and soon came
to it. A well-defined trail led up it. This was new

to him, and he followed it with his eyes. He saw the gate of a corral, and back of it, in the mouth of a little side draw, the upper part of the front of an adobe house. Fate at that moment took a hand in his affairs. His horse picked up a stone, and he had nothing with him for its dislodgment, not even his knife.

There was one thing to do, and only one. He dismounted and led the animal at a walk toward the distant building, and was halfway there when the door opened and a young woman stood framed by the casing. She seemed to be watching him intently. At that distance he thought her to be pretty, and each moment of progress made the thought more definite. She was pretty in figure, color, and features. He found himself smiling as he neared the door; and he was pleased, somehow, by the answering smile.

"Your horse is lame," she said, practically, sympathetically. "Stone?"

"Yes. Picked it up just below. I haven't a thing to get it out with. Even left my knife home."

"There's a box of tools in th' kitchen," she said, stepping back from the door as an invitation for him to enter.

The invitation given and understood, they remained as they were, looking at each other. Brown hair, and brown eyes. The figure had a moderate robustness that pleased him; it was sensible, strong, and sturdy. One experience with a delicate woman, his stepmother, had given him very definite ideas on this subject. He felt his face grow warm, and was guilty of a little tingle as he saw the blood deepen the color of her throat and cheeks. The horse moved restlessly and pressed against him.

"I'll look th' tools over," he said.

There was nothing coy about her, nothing affected. Her eyes did not evade him, and she faced him squarely. Her color deepened still more, and her eyes were glad. Without a word she turned and led the way.

He found the hook he knew would be in the tool box, and in a moment the stone was out. He stepped forward to put the tool where he had found it, but she smiled and held out her hand for it. Their fingers touched, and blood again surged into their faces. They made a pair to draw to.

"That's a beautiful horse," she said, looking over his shoulder at the restless and mettlesome animal.

"Yes, he is; he's near as good as th' roan," gravely answered Corson. "His mother came from below the Rio Grande, and his father is blooded stock."

"You're sure he's all right? All right to be ridden right away?"

"Yes." He glanced around slowly and curiously. "I didn't know anyone lived up here; but then, th' last time I was through here was years ago."

"This is the JM," she volunteered, a little hesitantly, and with the barest suggestion of defiance. Her lips compressed a little, and a vague expression came

into her eyes, an expression which sobered him. It
suggested fear.

Corson was a hard-boiled cowman, a good mixer,
handy with gun, rope or cards; and a relentless peace
officer. Where women were concerned he was a gen-
tleman. If his presence bothered her, and now it looked
that way, he knew what to do. He nodded, thanked
her, and swung into the saddle. He picked his hat off
the pommel and turned the horse. For a moment their
eyes met, and there was something in hers that hurt
him.

He touched a heel to the bay's flank, and was riding
past the corral gate almost before he knew it. He
turned to the right when he came to the arroyo,
crossed the Gap and the main road beyond it without
more than noticing them. He reached and followed
the river and had passed Green Canyon before he
remembered that the round-up crew and wagon lay
in the other direction.

The Kiowa was low, and in some places not ankle
deep. There had been no freshets to stir up the soft
bottom, and a man could cross it almost any place
without danger from quicksands. A glance at the sun
told him that he could get to the wagon before dark
if he rode hard; but he would have to cross the intervening hills and ridges by canyon trails, rough, steep,
and tortuous, and the horse had covered more than
its share of miles. He shook his head and followed the
river. Just south of the Bar W ranch houses he cut

close to the hill and turned up Coppermine Canyon. It was not long before the little town of Willow Springs came into sight, and he was practically home.

He passed the hotel, the stores, and the frame bank building, stopping finally before the Cheyenne, the rendezvous of the range. The proprietor and bartender grinned as the sheriff stepped through the door, slid the bar cloth from the right to the left hand, and kept up the senseless polishing.

" 'Lo, Bob," he said. "Reckoned you was roundin' up."

" 'Lo, Steve," grunted Corson, absently, dropping into a convenient chair. He studied his boots without seeing them, and then, glancing around the room, looked at the placid bartender.

"You ever hear of th' JM?" he asked, casually.

"No," answered Steve, showing interest. "What have they up an' done?"

"Nothin'."

"Huh!" said Steve, speculatively.

A horseman clattered past the door, a curling finger of dust drifting in through the opening. The distant and mournful squeak of a wagon sounded loudly in the silence. Steve meticulously straightened three piles of sacked tobacco on the back bar and slapped lazily at a loudly buzzing fly.

Corson abruptly arose, turned on a heel, and stalked from the room. The sharp, sudden beat of hoofs told of his departure. Steve closed his mouth, gently scratched above an ear, and shook his head suddenly. Something was in the wind, and he would keep his ears cocked.

Out on the JC ranch Shorty was arguing with the cook, both draped lazily on the wash bench just outside the bunkhouse door, when Corson rode into their sight on the Willow Springs trail.

"Bob," said Shorty.

"Yeah," said the cook.

"Been to town," said Shorty.

"Yeah," said the cook. He brightened suddenly. "He can tell us somethin' about this new-fangled round-up."

"Yeah," said Shorty, and continued the argument.

Corson kept on past the ranch house and the bunkhouse, unsaddled at the corral gate, turned the horse into the enclosure, and walked slowly toward the bunkhouse, lugging his heavy saddle.

"How they comin'?" asked Shorty, curiously.

"Who?" demanded his boss.

"Th' wagon. Th' round-up. What th' hell you reckon I mean?"

"Don't know."

"You don't know?"

"No. Been off servin' a writ."

"Sheriffin' don't amount to much these days," volunteered the cook, pessimistically. "It's all paper work, now. There was a time when it was mostly lead."

"Yeah? That so?" snorted Shorty. He had vivid

recollections of several jobs handled by the sheriff's office not too long ago, when the only paper involved might have been gun-wadding; only nobody used that kind of guns any more.

"Shorty," said the sheriff, "you ever hear of th' JM?"

"Cows or cigars?"

"Cows!"

"Needn't go on th' prod. No, I ain't never heard of it." He studied the solemn countenance of his boss and best friend. "Why?"

"Nothin'," said Corson, executing an about-face and walking off toward the ranch house without another word.

Shorty stared after him and then slowly turned his head and regarded the cook with triumph.

"Mostly paper work, huh?" he said, with quiet satisfaction. Again he watched the ranchman until the ranch-house door hid him from sight. He nodded wisely and slowly got up from the bench to wrangle in the night horses.

Suppertime came and went without Corson putting in an appearance. This was against his custom, for he usually ate in the bunkhouse. The light in the kitchen went out earlier than usual, but the glow of a cigarette on the back porch told Shorty that his boss had not turned in. When the boss herded by himself like that, after dark, it could be taken as an omen and a portent. Mostly paper work, huh?

When the cook shouted his breakfast call in the morning it was not answered from the ranch house, and a glance at the corral showed one saddle horse missing. Corson's saddle was not on the rack.

The horse that was missing was the bay, a first-class cow horse, a well-trained cutting-out horse, shod especially for that kind of work. Shorty knew how well his boss liked that horse and he had stall-fed it the night before, instead of turning it out on the range, on the off chance that Corson might want to go on to the wagon and join the boys in working the cattle. Shorty turned and went back toward the bunkhouse to continue the argument with the cook.

CHAPTER II

IT WAS the seventeenth day of the round-up, and Corson knew that the JC wagon should be up on Jimmy Branch, near the alkali holes. The outfit was working the country west of the brakes, having already cleaned up the western part of their allotted section.

It was the first year of the Cattlemen's Association and, therefore, the first round-up run under its supervision. In this section alone there were nine wagons out this spring, and the range was being combed as it never had been combed before. At most, the number of stray men in previous years with his wagon had been four; this year the number was eight, and he had the same number of JC representatives with the other outfits, a man to each wagon.

He followed the trail which led from the JC ranch houses up through Horsethief Gap, climbed up the long slope on the north side of Saddle Pass, and dropped swiftly down the steep pitch leading to the alkali ponds. It would be good to join the boys and work with them again, good to keep his hand in with horse, rope, and iron. He was riding the best cutting-out horse on the ranch, especially shod for the hard, fast work with range cattle. The animal was not young, not as good cutting-out horses went, but its forefeet were swift and sure, its shoulders flexible. It was still good for a considerable number of years at this hard and punishing work.

Around the shoulder of the ridge, just east of the holes, he located the looked-for dust cloud. The chuckwagon, he knew, would be at a little spring on a feeder to the branch. He came to the fork of the trail and followed the road leading to the Turkey Track, Owen French's ranch to the east. French had been assigned the country east and north of his home ranch, which included the desert stretch. Most of his gathers necessarily would be light, and while he had more country to cover than any other wagon working the range, it was much flatter.

Corson rode around the shoulder of the ridge and saw the wagon halfway up the little draw. The great circle of riders was cleaning up the basin, and had constricted about halfway. Cattle were popping out of the draws and thickets before its advance. The day herd, off to the right, was being held on the far side of the draw by two men; and a beef herd, all JC steers for the filling of an unexpected order, was farther up the draw, with two men holding it in loose formation.

He dismounted at the wagon, tossed the reins over his mount's head, and nodded to the cook.

"Howd'y, sheriff," said that important person, deftly slicing a number of steaks from a hindquarter of beef on the tailboard. He silently counted them, his lips moving, glanced speculatively at the JC owner, and forthwith cut off two more.

Corson passed between two sizzling Dutch ovens and seated himself cross-legged on the sand in the scant shade of the chuckwagon. It was like old times, and he was eager to take part in the afternoon's work and to get his rope arm limbered up. The calf round-up was the highlight of the whole year's work, and its tally sheets would tell a man pretty near where he stood in his business. Up north a man had to cut hay all summer and stack it against the winter's demands; down here the cattle rustled for themselves all year around. Both ranges had spasmodic outbursts of cattle-stealing; but, he chuckled, that sort of thing had been cleaned up and stopped in his country and county.

"I see th' boys are workin' right to th' schedule," he said, his eyes on the distant, dust-wreathed slope.

"Yeah; an' so am I," growled the cook, with the traditional range cook's pessimism.

"Yeah?"

"Yeah. Great Gawd, Corson! Eight stray men to feed, three times a day. An' eat! I suspicion they never had a square meal between 'em till they hooked onto this here wagon."

"You oughta have lots of help, an' have things right easy, with eight men to bully," countered the JC owner. "Let's see, now: no firewood to rustle, no dishes to wash, no water to tote; an' a man as wise as you

are shoulda broken one of 'em into gettin' th' breakfast fires goin' so you can sleep a few minutes longer
in th' mornin'."

The cook's answering grin forthwith pleaded him
guilty on all four counts.

"Th' boys turned up a new brand," he said, adding
fuel to the third oven. He glanced at his alarm clock
and fell to putting lard into the ovens. It sizzled and
crackled at a furious rate and the cook scraped away
some of the glowing embers.

"That so?" asked Corson quickly, his questioning
gaze on the placid cook.

"Yeah," said the cook. "Yesterday, over in Bull
Canyon," he amplified. "Nueces was figgerin' on
sendin' in a man with th' news, if you didn't show up
today."

"Bull Canyon," mused Corson thoughtfully. If he
had taken the right-hand trail at the fork, instead of
the one leading east to the Turkey Track, he would
have passed the mouth of the canyon. "What's th'
brand, George?" he asked.

"Hoss-shoes."

"Horseshoes?"

"Yeah; but they warn't on no cattle," said the cook,
realizing his importance.

"Horses?" asked Corson, a little mystified.

"Nope. On th' ground."

"What you drivin' at?" demanded the sheriff,
shortly and a little brusquely.

"Why, they found forty-two yearlin' steers holed up in th' canyon. Slick-ear mavericks, all of 'em. There was two down trees acrost that narrow place, that closed it tight; an' there was hoss-shoe tracks in that soft dirt near th' spring."

Corson glanced at the alarm clock, found that it was facing away from him, and pulled out his watch. Verifying this by a glance at the sun, he again leaned back against the wagon.

"Seems like we musta been right careless in our round-ups," he said. "Last year we musta been extra careless."

"You figger they're all JC critters?" asked the cook, popping steaks into the furiously noisy grease.

"Huh! That's right," admitted Corson, slowly. "Nueces recognize any of 'em?"

"Nope; but that don't mean nothin' definite."

"Shore. I know that; but sometimes a man sees a critter that he's seen before."

The moving circle of riders out in the basin was now drawn close, the herd loosely gathered in the center of it. One rider flung up his arm. The circle stopped. The horse wrangler began to bunch up his herd a little. The cook began to slice bread and pile it on three plates on the tailboard. Corson arose, vaulted into the saddle, and rode at a walk to meet the incoming rider.

Nueces grinned cheerfully, wiping dust and sweat from one side of his face to the other.

" 'Lo, Bob."

" 'Lo, Nueces. Heavy gather."

The boss of the wagon and foreman of the JC glanced over his shoulder at the herd behind him and nodded briskly.

"Yeah. Been havin' heavy gathers right along. I got th' beef cut out, over yonder. Reckon I'll have a couple of th' boys start it in for th' ranch after dinner. Sooner I get it off my hands, th' more riders I'll have. I shore need them two fellers."

"Good idea. Throw 'em into th' big pasture."

"Yeah," grunted Nueces, who was also a deputy sheriff and a good one. There was a rumor that the new Cattlemen's Association wanted to use him in another specialized capacity. "After dinner, Bob, me an' you'll take a little ride. We didn't bother 'em when we found 'em, because we wanted you to see how nice they was holed up. Be a damn' shame to slap th' Association brand on *that* bunch. In th' old days we woulda divided 'em up between us an' the Turkey Track an' th' Bar W. Accordin' to th' breeds, we oughta divide 'em between us an' th' Bar W. Don't know but it would be a good idear to do it anyhow. Most of th' stray men feel that way about it."

"Mavericks will carry th' Association brand," said Corson. "We accepted th' new rules, an' I helped to make 'em. So did th' Bar W an' th' Turkey Track. You recognize any of 'em?"

Nueces shook his head.

"No; but that don't mean a thing," he growled.

"There's a hull lot of cattle on this range that I've never seen, or would know again if I had seen 'em."

"Any of th' stray men recognize 'em?" persisted Corson, with deep interest.

"Yeah," answered Nueces, slowly. "That Baylor Ranch rider says he's right shore of three of 'em. Wanted to slap th' BLR onto th' hull bunch." He laughed sarcastically. "I up an' handed him a two-bit piece as a medal for bein' th' galliest hombre north of th' Rio Grande. He got mad an' thrun it on th' ground. There was just enough Scotch in me to pick it up ag'in."

They saw the cook throw his hat in the air, and it seemed to be the signal for a race, and a race it became. The circle of riders around the loosely held gather had gradually become lop-sided as they forsook their places and worked around to the camp side, leaving the cattle in the care of two men. Now the lucky first-to-eat energetically threw the dust behind them and strung out on a bee line for the chuckwagon. Their position in the race depended on their start and on the speed of their mounts.

Nueces and Corson drew rein and let them stream past. A good straw boss thinks first of his horses, the quality of the food, and the welfare of his men. The eager riders raced past, caring nothing about saving their tired horses, since they all would have remounts after dinner. They shouted loud greetings and quips, and stopped just short of the sacred wagon. When the two bosses finally rode in, the hungry line-up was already in motion past the tailboard and the hot ovens.

"There's too damn' many cucumbers in these here pickles," growled the BLR rider, finding the cook's stern and unrelenting eye on his fishing. He kept what the fork had stabbed, not daring to fish again, and left the pickle barrel to the next man in line, growling that he never did have any luck, anyhow.

Nueces and Corson each took a plate and cup, bread and pickles, and finished loading up at the crackling ovens. They joined the seated circles, crossed their legs, and aided in maintaining a high-tension silence. After a few moments a gusty exhalation announced the finish of the first heat, and a cheerful man, cleaning the last drop of sorghum from his plate with the last bit of bread, placed his empty dish beside his empty cup and reached for the makings. The man on his right got up stiffly, deposited his plate and knife in the big pan, and, meticulously wiping the bottom of his cup on dusty trousers, bailed himself another serving of coffee. He drank it standing, put the cup in the wreck pan, and rolled himself a smoke.

"Santa Claus left us somethin', over in Bull Canyon, Bob," said Big Jim, shoving the glowing match deep down into the sand. He glanced out of the corner of his eye at the BLR rider, who was showing interest.

"Yeah, so I heard," said Corson. "Throw th' CA Circle Star irons in th' fires this afternoon, an' I'll take a couple of th' boys an' go after 'em. Cook says forty-two head."

The BLR representative stirred restlessly and spoke. He seemed to be a little nervous.

"I say it's a damn' shame to give all them cattle to th' Association," he declared. "We all know they came from this section of th' country. Stands to reason they belong to somebody down here."

"That's shore right," said another voice.

"Rules is rules," snapped Nueces, finding nothing strange in his swift change of front.

"Three of them yearlin's came from our range," persisted the Baylor rider. "I've seen 'em a dozen times."

"You'll shore see 'em ag'in this afternoon, an' then you can kiss 'em good-bye, if you wants," countered Nueces, swiftly. "They're Association animals an' they're goin' down th' river."

"Looks to me like some thrifty hombre was layin' 'em away for a rainy day," said the Turkey Track man. He chuckled. "Hell, they never figgered that it don't never rain down in this country. You got any cigarette papers, Jim?"

"Yo're shore right, Turkey," said the cook, his cold eyes resting on the smiling face of the stray man. "It never rains. That means that there ain't no water in my barrels. There's two buckets under th' rear axle, an' th' spring is just exactly eighty-one paces from th' wagon tailboard."

"Yo're plumb wrong," contradicted the Bar W rider. "It's seventy-eight. I counted 'em, myself, this mornin'."

"Eighty-one is right," said the cook, flatly. "Yo're laigs is too long."

"How in hell do *you* know how many steps it is?" asked the Baylor man, nastily. "You never got close enough to that spring to do no countin'."

"I'll tell you how I know it, Cucumber!" retorted the cook. "I allus take a good look at any water I'm usin', in case it has to be skun; an' eighty-one is plumb official."

Turkey Track arose, walked to his saddle and fumbled with it a moment. When he returned he gravely handed the peeved cook a first-class big piece of pitch pine which he had that morning picked up on the mesa, and then he resumed his seat with an air of confidence. It was justified.

The cook looked at this precious chunk of tinder, glanced at the small piece near the rear axle, and turned stern eyes on the BLR rider. That new tinder had been like a gift from heaven.

"Yo're dead right, Baylor," the cook slowly and meaningly admitted. "But I figger on checkin' up on you when you start, which will be right soon. Eighty-one is wrong; seventy-eight *might* be right; but we'll count yore laigs, both comin' an' goin', an' call th' figgers final."

A man from over Iron Springs way sauntered to the

wreck pan and reached for a dish cloth. The BLR rider picked up the buckets and slouched off toward the spring. Belts were being retightened. Nueces watched the day wrangler stop the cavvy just the other side of the wagon, and looked meaningly around the small circle. Man after man went off to pick out his best cutting-out horse. They saddled up and hastened toward the herd, to relieve the two hungry men with it. Nueces called to the last pair that rode away, and motioned toward the beef cut, up the draw. He swung his arm in a half-circle as he called out to them.

"Take that bunch to th' ranch an' turn 'em into th' big pasture. Get back as soon as you can."

They nodded and loped away. The straw boss and Corson waited for the wrangler and the four herd riders to eat, and then helped the former drive off the horse herd, going with him for a short distance. All the horses were well broken, and once started, knew what they were expected to do.

Swinging around, the two men were about to start for Bull Canyon to look over the cached herd of yearlings, when Nueces chanced to glance back at the wagon. He saw the Baylor rider slam down the buckets so hard as to slop water on the cook's boots. They were too far away to hear what was said, but the gestures were emphatic.

Nueces glanced at his companion.

"Kinda sorehead, he is," he growled. "Cook can handle him part way; if an' when he gits past that mark, *I*'ll take him over. Seems to reckon common punchers are right scarce, an' good range cooks plentiful. I'll lay that hombre out as straight as a wagon tongue if he lifts his front laigs *too* far off th' ground!"

"He's sore about them three yearlin's he said he recognized," said Corson, shortly.

"He was damn' sore about somethin'," admitted the straw boss. "Sweet as black-strap, he was, till we come onto that little bunch in th' Bull. He went sour right then an' there, an' he's been gettin' worse steadily."

"Still," said Corson thoughtfully, and after a moment's silence, "he wanted to brand 'em in Baylor's mark; an' once that mark is on a hide, it can't be made into anythin' else that's reasonable. It would just be sayin' good-bye to 'em."

Nueces was studying his friend and boss.

"Yeah?" he asked, slowly. "You mebby figgerin' he knows somethin' about 'em?"

"No. I mean it looks like he's loyal to Baylor; but still, he mighta wanted to play safe on his own account. Huh!" he mused. "Bull Canyon!"

"Shore, an' that's th' hell of it," growled the straw boss. "It's right smack into our territory, with th' Chain outfit workin' th' territory south of us. Why, four days ago we was close enough together to see each other's dust. Why would anybody cache that bunch of yearlin's right plumb into th' thick of th' round-up, with two wagons workin' all around 'em? They might know them yearlin's would be found. An' they mighta knowed that they couldn't drive em off with us on one side an' th' Chain outfit on th' other. It looks locoed to me."

"Mebby there's an explanation," said Corson, a light suddenly breaking through his cogitations. "I said *mebby*."

"Yeah?"

"Yeah. You know what th' original plans were?" asked the sheriff, and then answered his own question. "Th' Chain wagon was to start where it is now. We were to work th' north section first, an' come down this way. All that time th' Chain would be workin' south, away from th' Bull. After four, five days, th' Chain would be outa th' way, an' we wouldn't be nowhere near that canyon. That would give 'em a chance to drive east or west. Now wait a minute! Baylor's wagon woulda been over on Crooked Creek, an' th' Turkey Track would be workin' away over across th' Wilson Trail, other side of th' desert section. But shucks: that don't tell us anythin'. They could have driven that bunch west, east, or south. Th' Bar W, bein' on th' river, wouldn't have let them through in that direction. It don't tell us where they came from, or where they was goin'; but it does tell us that changin' th' round-up layout at th' last minute made their hand into a four-flush. Let's go an' look at 'em. There'll likely be somethin' worth seein'."

CHAPTER III

ALICE MEADOWS put away the last dish and turned to look out of the window, through the strong evening light, at the corral gate, visible at the mouth of the little side draw. Four saddles and other riding equipment lay close up against the base of the pickets. Her stepfather and stepbrothers were inside the corral, out of her sight, selecting saddle horses from the remuda they had just driven in. She well knew the animals they would choose: the best and surest mounts, trained and tried night horses, as expert in handling cattle, almost, as the men who rode them. If the quality of the JM cattle was equal to that of some of its horses, it would be a better thing for the ranch.

The frown on her face deepened, and she sighed as she started to tidy up the small room. The men folks had been in an ugly temper during the last two weeks, and she most fervently wished they would do their riding in daylight. When they got home around dawn they expected breakfast to be ready, and that meant early hours for her. Well, there was one consolation: the moon was dark part of the time, and that cut down a deal of their nocturnal riding.

The little house was anything but pretentious. It was

just a four-room adobe building, squat, square, ugly, and gray, and it matched the color of the draw in which it stood. Any stray riders going along the little-used trail up the arroyo might easily overlook it. No whitewash ever had been used on it. Its hard-packed clay floors were bare of any covering.

Her stepfather and his sons had four bunks built against the walls of one room. The cubbyhole next to them was her own. Then came the sitting room, and lastly and most important was the combination kitchen-dining room, the heart of the establishment.

Around the shoulder of the main arroyo, and a few miles to the east, and at a much higher level, lay Packers Gap. Traces of the old trail were still to be seen on both sides of it, where camps had been made in the old days. Picturesque and slovenly Mexican, Indian, and breed muleteers had found that way to the far distant settlements of the Mississippi Valley, all hungering for the profits to be found on the rough frontier of a mightier nation and an alien race.

Then had come the hardy plainsmen and moun-taineers, packing in powder, lead, tobacco, and cotton goods on the westward journey, and peltry and Spanish dollars on the eastward. They slowly passed out of the picture as wheeled vehicles came in, drawn by mules and later by oxen. The great wagons had found the Gap too hard a nut to crack, unless they had to crack it; and forthwith discovered an easier and more prac-tical way. Any breed of men who could take wagons over Raton Pass could have mastered the Gap with much less effort; but the same need did not apply at the latter. A little more than five miles north and east was Saddlehorn Mountain, and here the wagons had quickly found a better way. This old road was still much in use and took its name from the mountain above it. Packers Gap, almost overnight, had become nothing but a local, short-cut trail, and was now scarcely ever used except by the girl's menfolks and their infrequent visitors. And the more infrequent those visitors were, the better she liked it.

The Meadows herd, branded JM on the left hip, was too small to have supported five people, but in this regard they were fortunate. Black Jack Meadows had a small inheritance invested securely somewhere in the East, and four times a year an important envelope reached the post office at Bentley, to find that it was being waited for impatiently. The check made a drawing account in Bentley's one general store, to be taken out in trade.

The JM cattle were of small account, and in such an out-of-the-way part of the country that they practically were forgotten by all but their owners except when some round-up crew was foolish enough to sweep across their high, rough range.

For the last few months her stepfather had spoken vaguely but hopefully of a lucky turn which had increased his invested capital, and he was looking forward eagerly to the day when they all would be able to leave this part of the country and enjoy a more pleasant existence. She most fervently wished that day godspeed, for it could not come too quickly for her.

She heard the clatter of hoofs at the corral. They sounded for a few moments and then abruptly died out as the shoulder of the main arroyo was passed. This told her that they were riding east, headed for the Gap. When they rode westward toward Bentley the sounds of their horses died out gradually, and at one place were thrown back loudly and unexpectedly by an echo.

She turned to look around her for one final check-up on the tidying, and her gaze finally settled upon an iron hook lying on top of the tools in the box against the wall. Instantly it brought a picture to her mind that was clear and sharp.

She stood motionless, jealously reviewing each detail, each word. He had been as a man should be, straight, lithe; frank and calm and assured. There was nothing furtive about him in looks, words, or actions, which was something of a treat to her after the months she had lived in this house. At last she sighed, turned reluctantly away, and picked up a homemade willow basket filled with darning. Stepping through the kitchen door, she looked down the trail for a long moment, closed her eyes for an instant, and then sought the box up-ended against the outer wall of the house, to take up the darning where she had left off and to utilize until the last moment the slanting rays of the sun, now passing over her head to paint the top of the ridge until it resembled molten iron.

Nueces and Corson glanced again at the wagon and saw the Baylor rider going toward the herd.

"Yo're all through here," said Corson, looking out over the range.

"Yeah," answered the straw boss, thoughtfully. "Th' wagon will move on to th' spring on that bench in Horsethief Canyon, about halfway between here an' where th' branch trail turns off."

Corson knew the round-up itinerary by heart. He rode stirrup to stirrup with his companion, puzzling over the problem presented by the cached herd of maverick yearlings. They cut and followed the branch trail where it started to climb up over the watershed, and then forsook it to enter Bull Canyon. The rise was sharp, so sharp that it masked the canyon entrance to anyone riding carelessly along the trail below it; and so sharp that it brought back to the mind of one rider another steep pitch, and what it had led to.

They pushed on, past a pocket in the east wall, and soon swung to the left and entered the narrow, steep-walled portals of a side canyon. Two trees deftly felled on opposite sides of the narrow opening effectively blocked it. The two riders pulled up close to the barricade and looked through it.

"Slick-ears, an' yearlin's, at that," muttered Corson.

"That shore makes 'em mavericks, accordin' to my dictionary." He paused for a moment. "They're a mixed lot, too. Some straight longhorns, some Herefords, an' some Durhams."

"Th' feed in there is mighty near done, too," observed Nueces, his practical cowman's eyes sweeping over the little canyon. "Now if you or me was to throw a bunch like this into a place like that an' block 'em in, we'd shore figger on gettin' 'em out ag'in purty soon, unless we wanted 'em to starve."

"Yes," replied his companion, slowly. "A cowman shore would think of that. Most fellers down in this part of th' country are cowmen. They would think of that. Th' fellers that threw this herd together was cowmen: they would think of that. This bunch shows careful pickin'. All of which means that they never intended to hold this bunch in there as long as this. An' what's th' answer to that?"

"Somethin' shore as hell interfered with their plans," growled the horse-faced straw boss. "Somethin' they just didn't figger on. You was right, Bob, about th' round-up shift."

"Reckon so; anyhow, it looks that way," said Corson. "I ain't got much to go on, except what we find right here; but as it stands, I'm willin' to believe that these animals were driven away from their mothers, holed up somewhere until they was weaned, an' then pushed across th' range at night, and left here, temporary. If I believe that, then I won't get a chance to work with th' oufit. If I believe it, then that means other kind of work for me. Every dollar I've got is in th' cattle business, an' I was elected sheriff of this county to protect th' belongin's of every man in it. Changin' th' round-up layout raised hell with their plans. They didn't dare try to get this bunch out of here an' on its way. That seems to be right plain."

"Yeah, shore does," said Nueces, loosening his rope. "No use goin' after any of th' boys to handle this bunch. Me an' you'll drive 'em. We'll slap th' Association brand on 'em an' send 'em down th' river. When these are thrown into th' Association's herd, there'll be quite a bunch for somebody to bid in."

He dropped his rope over the stump of a shattered branch, his companion's rope following his own. The two horses turned, headed in the other direction at a sharp angle, and pulled. One of the two trees swung slowly, as if on a pivot, and in a moment was dragged aside, and the portal cleared sufficiently. A few minutes later the little herd was moving toward and through the opening, and then down the sloping floor of the main canyon. They crossed the Branch trail, followed it down, rounded the edge of the ridge, and stopped between the wagon and the scene of the branding operations. The little herd had been checked on good grazing ground, and almost immediately fell to grazing.

Nueces faced the distant fires, raised his hat, and moved it to his right, twice. Two men left the gather in the basin and rode swiftly to answer the summons. They approached the herd at a walk and stopped at the side of the straw boss.

"Take over this bunch," ordered Nueces. "Th' Association's rules are to brand th' mavericks first, out of every gather. These didn't come out of this gather, an' we can't mix things up an' mebby chouse th' herd. You boys hold 'em here until we've cleaned th' main herd, an' then push 'em down to th' fires, an' we'll slap th' Association mark on 'em an' push 'em down th' river for somebody else to herd. Mebby th' Bar W wagon is holdin' a bunch of 'em. If they are, throw these in with 'em an' come back. Get a receipt for 'em."

"Somebody shore is goin' to miss this little bunch some moonlight night," said the first rider, grinning.

"Yes; except that th' news will spread, an' nobody come after 'em," said Corson. "I'm right sorry that we missed th' somebody that put 'em in there," he added, grimly.

"How's that Baylor rider actin'?" asked the straw boss.

"Just about as sweet as that cucumber pickle he speared at dinner," answered the first of the two riders.

"Jed missed three throws in succession, an' th' Baylor rider has been bawlin' him out ever since," said the second man. "He's now askin' heaven an' hell for a roper that can rope. Somebody's shore goin' to tie a knot in his *tail*. He's a damn' trouble-maker."

"First thing he needs is a little slack," growled Nueces. "Reckon I'll give him some an' see how he uses it. You comin' with me, Bob?"

Corson was. There was something in his companion's mind that he did not wish to miss, and he thought he knew just about what it was. Nueces was a bad man to prod, and anything that interfered with the smooth working of his outfit prodded him.

They stopped not far from the nearest fire, where the Baylor rider was one of two flankers. Jed was doing the roping, and his cast fell short again, and the calf had to be chased back to him. He was seething with anger, but holding himself down remarkably well, so far as his tormentor was concerned.

"I've seen some damn' rotten ropers in my life," growled the Baylor man, "but you shore win th' diamond-studded hoss-shoe. What th' hell's th' matter with you? Give me a *real* roper, an' I'll make him sweat!"

His fellow flanker was about to take Jed's part, but chanced to glance at the straw boss, caught the motion of Nueces' head, and turned on his heel. He walked to the fire without a word and moved the irons about in it.

"Where th' hell *you* goin'?" snapped the Baylor man, and then found himself to be the focal point of the straw boss's eyes.

"We're runnin' one rope, one flanker, an' one iron at this fire," said Nueces coldly. "I want to see an expert work. A man like you is too good a flanker to be pestered with a poor roper. One expert shore oughta have another."

"What you mean?" asked the Baylor rider, suspiciously.

"I mean that I'm goin' to give you a roper that don't miss three throws outa four: th' kind you been askin' for, an' a feller that don't miss his casts when he gits mad," answered the straw boss, smiling pleasantly. His face was friendly and sympathetic, and he kept it so as he turned to the discredited roper. "Jed, take that leaky rope of yourn an' go over there an' relieve Bludsoe. There ain't no cucumber pickles at that fire, an' there ain't no likelihood of some flanker gettin' shot. You tell Bludsoe I said for him to swap fires with you."

Corson kept a straight face, but with some difficulty. George Bludsoe was the best calf roper he ever had seen, and he had seen some good ones. Bludsoe was the best one-man tier-down on the whole range. He could work and braid rawhide into the finest ropes and hackamores that a man ever saw. His gun was as good as his rope. He could handle green horses like soothing syrup, which was a distinct asset. He had been brought up in that old Texan school, where a dollar was a dollar, except that it was never around to be one; where sheer, undeserved poverty had turned out a breed of men, and women, who did things for themselves that but few others could do. Whenever Bludsoe missed a calf, they tolled the bells, down in Texas; and it was said that Texas bells had not been tolled since the Alamo.

Bludsoe pulled up in front of his straw boss with a smile and a nod for Corson.

"You wantin' me?" he asked.

"Yeah," answered Nueces, one eyelid faintly flicking. "That there Baylor rider shore hates to work with a bungler, an' I don't blame him. He has put hisself on record, free an' voluntary, to hold up his own end if he gets a good roper. We got to use what we have, an' yo're a fair man with a rope. You'll have to do, anyhow. Go to it, Gawrge. *Hi!*" he shouted at the hard-working cutters-out in the herd. "Why don't you push out more on *this* side? Yo're holdin' up this fire." He faced the riders outside the herd and got their attention. "Shoot more of them calves this way! Our irons are gettin' too hot over here!"

The Baylor man suspected that he was in for something, but he was too sore and too game to quit. He was a chesty person, and he had gone on record. He glared at Bludsoe.

"If yo're all through cuttin' yo're fingernails, let's start!" he snapped.

"Gosh!" exclaimed Bludsoe, contritely, "I plumb forgot all about you." And he went to work.

He went to work with the neatest four-strand, braided rawhide lariat a man ever saw. It was thin, tight, and close, slick with tallow; and it had a wall-

and-crown knot at one end and an eight-strand, flat-braided hondo at the other. You and I would have broken that rope with the first plunge of even a half-grown yearling; but Bludsoe let it slip around the saddlehorn with practised ease. It is doubtful if the rope ever had received a threatening strain in its existence. It was not a long rope. At a guess I'd say forty feet. George had three ropes, and one of them was a full sixty feet of six-strand braiding that was almost as strong as a fiber rope one size smaller. And he could throw it the full length, which took skill as well as strength. This rope was tied on the other side of his saddle. The third, an extra, was in his war-bag at the wagon. It also was braided rawhide.

George was not using a three-eighths-inch rope to-day; neither was he using the six-strander. The tool in his hand was hardly more than five sixteenths of an inch in diameter, light, beautifully flexible, and just right for him for the job on hand. He called it his calf rope, and when it left his hand it whistled through the air, smacked around a calf's neck with a remarkably small loop, and the flanker forthwith had a job to do.

The calves began to come faster. Bludsoe's rope whistled more rapidly. The iron men came to life, and the Baylor man's helper generously let him do all the grab and knee work. Playing his part in the game, he took the flanker's bawling out with good grace, and winked at the straw boss.

"Why don't *you* go down th' rope once in a while?" shouted the Baylor rep., angrily.

"Never like to muss up no purty exhibition like yo're showin' us," panted the partner. "I never saw such flankin'. You'll wear that roper out. Look at him sweat! First time *I* ever saw a flanker flop 'em so fast that his roper fell behind. My money's on you."

The Baylor man was exceedingly busy. He was entirely too busy to waste a glance at his roper, but he hoped that his partner had spoken truly. He'd show up the damned Texan! The calves came in a stream. Nueces left the saddle and took a hand in pinning them down after they flopped. The iron man was on the jump. Minutes passed, but the Baylor man began to reckon them as much longer intervals of time. He stood up, eased the crick in his back, and was about to speak his mind when the roper forestalled him.

"Yo're turnin' my rope loose too fast," complained Bludsoe, with a straight and worried face. He had his eyes on two calves, coming up almost together, on an angle which would bring them together at just about the right place. He motioned to the following riders, and they nodded and laughed softly.

Bludsoe carelessly loosed the other rope, threw the knot end over the horn with a clove hitch. His right arm rose, and the little rope whistled again. It fairly leaped over the head of the first calf, and was hardly set before the second rope whistled through the air like a blade, slapped swiftly around the neck of the second calf, and both ropes pulled tight.

The Baylor man, reaching up to grab the first rope and run down it, had to grab the second to keep it from catching him under the chin. As his left hand closed on it, the first calf suddenly decided that this was a most auspicious occasion to do something on its own hook. It darted sideways and then plunged forward. The slack of the swinging rope dropped below the flanker's knees, tangled with one spur, and then straightened out like an iron bar as the calf whirled and darted back again. The flanker's feet went out from under him and he found himself on his back in a little cloud of dust.

He rolled swiftly on his side, twisted his foot until the spur was free from the rope, and then his right hand streaked toward his holster. It stopped there, motionless, for he found the roper's gun squarely on him. It was no secret on the range that George Bludsoe was a killer. If he had not been a killer he would not have been living at this moment. The flanker's hand forsook the holster and pressed against the ground to help him get to his knees. As he slowly stood erect, the roper's gun slipped back into its sheath.

"What you reckon yo're doin', Bludsoe?" demanded the dust-covered stray man, ominously. Rage glinted in his narrowed eyes.

"Just seein' if I could get th' rest of th' wind outa

you before you used it all up for grouchin'," retorted
Bludsoe, evenly. "I might say it was th' calf that done
it; but I ain't slippin' outa nothin'. You sweeten up,
an' you'll find this outfit's th' best you ever worked
with; stay sour, an' you'll wish you was never borned.
It's yore deal."

The Baylor man faced the straw boss, his face flam-
ing. Then it went white, as white as dirt and tan would
permit.

"Is this th' way you run yore wagon?" he demanded, almost in a whisper.

Nueces carelessly shoved his Stetson hat up the frac-
tion of an inch and looked the enraged man squarely
and calmly in the eye.

"I've allus found th' best way to run an outfit, if
you've got a good one, is to let it shake itself down
an' run itself," he slowly answered. "I got a good
one, a damn' good one. It works as slick as tallow on
rawhide. You been askin' for trouble th' last couple
days. You been like a burr under my saddle. You been
ridin' th' cook. You got Jed so riled up that he missed
his throws. Well, you got what you looked for: *some*
of it. There's more left if you want to look for it.
Now you can get sweet, or you can pull yore drag. Th'
next man that talks to you will be me. I'm lettin' you
write my speech for me."

"All right!" snapped the stray man. "I figger I've
been mistaken. I kinda reckoned this was a real cow
outfit. I'm pullin' my drag, an' I'm doin' it now. Next

time some of you fellers see me you mebby won't be so damn' cocky. So-long, th' lot of you: an' go to hell!"

"I'll go to hell with you as far as th' wagon," said Nueces, stepping swiftly toward his horse. "Good cooks are right scarce, an' we ain't figgerin' on buryin' ourn, or even huntin' up a new one. Cook ain't as young as he used to be, but his temper's got worse steady right along. He might answer you sassy. Come on: get yore hoss an' start. Th' sooner you cut yore string, th' sooner I can get back here."

Bludsoe's long rope was again fastened to the saddle. He hung the pet calf rope over the pommel and grinned at Corson. The four men holding down the double catch were calling for the irons. Corson grinned, and then turned to scrutinize speculatively the back of the departing stray man. He groaned, shook his head, and rode slowly toward the wagon.

CHAPTER IV

THE cook's clock, the curse of a round-up camp, awakened Corson and he saw blankets squirm or heave, according to the nature or present feelings of the men under them. Somebody swore softly, another muttered, and both went to sleep again to steal a few more minutes of oblivion. The cook turned off the alarm as the Appleton representative threw off his blankets and matched his yawn with his stretch. This was his morning to pamper the cook.

Corson chuckled and, because he was wide awake, watched what was going on around him. Old George Appleton owned the GA brand and was not nearly as old as the cognomen suggested. The GA stray man, drawing on his boots, moved over to the Dutch ovens, scraped the ashes from them, found live coals beneath, by some favor of Providence, and began to pare splinters of tinder from the cook's much prized pitch pine. The cook, himself, observing these activities, turned over for another precious forty winks. No one could say that he did not know how to train stray men, and the strange part of it was that most of these stray men rather liked it.

The GA rider fanned the coals with his hat and

was soon rewarded by a little blaze, which he fed sparingly and judiciously with bits of wood. Every fire going to his satisfaction, he picked up the buckets and headed for the spring, gently kicking the pitch-pine chunk against a rear wheel of the wagon. This was a mild declaration: if the cook wanted that hunk of resinous wood in the wagon, let him put it there himself!

Nueces had been turning loose the JC animals, since the outfit was on its own range, as fast as they had been worked. This meant that the stray herd was greatly reduced in size; but it took two men, just the same, to night-herd it. In it were the cattle belonging to the ranches represented by the various stray men with the wagon. The Baylor gather had been cut out and started for home, together with the Baylor remuda, by the angry representative from that ranch.

The cattle would come fast and thick from here on to Horsethief Creek. The JC beef cut had been sent home to the ranch the day before, and was now out of the way. There would be no more beef cuts until the fall round-up, which was strictly a beef affair. The maverick herd had been marked with the Association brand and thrown in with the like gathers of the Bar W, down on the Kiowa. The cavvy, over a hundred and fifty head, grazed along the far slope of the draw, hobbled but contented.

The GA rider returned with two buckets of water and with sufficient data to stage a dispute. The spring

was neither eighty-one nor seventy-eight paces from
the wagon: it was eighty-three. He put the buckets
down handy to the tailboard, hurriedly added more
fuel to the fires, and then went to the wagon and
pulled a hindquarter of beef out of it, stripping off the
protecting flour-sack covering.

The cook's blankets stirred again, and that worthy
monarch of the open range deigned to throw them off
and to sit up. The tinny clatter of the washbasin told
that the stray man had taken it from its nail on the
wagon box and was performing his morning ablutions.
He puffed and slobbered like a grampus, if a grampus
puffs and slobbers. He wiped his manly countenance,
carefully slicked his hair, and turned to face the rising
cook.

"There, —— —— you: do th' rest yoreself," he
said to the dough expert, with a grin.

"Thanks, Curley," grunted the cook, heading for
that same washbasin. "Yo're daddy's good little boy."

"Go to hell," said Curley.

Nueces sat up and threw off the blankets. He was
the skipper of this ship on wheels, and he liked to be
on deck early. He glanced at the cook, at the tarpaulin-
covered figures, and out over the range. The stray
herd was already on its feet, placidly grazing, the two
riders with it loafing in their saddles, their eager eyes
on the signs of life at the distant wagon. His gaze
flicked to the grazing saddle horses and passed on.
The night horses near the wagon were searching for

feed at the ends of their picket ropes. He looked at the figure at his side and grinned as he found Corson's wide-awake eyes on him.

"Mornin'," grunted the straw boss. "Find th' ground soft?"

"It would have been, only th' stuffing in this damn' tick got worked all out of one place," replied the owner of the JC. He glanced at the picketed night horses, idly reading the brands. "Hey! Nueces!" he said suddenly. "You ever hear of th' JM?"

"Yeah. They run a few head over Packers Gap way. Two-by-nothin' outfit. They did some ridin' for th' Baylor outfit, too. Why?"

"Nothin'. How come you heard of 'em?"

"Range gossip, I reckon," answered the straw boss. "I hear lots of useless things."

"I know you do, you long-headed old maverick," replied Corson with a grin, "only there's a lot of it that ain't useless. You ain't figgerin' on cleanin' up that whole Horsethief Creek section today?"

"No. We work from here to th' wagon this mornin'," said Nueces, stretching his long arms. "This afternoon we go on north to th' trail fork, an' then work back to th' wagon. Can't go chousin' up that section an' throwin' back branded calves to be rounded up ag'in. Tomorrow we cut th' herd in two an' clean up one half after th' other. Don't know any better way to handle it."

Blanket after blanket heaved, erupted, and shelled

out its inmate. Tantalizing odors filled the air. The cook knew his business down to the last brass tack; and he should have, for he drew down heavy pay. Sizzling steaks, strong coffee. The sliced-bread edifice on the tailboard grew story by story, a little white monument against the darker background of the hills. There was brisk activity around the washbasin, and a sudden burst of talk.

"That red-an'-white bounced plumb into th' air, turned in my holt, an' lit back on all four laigs," laughed a flanker of the day before. "He butted me so damn' hard I was cross-eyed for a minute."

"He's goin' to be th' boss of th' range when he grows up," said a companion, chuckling.

"Hey, Gawrge! What'll you take for that calf rope of yourn?"

"More'n you'll ever have," replied Bludsoe.

". . . so I took three cards, an' slid th' last of two months' pay plumb in th' middle of th' table. 'There,' says I. 'How you like th' looks of that?' "

"We oughta save out some old cows for a bait herd, when we work that chaparral country, up north."

"Grup PILE!" shouted the cook with unnecessary loudness, and easily had the last word.

Another good meal had joined the pleasant things in the yesterdays, and tobacco and papers put a period after it. The big dishpans were filled, and a softly whistling stray man, who would rather wash than wipe, was helping the cook get rid of their messy contents.

"Is there anythin' better'n a good steak, fried brown in batter?" asked a chuckwagon worshiper.

"Hell, yes! Ham'n aigs!"

"You fellers ever hear tell of th' two Texans that dropped in on old Judge Bean, th' old moss-head that claimed he was th' law an' order west of th' Pecos? They——"

"There's two hungry boys out there with th' herd," said Nueces, abruptly. "An' it's gettin' later every minute. First thing we know it'll be noon an' nothin' done. Let's get th' hosses an' roll along."

They left camp in a noisy bunch on the night horses. They took the hobbles off the cavvy, drove it in and up to the wagon, made a flimsy corral with lariats running out from the wagon, and began to pick their mounts for the day's work.

"We got right rough goin' today, an' hard ridin'," said the straw boss, slowly. "Pick out yore best runnin' hosses for th' circle. Curley, you an' Bill have been on th' outer circle too blame' much. Swap places today with a couple of th' lazy hounds that have been huggin' th' middle of th' line."

"Just you wait till we get down into that *real* country," replied Curley, grinning. "You'll see me in th' middle there, all right."

"That won't be long," said the Iron Springs rider. "Damn th' chaparral."

"There won't be much of it," said Nueces. "They changed th original round-up plans an' gave us th' best of it."

"You oughta be glad it ain't th' beef round-up," chuckled a companion. "It's a case of too much ropin' an' tyin' then. We got it easy now."

The day wrangler was once more in charge of the cavvy, now minus the cook's four work horses, and he drove it off toward the next wagon stop, grazing it as it went. The others saddled up, swung away from the wagon, and rode briskly down the draw, headed north, toward the scene of the day's work. Two men rode off at an angle, to take over the day herd and to relieve the last night guard. As the latter rode rapidly toward the wagon for their breakfast, the day herd was moving north, spread out and feeding as it went. The two riders would help the cook load his wagon, hitch up, and start him on his way to the next camp spot. He was to be there in time to bake a batch of bread and have dinner ready for the hungry riders. It behoved him to waste little time.

Corson and the straw boss rode ahead of the outfit, setting a brisk pace.

"How are they comin'?" asked the former, a question he would have asked before, except that he had had other things on his mind. The placidity of the straw boss had been a tacit admission that nothing of any consequence was wrong.

"Tallyin' good," answered Nueces, feeling in a

pocket and digging out some folded sheets of paper. He handed them to his companion. "We've branded near fourteen hundred in th' JC mark, includin' up to last night. Accordin' to th' number of cattle in our brand, 'specially th' cows, there's about seven hundred more to come. That's a rough guess, kinda. We're two-thirds through, as far as JC numbers are concerned."

Corson nodded, glanced at the sheets, and gave them back to the straw boss. Knowing that there were roughly twenty-five hundred cows in the JC brand, and estimating eighty-four per cent of them would bear calves that would live, he found his companion's estimate about right.

He pictured the cacnea herd, and wondered if anyone was working his range, driving calves from their mothers before they were weaned. The only proof of ownership to a calf is its presence with its mother, whose brand covers both. If the calf is weaned before branding time there is no indication of ownership. If anyone was working his range they would not gain as much by this practice now, if the Association rules were strictly carried out; unless they herded the newly made mavericks and hid them better than they had hidden this little bunch. Well, he would have a better knowledge of this phase of the cattle business after he had obtained the complete calf tally for entry into the tally book at the ranch.

He raised a hand in salute and turned off to the left in the direction of the ranch.

"So-long, Nueces; so-long, boys!" he called.

He did not go to the ranch, however, but circled the buttes and ridges and swung around them back through Horsethief Gap. At the entrance of Bull Canyon he stopped and rode in a steadily widening circle, closely scrutinizing the ground. He had little hope of picking up any signs that would tell him anything: too much time had elapsed.

Riding into the canyon, he examined the tracks in the now dried mud near the little spring. Nueces had protected them with a barrier of stunted piñons and brush. They were on the far side of the spring, in a small V-shaped opening between two great rocks, which accounted for the cattle not having trampled them out. They were in a good state of preservation, and he dismounted to study them better. After a few minutes' close scrutiny he believed that he had memorized them as well as it was possible to do; and he found no particular satisfaction in that: there was nothing distinctive about them, and the riders who had made them would have more than one riding horse in their string, and would not have to ride the same animal all the time. If they wished to play safe, they could rip the shoes off and throw them away. Outside the canyon he felt there would be little hope of being able to track them back the way they had come: the round-up would have obliterated such signs. He mounted, wheeled, and rode down the canyon, thinking things out as well as he could.

The JC wagon had the territory running west to the top of the divide between Coppermine Canyon and the Kiowa, beyond. The Bar W had been assigned the entire watershed of the Kiowa. The BLR outfit was responsible for the territory between that of the Bar W and Crooked Creek, running north to the road through Saddlehorn Pass. They had Durhams on their north range and Herefords on their south.

Baylor's range-bred Herefords had begun to run small of bone, and he had been tipped off regarding a foreclosure sale in the next county west, where he had bought his Durham sires at a price which made them a bargain, especially to a man whose one hope was to improve his original breed by crossing. The basis of his herd had been at the beginning, of course, a trail herd up from Texas, a trail herd of mixed cattle for range stocking. It was possible because of the nature of the country around his ranges that the longhorns had not all been combed out by his round-up crews, and that some of the original longhorn strain persisted unchanged.

The Turkey Track believed in Red Polls, a breed new to that whole section of country, and Corson doubted if there was a single longhorn bull or steer left on its more open ranges. The Bar W were running Herefords, and the new syndicate had been thorough in its round-ups and breeding. Corson himself had Durhams; and it had been a long time since he had seen longhorn steers or bulls on his ranch. The Chain's herd had been bred up by Angus bulls.

The Baylor rider's unreasonable demand came to him. If the Baylor outfit had been concerned in the handling of that cached herd, then the cattle had not come from the west. He had never heard anything to make him suspect the BLR. If a rider or two from that outfit was on the rustle, then it was possible for the thieves to have made up the little gather on their own ranges. Otherwise, the combination of the three breeds would have levied upon the Bar W for the Whitefaces, the JC for the Durhams, and some wild, rough country for the longhorns. It was all very plain as far as it went, but it did not go far enough.

He left the canyon and struck straight for the escarpment which lay a mile or more on the other side of the Branch Trail. Any cattle coming in from the south, southwest, west, or northwest would have had to pass between the mouth of the canyon and the slope of detritus at the foot of the sheer wall behind it.

Reaching the escarpment, he rode a zigzag course from one side to the other, and then back and forth until he came to the canyon through which the Jimmy Branch flowed and the trail ran. There were no readable signs suggesting that the cached herd had passed this way, and he swore under his breath at the interval of time which must have elapsed. The round-up had not helped to preserve any tracks.

Well, there was Bull Canyon and its branches. The rest of the day would give him time enough to examine it thoroughly. Examine it he did, found nothing of a positive nature, and at last looked back and down into it. He was upon the mesa beyond its head. It was twenty miles to the JC ranch houses, and nearly that far to the JC wagon. South of him was the Chain wagon, and he began to figure out its probable location. It was late afternoon now, and he had to make up his mind quickly. He swung his horse away from the canyon's edge and pushed it to the top of the ridge, the highest point on the mesa. Looking southwestward, he saw the faint dust sign which told him where to find the Chain outfit. Judging from the dust, they must still be working the herd. He wanted to have a talk with its straw boss, anyhow, and to do so now would be to cut his necessary riding in half. He kneed the horse and rode down the southern slope.

The Chain outfit had worked their gather by the time Corson rode up to their wagon. Franchère, the JC representative with this crew, was the first man to come in. He swung off his tired cutting-out horse and smiled at his boss. The cook gave the visitor hearty welcome without pausing in his duties. Franchère walked to Corson's side, to drop prone on the earth and relax.

"You see any signs of a forty-head steer herd, comin' in from th' west?" bluntly asked the sheriff.

"No," answered Franchère, rolling over on his side to look at his boss. "Why?"

"You worked that part of yore territory th' first week, didn't you?" asked Corson.

"Yeah," replied the rider. "They coulda come in through Horse Canyon without leavin' any sign. It's a reg'lar runway."

Corson nodded.

"Whiteface, Durham, an' longhorns. Yearlin' mavericks, an' right well selected. There was nothin' accidental about it."

Franchère showed more interest.

"Durham?" he asked.

"Yeah."

"Then that means Baylor, or us," he grunted, speculatively. "You see 'em, or just hear about 'em?"

"Saw 'em. Cached in Bull Canyon. They're Association cattle now."

"Damn shame!" snapped Franchère, and then explained himself quickly. "Some of them Durhams was ours."

"How you know?" asked Corson, looking curiously at his rider.

"Bull Canyon's on th' fringe of our range," explained Franchère. "If any bunch are throwin' a wide loop down in this country, they shore ain't workin' one range steady. Look at th' layout: Whitefaces an' Durhams. Whitefaces from th' Baylor herds or th' Bar

W; Durhams from th' Baylor cattle or our own. No Red Polls or Angus among 'em?"

"No."

"That tells us somethin'. They ain't botherin' th' Chain or th' Turkey Track: too far away, mebby." Franchère thought for a moment. "Them Maverick Whitefaces, now, they look small of bone?"

"No," answered Corson. "An' they didn't have any Durham blood in 'em. Yo're thinkin' Baylor. So did I. But there are yearlin' steers on th' fringes of his range that ain't Durham crosses, an' some of 'em are right big cattle. All these yearlin's were right well selected. Baylor's got some heavy yearlin's on his range, an' some of 'em are straight Hereford crosses. I thought that all out when I saw th' herd, an' I'm keepin' it in mind in case I find another cache. There's plenty of brains back of this business."

"Uh-huh," grunted Franchère, sitting up. A string of riders was leaving the herd and heading for the wagon. "Here comes th' boss an' th' boys."

"You ever hear of th' JM?" asked Corson, carelessly.

"No," answered Franchère, getting to his feet and moving away.

The tired riders dismounted near the wagon and soon flung themselves on the ground, nodding a grunted welcome to their visitor. Rube Shortell spoke to the cook, glanced around, and walked over to the sheriff's side, where he sat himself down cross-legged.

"How you boys makin' it?" he asked.

"Heavy, on our own range," answered Corson.

"By Gawd," said Shortell, "we had one gather that we had to split in two before we could work it, an' up here that's remarkable."

"Many strays?" carelessly asked the sheriff.

"That's funny," said Shortell. "Third day we was out, near th' head of Horse Canyon, we run into a bunch of Whitefaces. Cows an' calves. Holed up slick and purty in a side draw, over on th' west end of th' circle. Three of my boys found 'em, an' I was savin' up th' news for you." He shook his head. "Th' cows wasn't branded."

"Look like Durham-Hereford crosses?" asked Corson.

"No, sir! Straight Herefords, an' heavy!"

"My head's beginnin' to go around," said Corson. After a moment he spoke again. "That's a long way from th' Bar W," he growled. "More so, when you consider that our range lies plumb in between." He thought again. "No Durhams with 'em?"

"Not nothin' that looked like one," answered Shortell, "in *that* bunch; but I can tell you somethin' funny."

"I'm listening," grunted the sheriff, idly watching the men at the washbasin. He saw Franchère take his turn after a bit of horseplay with the next in line.

"Two of my boys routed out a bunch of calves an'

drove 'em on in with th' other cattle. They didn't have no mothers; but by the time th' herd quit chousin', an' settled down, they had all been smelled over an' adopted!"

Corson swore under his breath. Here was a strong indication that forced weaning was being done. Someone was heartily cursing the reallotment of the round-up wagons.

"Rube, will you keep all this under yore hat?" asked the sheriff, suddenly.

"Shore. Them boys of mine are close-mouthed, too. You smellin' somethin'?"

"Ain't you?" countered Corson.

"Kinda," grunted Shortell, thoughtfully. "What brought you down here, Bob?"

"Th' smell."

"Uh-huh. Well, grab yore plate an' fill yore belly."

CHAPTER V

As THE crow flies it was forty miles from the Chain wagon to the Baylor ranch. As a horse traveled, it was seventy, up and down, here and there, as the crooked canyon trails led. From the BLR ranch to their wagon, operating down on Crooked Creek, it was another twenty miles, and this twenty lay at right angles to the first course.

Corson could take the trail leading over Saddle Pass, cross his own range, ride through the town of Willow Springs and on to the Bar W, spend the night at that ranch, and make the rest of the journey on the following day, and save thirty miles. These thoughts were running through his mind as he lay in his blankets, listening to the tinny rattle of the cook's alarm clock. The strident bell had awakened him, and his mind was too busy to let him fall asleep again. He was conscious of a restless movement on his left: Franchère was moving under his covering. Corson sat up, throwing the blanket from him, and felt as a matter of habit for papers and tobacco. He turned his head suddenly and found Franchère watching him, and the puncher's grin came a little late.

The circle horses were being rounded up and driven

in, the cook was making certain preparations toward moving the wagon after breakfast was over, and the straw boss was looking over the tally sheets of the day before. Breakfast was soon out of the way.

Corson got his horse, coiled the picket rope, and threw on the saddle. Rube Shortell drifted over to him, his eyes on the hackamore.

"That's a right neat piece of work," he said. "Make it yoreself?"

"No. Bludsoe braided that," replied Corson. "He's right handy workin' up rawhide. I'm headin' north, Rube. Would you mind gettin' right suspicious an' keepin' yore eyes open? You can get word to me through Shorty, at th' ranch."

"I don't have to get suspicious, Bob; an' I only close my eyes after I pull th' tarp over me at night."

"If anybody should speak about it, I just drifted down here to pay you a neighborly visit," prompted the sheriff.

"Uh-huh. Drop in ag'in, any time," invited the straw boss.

"Reckon I'll head back for my wagon an' drift down to Cactus Springs," said Corson.

"Give my regards to Zeke Pike," said Shortell.

"I will if I see him," said Corson, swinging into the saddle. He looked around and saw Franchère saddling up not far from him. The two men exchanged nods, and Corson rode away.

He soon struck the north trail that led around Bull

Canyon on the east and joined the Jimmy Branch trail just below the entrance of the Bull. Half a mile farther on he had the choice of taking the trail over Saddle Pass and straight on past the JC ranch, Willow Springs, and the Bar W; or of following the Jimmy Branch trail down through Horsethief Valley, past his own wagon, and then a further choice of turning to the right for Cactus Springs, or to the left for his own range, Willow Springs, and the Bar W trail.

He had had no intention of visiting Cactus Springs when he spoke of it, back at the Chain wagon. Some streak of caution had made him speak as he had. Well, it was often good to carry a pretense a little farther. He would head for Horsethief, by way of the wagon, and then, instead of keeping on toward Cactus Springs, turn left, pass the JC, and go on to the Bar W.

It was mid-forenoon when he reached the wagon, and he drew up to speak to the cook.

"Got any word you want to send to Zeke Pike?" he called, forgetting that there was no love lost between the two men.

"Nothin' except to tell him to go to hell!"

"Oh, I plumb forgot!" exclaimed Corson, grinning apologetically. He looked out over the hilly range, now wreathed with dust. The gather of the day before was a little south of him, spread out and grazing placidly under the watchful care of two riders. "Well," he said, moving on again, "give my regards to th' boys. I'll tell Zeke what you said, if I see him," and then chuckled at the cook's reply.

He turned off the trail so as to go well around the outer circle rider, passed him, and went back to the road again. When sheltered by the shoulder of the butte, he swung left and headed for Willow Springs; but instead of riding through the town, he went around it on the south and, five miles farther on, dismounted before the Bar W ranch house, located on a bend of the Kiowa.

Red Perdue was loafing on the porch, his right wrist and hand hidden by bandages. He raised the left in grave salutation and grinned foolishly.

"What's th' matter with you, Red?" asked the sheriff, his eyes on the bandages.

"Wrist all sprained to hell an' gone," answered Red, cheerfully. "I was goin' down th' rope, looked backward like a fool, an' th' damn' calf acts up, an' th' rope took a loop around my wrist. How's things comin' over yore way?"

"Right good. Is th' foreman here or at th' wagon?"

"At th' wagon, but he oughta be ridin' in before long," answered Red.

They talked of this and that until the foreman hove into sight and passed the corrals. Corson swung up in the saddle and rode off to meet the newcomer.

" 'Lo, Bob. Visitin'?"

"Yeah: kinda. I've only done thirty-odd miles of ridin' today, an' I'm feelin' right fresh. What you say we keep on goin' an' visit yore wagon?" suggested the sheriff.

The foreman's face became suddenly grave.

"Anythin' wrong down there?"

"No," answered the sheriff. "I just want to talk to you where no long ears can overhear us."

"There ain't nobody in th' bunkhouse but th' cook," said the foreman.

"Who's th' BLR stray man workin' at yore wagon?" asked the sheriff.

"Young Baylor."

"You seen anythin' a mite suspicious since you started this round-up?" persisted the sheriff.

"How you mean?"

"*Any*thin' at all: funny actions, strange tracks, cached cattle, extra large number of yearlin' mavericks: anythin' at all."

"No, I haven't seen anythin' special; but you fellers must have, judgin' by that bunch of Association mavericks you threw in with ourn," said the foreman. "It's a howlin' shame to turn over all them yearlin's to th' Association."

"Yeah; but it's done."

"Just what's on yore mind, anyhow, Bob?" asked the foreman, curiously, looking closely at his companion.

"Take a ride down th' river a little way, an' I'll tell you," answered the sheriff.

"Well, I just come from down there, but if I must, then I must. All right: come along."

They got back to the ranch an hour before supper-time, and the foreman was very thoughtful; but they sat on the washbench near the bunkhouse door and talked of those things they would have talked about ordinarily. Supper found them hungry and wordless, and after they had left the table they sat in the bunk-room with Red Perdue and another puncher and talked some more.

On the following morning Bob and the foreman were the last to leave the table, delaying purposely. When they were alone they walked into the kitchen, and the cook casually gave the sheriff the bundle of food he had been told to get ready for him. There were no restaurants where Corson expected to be that afternoon and night. If his plans were changed later in the day the food would be a small loss.

It was noon when he reached Packers Gap, which, he assured himself, was as good a way to ride as any in the direction of Crooked Creek and the territory of the Baylor wagon. The truth of the matter was that he wanted another glance up that side draw, below the Gap. He might see her standing in the door of the little adobe, and any extra riding would be justified by that. He would not force his presence on her, of course; but a man never could tell, beforehand, just how his luck happened to be running.

He held the horse to a walk down the steep pitch

of the trail on the west side of the Gap, and when he
reached the entrance to the side draw he turned and
rode part way up the incline, and stopped. Two saddled horses were standing before the corral, and a
horseman was slowly riding toward the house. The
figure was very familiar, even at that distance. The
man had certain tricks, certain peculiarities and
mannerisms that proclaimed his identity. It was the
Baylor rider who had quit the JC wagon. What was
he doing up here? The round-up was a very busy time,
and a man should be out on the range with the cattle.
The answer was not a pleasant one. That woman was
downright pretty, and a pretty woman is a mighty
strong magnet on a cattle range.

He felt a surge of resentment and had kneed his
horse and sent it forward, when the door of the house
opened and the woman suddenly stood in the opening.
The Baylor rider took off his hat with a flourish, and
Corson, strangely vexed, removed his own to keep
things even. The Baylor rider's back was to him, and
Corson suddenly yielded to an urging for caution and
backed down the slope. While he was doing so the
woman raised her hand in a swift gesture, and he
raised his own in reply. That Baylor puncher thought
that she was gesturing to him, the conceited damned
fool! Again she raised her hand, and Corson's spirits
fell as swiftly as they had risen: the gesture was un-
mistakable—she was warning him away! Oh, well:
that was all right, for the moment.

He had sense enough left to him to turn the horse and push on past the entrance of the draw; but, once out of sight of anyone at the house or the corral, he swung from the saddle, cached the horse behind a huge mass of boulders, and worked back on foot. He wasn't on any man's payroll, and he had a right to waste a little time if he wanted to, if it could be called a waste of time. He was finding that he had a lot of interest in the Baylor sorehead.

He saw that interesting person stop before the door of the house, tuck his big hat under an arm, and turn sideways in the saddle; and then the pleasing figure in the doorway stepped back, and the heavy door closed solidly behind her. Corson felt like shouting. That was the proper treatment! By God, for a lead peso he'd —— Then he saw movement at the corral. Four men came into sight, two of them going into the enclosure. The Baylor rider waited a moment and then, with a gesture of anger, slammed the hat on his head, whirled his mount, and raced toward the saddled horses and their riders. Two more horses came out of the corral, were hastily saddled, and then the mounted group turned his way and rode swiftly down the draw. The sheriff slipped back into better cover, and soon watched them as they rode past him, down the arroyo.

"Why didn't you throw yore hat in th' door, Slade?" laughingly asked the oldest of the five.

"He shore didn't get a chance to, Pop," said one of

the younger men. "Alice called th' play before he made it."

The four riders laughed, but the Baylor man, whose name seemed to be Slade, was sullen and angry. He made a low-voiced retort and pushed on down the arroyo, bringing up the rear. Gradually the sounds of their horses died out.

"Alice," muttered Corson, smiling. He moved from his cover and led the horse out to the trail. "That's th' kind of a name for a woman: short, sweet, an' plain. An' *Slade:* huh!" He remembered that there had been a Slade before his time, a famous Slade, and a man who had been a man, until he had gone wrong. He had gone bad and had to be hanged. "Well, I'll mebby find out, some time, if this Slade is as good as th' other, as far as nerve is concerned. Come on," he said to the horse as he touched the saddlehorn. "We're goin' visitin'."

He saw that the door was open when he turned the corner of the arroyo and entered the draw. That meant that she knew he would not ride on without calling. How did she know that? There was a whole lot of difference between having a door slammed in a fellow's face and having one opened for him even before he came into sight. The thought made him laugh, happily, exultantly, and the surprised and indignant horse leaped forward under the roll of the rowels.

The bay's hoofs made a different sound from the hoofs of any other horse on that range. He was a first-class cutting-out animal, and he was shod especially for that work, for working with cattle, and according to his rider's own ideas. He was shod only on the rear feet. That meant that his shoulders were not crippled and stiff, that he was sure-footed, and that he did his stopping with his rear hoofs, throwing his weight where it belonged. When the round-up had started, Corson had shod him for working with the boys at the wagon, and then had found that he could not take a hand with the outfit, and since then he simply had neglected to shoe him all around.

The bay was like a cat, and now he stopped and swung like a cat, his hocks almost touching the edge of the porch. Corson's hat lifted, dropped swiftly, and came to rest on the horn of the saddle. He smiled down into the grave, wistful face looking up at him, and his blood was fairly leaping through his veins. Great land of cows! Nobody could blame that Baylor rider who carried a name right hard to live up to. In a moment he was standing beside her, and he checked his rising arms. If there was anything on earth that he wanted, he was looking at it now, looking at it with telltale eyes.

"But you shouldn't come here," she was saying in her low, even voice. Corson thrilled to it. "I motioned for you not to come. Strangers should keep away from this ranch, this draw. It's not safe."

"Yes: you motioned for me not to come; but you *knew* I would!" he answered, swiftly, tumultuously.

His voice, somehow, did not sound like his own. "You knew I'd come! You knew I couldn't help it, that I had to come!"

"But you shouldn't!" she replied, bravely; and it took courage to tell him that. She would not try to fool herself, for she well knew how she felt toward this man, and was glad of it; glad of it even if it meant pain and sorrow at the same time.

"Why?" he demanded, quickly, taking a short step forward as she stepped back. "Why shouldn't I come?"

"It's not safe. Strangers have no business here."

"Then that's easy! I'm no stranger. My name's Bob Corson, of th' JC, over east of th' Coppermine. I'll wait right here till th' family's all together, an' make myself known, an' also why I'm doin' it. If I can't come here just because I'm a stranger, I'll soon take care of that."

"Oh, please don't. That's just quibbling, an' this is no time for that."

"I'm sorry; but I was in earnest. I meant just what I said. I'm not goin' to be kept away from this house just because strangers ain't welcome here. I'm not goin' to be kept from seein' you just because it's dangerous! Let me tell you, Alice, that danger works both ways! An' I'm aimin' to stay right here an' meet it face to face when it passes that corral. Danger!" his voice rang out exultantly, rang out like the tones of a bugle. "What's danger, when a man can look at a woman like you?" He checked his arms again and held himself back by sheer strength of will. "You knew that I'd ride up this draw when I saw that th' door was open. You *knew* it!"

"Yes," she admitted, her eyes for a moment closing, but opening again to regard him evenly, levelly. She could feel the burning of her throat and cheeks. "I— I knew. Perhaps that was why I didn't want—didn't want you to come. And yet I did want you to. But you must not ride up here again. You *must* not! And now you must go on again. You must go back the way you came; over the Gap. Not the other way, after *them:* please."

"That man Slade," he said harshly, ignoring her words—those of them that he wanted to ignore. He was taut as a fiddle string, and near humming like one. "You don't want that man Slade an' me to meet!" he said, challengingly. Perhaps he was acting like a damned fool: all right, he was feeling like one and revelling in it.

She was gravely examining him, his tanned, lean face; his wide, sloping shoulders; his lean, small waist. The slick leather chaps came in for their share of scrutiny, but it was on his low-hung guns that her seemingly fascinated gaze lingered. Her face was flushed, her eyes alight; but her gaze was level and calm as she raised her eyes and answered him.

"No. I don't want you and him to meet," she said, simply, without emphasis. At his quick flush her lips straightened and a hurt look came into her eyes. "Please don't misunderstand me."

His next exhalation was a gusty one. To quiet the trembling of his knees, he spread his feet, and found that to be no cure. He took a half step forward, his arms swiftly going around her. For a moment she did not resist, or try to evade his lips; and then she slowly pushed free and held him back. Tears were in her eyes as she looked at his flushed and eager face.

"You—you shouldn't have done that. You had no right. I've asked you to ride on again. Won't you go, please?" She was calm again, externally, but her voice was low and hesitant. "I'm just selfish enough not to want you to ride into danger. You must not come here again."

He laughed grimly. Danger! Danger was only a price tag, and was usually a guarantee that the forbidden goods were well worth more than what was asked for them. He stepped forward again, but stopped against her open hand.

"All right! An' *that's* easy!" he said, his teeth flashing in a swift smile. Perhaps he was going loco, but it certainly had its compensations. "Instead of me comin' here, you go with me! Go with me to Bentley, Willow Springs. We can get married in either place, an' then go on to th' ranch. It's easy, Alice!"

She was studying him, reading him, and, somehow, not greatly surprised by his proposal; and she found a sudden joy in what she saw; but she slowly shook her head. Marry him? Take to the man she knew she loved the stigma of a dishonest father, of dishonest brothers? She had no proof of their dishonesty, but she needed none; for weeks she had felt it to be true. Go to her husband as the daughter of a thief? She closed her eyes to hide the pain she knew was in them, and shook her head again.

"I don't want to crowd you, Alice!" he pleaded. "Mebby I'm not doin' this right. I don't know. I never played a hand in a game like this, an' I don't know; but I'm tellin' you that no matter how strange it is to me, I aim to play it through, an' to *win* it—to win it for *both* of us!"

"Please, please go," she said, her words hardly audible. "Don't make it any harder than it is. Please!"

"We don't have to go to town an' get married right off," he said, eagerly, hopefully trying another lead. "There's Mrs. French, over on th' Turkey Track. I'll take you there, an' you can stay with her, an' make up yore mind when you want to!" He laughed again, ringingly. "There never will be any danger to me in ridin' up to th' Turkey Track! I told you we could get it all figgered out! I'll saddle you a horse, an' we'll go to th' Turkey Track. Alice, I love you; an' I got a right strong feelin' that you love me. I'll go saddle th' horse."

"No! No! Can't you understand? Won't you listen to me? I—can't go with you. I can't leave here. Why do you torture me? Won't you please go?"

"Alice, I don't know yore cards or yore play; but I don't question them. Not nohow. I don't want to make trouble for you, but I can't keep from seein' you. I can't keep away from here as long as you are here. But I will try to use my head. An' I've taken th' right to ask you a question; an' I believe that yo're fair enough to answer me fairly: is that Baylor rider botherin' you?"

"If he is, I have a father and three brothers," she answered, and then flushed. "I didn't mean it that way. I didn't mean to be impolite. You must know that. But again I tell you to stay away from here."

"Why?" he blurted, and then raised his hand swiftly. "Don't answer that. I didn't mean it. You'll tell me, of yore own accord, some day. I'm makin' that a promise. An' some day you'll tell me somethin' more than that! An' *that's* a promise, too. There never was a bigger promise than that in yore life or mine! Next time I ride past, open th' door an' I'll turn in; keep it closed an' I'll keep on goin'. I promise you that. I don't want to worry you. I wouldn't worry you for——" He cleared his throat and felt like a glorious fool. "Good-bye, Alice!"

She did not answer. She could not answer. She just stood there and watched him mount and wheel and ride away. She feared that she would choke. He passed the corral, dropping steadily down the slope, and then he was lost to her sight. She waited for the abrupt dying out of the hoofbeats, the strange hoofbeats,

with the peculiar softness of two of them. She had
never before heard hoofbeats that sounded like those.
They did not die out abruptly; they slowly faded and
at last ceased; and then she waited almost breathlessly
for an endorsement that she did not need. It came, the
clear, loud echo that told her he was not going back
the way he had come; not going over the Gap as she
had asked him to; he was riding down the arroyo
toward Bentley, following the five riders who had just
gone that way. She bit her lip, slowly shook her head,
and slowly, almost reluctantly, crossed the porch and
entered the house; but for some reason she did not
close the door behind her. It stood wide open, in view
of the arroyo trail.

CHAPTER VI

CORSON's ride down the draw was an incident which he never clearly remembered, a vague haze of motion which meant nothing. He did not remember turning into the arroyo or heading down it; but with that steep slope and the difficult trail up it well behind him, the horse preferred to leave it that way, and to take the easier trail. The animal had been to Bentley more than once, the way was familiar and all downhill, and the hotel oats were good. For these reasons the sheriff was riding to town instead of somewhere else, and in his present state of mind one way was as good as another.

Gradually he came back to the present moment and began to get command of his wild and intoxicating thoughts; and, as his command grew, his thoughts reached out more and more and finally caused him to remember the riders who had gone down the trail ahead of him. Here was a possible menace, and he shook himself out of the pleasant land of daydreams and gave a growing attention to his immediate surroundings and the status of his affairs as an official.

His mind ran back in time and showed him the trail which lay ahead. The bends were not sharp, and thus somewhat cut down the possibilities for ambush. Then he smiled to himself: it seemed that a man in love could be a damned fool. The riders ahead of him had no reason to be thinking of ambushes. They were totally unaware of his presence in the arroyo. They had no reason to suspect that he was anywhere in their vicinity. He bent his mind on sterner, although hardly more treacherous to a single man, things than love. Black Jack Meadows, his three sons, and Slade were riding ahead of him toward Bentley. Alice's fear for the safety of strangers around the JM ranch must have a foundation. What, exactly, was it?

His mind seethed with possibilities; possibilities which he felt, lacking proof as he did, to be probabilities. They were nebulous, vague, without form or substance, but they were there nevertheless. They mixed and merged, stood out clearly for a moment, shifted tantalizingly, and mixed again to form a new combination, to become a bewildering, chaotic mental cloud. What were some of them? What did they mean, individually and collectively? Then he remembered the look in Alice's eyes, and came perilously near getting off the mental trail, which was an easy thing to do.

A cached herd of yearling mavericks, of three distinct and easily recognizable breeds. A sequestered bunch of cows and calves, all Whitefaces. An isolated group of calves, so freshly separated from their mothers as to be quickly claimed by them when thrown together with them in the herd. Weaning took about

two weeks—that was close enough as an average time
—so they could not have been separated for very long.
A bunch of Durham calves being weaned on the Chain
range, where no one but Chain riders ordinarily rode,
and on a part of that range where even Chain riders
seldom went. Whiteface cows and calves holed up on
the Chain range. There were the actions of the Baylor
stray man. There was the JM outfit, which almost no
one seemed to know much about. It was up in the hills
near Packers Gap, off the little-used trail down Lucas
Arroyo, and right handy to the Kiowa and Crooked
Creek watersheds. These were the discrete facts from
which he had to evolve the proper pattern.

The Baylor stray man had been at home, seemingly,
on the JM ranch. A little outfit like that would be
forced to work out, to earn money riding for other
ranches. The meager returns from its own beef would
not support it, and to eat its own beef, or to sell them
off, would be to destroy all hope of increasing its
herd: the steers would be too few in number to depend upon. It had to get outside money to eke out its
existence. If it did not work for that money, then it
had to obtain it in some other way. How? That was
the question. And the answer: theft? Perhaps either
theft, or gambling, or both.

He kept on down the trail, the fresh tracks of the
five riders plain to be seen. The trail slanted down the
arroyo, running along the south slope; and where the
arroyo finally opened out, fan-like, the trail crossed

over, turned north, and dropped down the benches toward the little frontier town of Bentley.

He came to the cross-over and found that the tracks divided here. Four horses went on toward town, but the fifth had swung to the left, climbed the gently sloping shoulder, and headed up the valley of Crooked Creek. This lone rider, the sheriff thought, must be Slade, returning to his own outfit. What had the man done with his string of horses and his drag of cattle? When the stray man had left the JC wagon he had cut out and driven away all BLR stuff, both horses and cattle. Well, he would get the answer to that question later, and take the chance, now, of being able to find Slade when he wanted him. Right now he was going into town behind the other four horsemen, for he could afford to gamble on Slade, and he suspected that the others would be well worth watching a little.

Bentley had a peace officer, a sleepy-eyed, lazy individual who was very misleading; a shrewd, straight-thinking veteran of the old frontier, devious and wandering in talk, but disconcertingly direct and swift in action when action was needed. Corson had been able to do the marshal a few favors in the line of duty and, naturally enough, expected a few in return, upon demand; but if he could get the information by roundabout means rather than by direct request, he could cover his plays a little better and save up the demands for later use. It never was wise to shoot all one's cartridges away at one time.

The sheriff pushed past the general store and dismounted before a low, adobe building. This had two
rooms, the second and rear of the two being lined with
two-inch hardwood planks, and floored with the same.
It had one window, now open, which was segmented
by iron bars. A sun-bleached, faded sign on the front
of the building made a blunt statement: CITY
MARSHAL. Across the street the earth sloped upward in a low ridge which shut off the view of the
wagon road leading up over Saddlehorn Pass.

Corson swung down from the saddle and entered
the small, cool room. The marshal's legs rested on a
second chair, the heels of his boots projecting out past
the far side of the seat to give clearance for his spurs.
He looked up slowly, his sleepy eyes resting casually
on his visitor's face.

"Set," he drawled, nodding toward a chair.

Corson obeyed, dropped his hat on the floor, and
drew a sleeve across his forehead.

"Cool in here," said the sheriff, relaxing gratefully.

"Y-e-p."

"Town peaceful?" asked the visitor for the sake of
making conversation.

"Y-e-p. Th' Baylor wagon's gettin' closer every day,
however, an' th' boys'll be driftin' in to raise a little
hell; but I'll straighten 'em out if they gets real ornery.
It'll be a kinda change for me."

Corson scooped up his hat and arose.

"Well, what I wanted was a drink of water," he said, moving lazily toward a corked jug in the corner. He deftly threw it over his arm and let it gurgle into his mouth. His thirst was no pretense, and he sighed gratefully as he put the vessel down.

"Ain't in no hurry, are you?" asked the marshal, showing a faint trace of alarm.

"No; not 'specially," answered the sheriff.

"Set down ag'in. You young fellers are allus workin' up a sweat an' a lather."

Corson laughed and sought the chair again. He passed a hand over his forehead, brushing back his hair, and looked at the marshal.

"A feller named Slade was ahead of me on th' trail down Lucas Arroyo," he said, carelessly. "Th' name struck me. Wonder if he's any kin to that Jack Slade that was hanged up in th' Montana gold fields, years back?"

"Don't know; but he's just as pizen," placidly replied the marshal, his eyes lighting up reminiscently. He liked to talk of the old days. "I knowed Jack Slade, knowed him well. His real name was Joe. I was freightin' supplies to th' stage stations when Slade come up from th' lower Platte, an' took holt of th' Rocky Ridge Division. He spent a lot of time at Julesburg, an' disgraced th' Overland at Virginia Dale. I saw him shoot a button off a teamster's overcoat. Brass button, it was. Mite careless he was with th' next shot

—on purpose. We buried th' teamster. This here Slade is a whelp of th' same kind, with none of th' other Slade's good p'ints, if any."

"Works for Baylor, don't he?" asked Corson, lazily, and with but little interest.

"Y-e-p. He wouldn't work for me very damn' long," asserted the marshal with a trace of vehemence.

"No?" asked Corson in mild surprise. "Why, he's a good man with cattle. He was one of th' stray men with our wagon."

"Uh-huh. He's too damn' good a hand with cattle," replied the marshal in a growl.

Corson let the ensuing silence continue for some moments, and then he looked up curiously.

"I came over Packers Gap just now," he said. "There's a new ranch up there. I never knew that before."

"Y-e-p," said the marshal. "Been there two, three years. Black Jack Meadows, three sons an' a gal. JM on th' left shoulder, run together. Scrub cattle, an' not too many of them."

"Huh," grunted Corson idly. "Didn't notice none."

"Ain't many to notice. They'd starve to death if they depended on their cattle."

The sheriff's desultory conversation was beginning to show results. He dug up a match and chewed thoughtfully on it.

"Well, I reckon there's plenty of work for 'em all, down in this part of th' country," he said. "Bein' so handy to th' Baylor ranch, I reckon they work there a little."

"Feller would reckon that way," grunted the marshal. He pulled out a stinking corncob and loaded it with straight leaf. The sheriff pushed back his chair to get the benefit of what air might be coming in through the window in the side wall. He knew that combination, and knew it well. He thought that it might possibly serve for a substitute for cattle dip. It stunk enough, anyhow.

"Has Baylor bred up th' size of th' bones of his Whitefaces?" he asked, not caring to crowd too hard along the main track.

"Y-e-p. He never would have had to breed 'em up if he'd a-listened to me, in th' first place," said the marshal.

Corson suddenly leaned forward and looked out of the opposite window.

"There's four riders on JM hosses," he said, carelessly.

"That'll be Black Jack an' his boys," explained the marshal without trying to see the men in question. "Hair-trigger, th' whole lot of 'em. Ornery, an' proud of it. Never show any of 'em yore shoulder blades if you have words with 'em. Which way they headin'?"

"This way."

"Huh! You watch. I'll show you somethin'," growled the marshal, slowly getting off his chair. He jammed the pipe into a pocket, slouched to the door, and stopped there, filling the opening, his spread elbows touching the casings on each side of him. Corson stepped a little forward, where he could see the street and still be vague and indistinct in the poor light of the room.

The four horsemen came steadily down the street at a walk, and as they neared the marshal's office the leader glanced at the occupied door, said something out of the side of his mouth, and the group forthwith spread out. They came steadily on, four pairs of keen eyes on that door opening. As they went past, their heads slowly turned to keep that door in sight, and it was not long before they had to shift in their saddles to keep it within their vision.

The marshal spat forcibly and contemptuously into the street and pushed back into the room, smiling significantly at his alert and surprised visitor.

"There," he said, lazily seating himself again. "Told you I'd show you somethin'." He nodded slowly and pulled the pipe out of his pocket. "That Slade hombre is a right close friend of theirs."

"They shore don't like you," said the sheriff with emphasis.

"Well, we're even up, on *that*," grunted the marshal, grimly.

"But how do they make a livin'?" asked the sheriff, showing a little interest now. After what had happened and had been said, he could show interest without exposing any part of his cards. It would naturally grow from what had gone on before.

"Re-mittance," grunted his companion. "Th' old man gets a check four times a year from th' East. He hands it over to th' general store an' draws supplies ag'in it."

Corson was picturing the physical appearance of the four riders.

"None of 'em are what you might call big men," he said.

"Downright runty," grunted the marshal; "but a side-winder is a kinda runty rattler. Unexpected reptile, too, throwin' hisself along like he does. But he shore is pizen an' mean. You busy sheriffin', these days?"

"Oh, I have a writ or two to serve," answered Corson, smiling. "Our cook said that sheriffin' was all paper work these days. Not like it used to be, when it was mostly lead an' powder smoke."

"Huh!" grunted the marshal. "Swear him in an' give him a badge. He might have to change his mind," said the town officer, his sleepy eyes on the younger man's face. He, the marshal, was no fool. In his generation, out in that country, fools usually died young; and not only was he still alive, but his age was respectable. So the sheriff rode over Packers Gap, did he? He saw Slade leave Lucas Arroyo, and then came into town almost in the dust of Black Jack Meadows and his boys. There was a lot of spread-out deviltry going on out on the ranges, if he knew anything; and he knew that Bob Corson was nobody's fool. Paper work? Hell!

"Many mavericks this round-up?" asked the marshal, after a short pause, his close-lidded eyes on the younger man's face.

"Why, yes. I reckon so."

"Old uns?" persisted the marshal.

"Why, no; not as many old ones as you might think," slowly answered Corson.

"You ever know prices for improved yearlin' steers to be any higher than they are right now?" hammered the marshal.

Corson thought for a moment and then shook his head.

"No. I can't say that I ever have."

"Most of th' improved stock all over th' West was built up from Hereford sires, warn't it?" demanded the marshal.

"No. I wouldn't go anywhere near that far," replied Corson; "but an awful lot of them were while th' Hereford craze was on, an' that's 'specially so in th' southern part of th' cow country. Herefords didn't do so good, up North."

"All right: we're comin' to some of that," said the marshal. "An' what happened to 'em, th' Hereford range-bred crosses?"

"They seemed to get lighter in th' bones," answered the sheriff.

"Y-e-p. They didn't just seem to, but they did. It'll take time to bring back th' weight, won't it?"

"Not so long if they use Angus or Durham," replied Corson. "Th' BLR are near back to weight, right now."

"Y-e-p. Heavy yearlin's will be worth more money every day they grow, won't they?"

"That's true of all cattle under four years old."

"Y-e-p, it is," admitted the marshal, and then abruptly switched the lead. "Some brands can't be changed right handy," he said.

"I've been changin' brands in my mind for th' last few days," replied Corson, frowning. "Two of 'em can't be changed into anythin' reasonable, an' th' others won't change right."

"You get any idears from that?"

"Too damn' many," growled the sheriff. He moved toward the door. "Will th' storekeeper talk to me?"

"Depends considerable on th' subject," answered the marshal. "He'll talk to *me*, though."

"I'd like to know th' size of that quarterly check that Black Jack Meadows gets."

"Two hundred an' twenty-five dollars, even," said the marshal. "That's six per cent on fifteen thousan'. Took me near a hull evenin' to get that figgered out, but I stayed with it."

"You reckon it's a trust fund?" asked Corson.

"What's that? What you mean?"

"I'm wonderin' if he owns th' fifteen thousan', **or** only th' interest on it," explained the sheriff.

"Don't know; but what difference does it make, anyhow?"

"Considerable," replied the sheriff. "He could get started in buildin' up quite a little ranch if he owned th' principal, an' make more than six per cent on it."

"Y-e-p; he could," admitted the marshal. "Well, that's what money he gets an' spends."

"An' it seems to be enough to take care of that family, if they're thrifty. They'll get *some* returns from their cattle."

"Y-e-p: smokin'-tobacco money," grunted the marshal. "You want to go over to th' store?"

"Not now," answered the sheriff. "I'm ridin' on. I want to see Baylor, or his straw boss."

"Their wagon's up on Crooked Creek, halfway between here an' Iron Springs," volunteered the marshal.

"All right," said the sheriff, nodding, and stepping through the doorway.

The marshal grunted and loafed after his visitor.

"There's lots of money a-passin' acrost th' gamblin' tables in this town," he said. "More'n I ever saw before."

"Well, that's worth knowin'," said the sheriff, swinging into his saddle. He nodded thoughtfully. "Well worth knowin'," he repeated. "Anythin' else you want to say?"

"Well," drawled the marshal, "I might say that gal's all right, but I wouldn't nest up with no family of side-winders. They're runty, but damn' deadly."

Corson looked down into the inscrutable old face and into the sleepy eyes, and found that the eyes had become blank. He also found that he had nothing to say, and he smiled, nodded, and rode away.

CHAPTER VII

CORSON rode at a lope along the Crooked Creek trail, looking to the right and left, but mostly to the left, at the great ridge dividing the watershed of the creek from that of the Kiowa; at the ridge whereon the JM was located. It was wild, rough country, with steep pitches, sheer walls, a tangle of brush and scrub, and twisting arroyos and deep, hidden draws. It was ideal country for the hiding of stolen cattle; but on that score the Bar W outfit had swept the Kiowa side, and the BLR had cleaned up the cattle on the western slopes, and turned them back again, notched and branded. Under these circumstances, no herd of stolen cattle could have escaped unseen.

Suddenly he realized that he was hungry and that it was well past noon, three hours past it, to be more exact. He had not touched the rations given him by the Bar W cook; and he would not touch them now. It would be better to eat hot food at the Baylor wagon.

He soon came to the ruins of an old trading post, destroyed years before by raiding Comanche warriors. Its adobe walls still stood above his head in several places, but the fallen roof had long since disappeared except for piles of broken adobe that showed how it had been torn apart for the sake of the firewood its long poles had provided. As he was about to ride past the ruins a vicious hum near his ear made him duck swiftly and slip from the saddle. Slade?

He quickly led the horse under the protection of the highest part of the wall, and then slipped along the base of it, heavy rifle in hand. The belated report of the shot had been faint and flat, and had come from the west, from the direction of the hard, flinty, Dry Arroyo country, where tracking would be difficult, and the possibilities for ambush without number. If Slade had fired that shot, he could get a fairly good line on him at the BLR wagon.

Corson crawled between the base of the wall and a pile of ruined adobe bricks, and a second shot showered him with dust. A third spanged from the top of the wall and whined into the sky. The lead was nearly spent, for it had travelled a long way before striking. The shots had come from three widely different points. Corson wriggled backward, around a corner, and smiled grimly. There should be a fourth, and if there was, it would tell him a great deal. There was a fourth, but it came from the direction of the first, and therefore told him nothing of value.

Was the fourth man present, holed up in another direction, in the direction which the sheriff would be expected to choose if he made up his mind to ride for it? Those shots had been fired at very long range, but they had come close enough, at that. They tended to awaken respect for the marksmen. If there was a fourth man, holding his fire, he likely enough would be the best shot of the gang, picked out to down the quarry when it had been driven his way.

Corson led his horse inside the rectangle. If they got the horse they would have a deadly advantage; and they had advantage enough now, considering the odds. This would be a good time to eat some of the Bar W cook's food; be damned to them! He'd eat hot grub at the Baylor wagon!

He cautiously slid his rifle out through a gap in the wall where a window once had been. Instantly another shot smacked into the adobe, not a foot from his head, and showered him with clay; but he saw no smoke, and he had been looking for that. These were black-powder days, and smoke should have been discernible. The marksman must have fired through a small opening in a heavy screen of brush and stood well back from the screen when he did so. Well, there were plenty of dry washes and draws over there whose banks were fringed with just such sort of screens. Another thought came to him: these men were using field glasses or telescopes on their rifles.

Why had they fired at such long range, when the odds were so great against making a hit? Because, perhaps, in failing to hit him, they might cripple the horse. Why had they taken cover so far from the trail, when they could have ridden in to the ruins of the old post and shot him down at point-blank range?

Why? He grunted. Was it because they had just then come up even with him? Was it because they had ridden out of Bentley the wrong way, had to circle, and then overcome the opposition of rough country while he had been loping along a level trail? It was a reasonable explanation, anyhow. He had seen Black Jack and his boys ride out of town toward the north.

He was hungry. If he wanted to eat with the Baylor outfit he would have to get started. All right. Perhaps they had fired at such long range to coax him into hunting down the marksmen, and what a fool he would be to ride up to the muzzles of three hidden sharpshooters! No, that would not do: they all would not have fired if they had hoped to lure him into a play like that. Only one man would have fired. Well, to hell with them: he was going to eat a hot supper with the BLR round-up crew. If there was a number four waiting for him to ride for it, he would give him a chance, but it would be a mighty slim one.

He swung into the saddle, bending as low as he could, and sent the horse through the door in a leap. For the next half-mile he zigzagged like a crazy man, riding at full speed, and on the best cutting-out horse he had ever owned. It was adept at dodging and changing course quickly; much better at this sort of work than the animal he usually rode. Gradually the zigzags grew longer and less jerky, and he took good care not to pass too close to dangerous-looking cover. A mile was added to the half, and he then let the horse ease up; and half an hour later he was rocking along at the regular trail lope.

The Baylor wagon was on a small branch of Crooked Creek for the sake of better water. At this period of the year the creek was very low, and the consequent concentration of iron was objectionable. Farther up, nearer to Iron Springs, one could see the rusty streak holding to itself in the clearer stream; but it slowly became diffused lower down and lost its identity. Crooked Creek had a strong trace of alkali which the addition of iron did not improve. The wagon was now working the west side of the valley, having cleaned up the other slope, and from now on to the end of the round-up its gathers would be light. The hard work was over.

The straw boss, riding in toward his wagon, saw the horseman leave the wagon road and head his way. A moment's scrutiny revealed the newcomer's identity, and the straw boss kept on past the wagon and went out to meet him.

Was the BLR mixed up in this range puzzle, actively mixed up in it? It was hardly probable, but it was possible. More likely, if it was mixed up in it, it was some of its outfit, individually, and not the BLR itself. A man never made a mistake in keeping his mouth shut. The straw boss, who was also foreman, could safely be told that which he already knew, or part of it, if he was mixed up in it. After all, Slade was a BLR rider.

"Hello, Corson," called the straw boss, smiling broadly.

"Hello, Jerry. I reckon th' worst of yore job's about over."

"Yeah. We'll gather light from now on. How're th' other wagons makin' it?"

Corson told him briefly, and a silence fell.

Jerry finally twisted a little in the saddle and regarded his companion levelly.

"Slade go on th' prod with you fellers?" he abruptly asked.

"Yeah, a little," answered Corson, promptly. "I got somethin' to talk about, off by ourselves. But first: is Slade out there with th' cattle?"

"Yeah."

"How long's he been here?" asked the sheriff, watching the other closely through half-closed eyes.

"Rode in just in time to eat dinner with us," answered the straw boss.

Corson grunted. Evidently Slade had not been with the ambitious sharpshooters west of the old adobe trading post. That made it one less to consider.

They rode slowly up the creek, toward the trail leading to the Baylor ranch, and while they rode, the sheriff told his companion about the cached herd in Bull Canyon, and nothing more. After listening to Jerry's comment, he asked a question, roundabout, putting it indefinitely in regard to identities.

"You hire any extra help on th' ranch before th' round-up started?"

"Why, yes. Black Jack Meadows an' his boys worked a little for us, helpin' to break in broomtails; but not as much as they did last year."

"You didn't find anythin' suspicious when you combed th' ridge yonder?" asked Corson, waving his hand toward the east. He began to feel that the straw boss was straight. He had never heard anything against him, and the man's looks and words and actions were straightforward. The question he had just asked was more in the nature of a feeler, and the way in which it was answered banished any lingering suspicions against the integrity of the BLR foreman.

"No," replied the straw boss, slowly. "I did reckon for a while that th' JM had more calves than nature intended for 'em to have; but th' next few gathers didn't give them any a-tall. They just happened to be all bunched up in th' first two."

"Many mavericks?" asked the sheriff.

"Yes, a few; th' reg'lar run for rough country."

"Everythin' looked all right on yore own range?" persisted Corson.

"Well, not exactly," slowly answered the straw boss. "You know, a bunch of cattle will kinda get to feel at home on one section of th' range. A man can go out lookin' for a certain bunch, an' know just about where to find 'em."

"Yes, if th' place is better than other parts of th'

range," replied the sheriff. "No, I won't even make that exception. It goes as you said it."

"Shore. Now," said the straw boss, "there's a little pasture at th' head of Broken Jug Creek where quite a bunch of Whitefaces, cows an' calves, hang out. They range through it an' around it, but if a man heads for there, it won't take him long, generally, to locate that bunch of cattle. An' they allus work back there to water."

Corson nodded understandingly but said nothing.

"One of my boys," continued the straw boss, "was ridin' there th' day before th' round-up started, comin' back from th' Kiowa. He had his choice of th' two trails around the butte, an' just for a change he took th' one goin' up th' Broken Jug. It was a little longer an' some harder, but he went up along it. When he got to that pasture he didn't see no cattle. Well, they mighta watered an' then drifted back, out of his sight. Cattle can get outa sight right easy, over there. He looked th' place over an' figgered they wouldn't stay away very long, because th' feed looked right good."

Corson nodded again as the straw boss paused, and again said nothing.

"Well, as a matter of fact," said the BLR foreman, "when he did speak about it, some days later, an' I got to questionin' him right close, he allowed that th' feed looked too damn' good; looked like nothin' had been in there grazin' for quite a spell. He didn't say anythin' about it when he got home to th' ranch that

day, because we was all lathered up gettin' ready to go
out with th' wagon th' next mornin'. He had been
loafin' on his breakin' job, an' had to put in most of
his time breakin' in th' green hosses that he'd drawed
for his string.

"When he spoke about it later, like I said, I didn't
work up no sweat over it. We were right in th' middle
of heavy gathers, an' I knew, too, that we would be
workin' that part of th' range inside of a week. Well,
we did work it, an' we reckoned that we got them
critters, but I'm gettin' less shore of that every day.
When we haul th' wagon back to th' ranch, I aim to
spend some time ridin' round over there. An' from
what you've just told me, I wish I'd done th' ridin'
round before now, round-up or no round-up. So far
as th' JM's concerned, you can ride easy: they ain't got
an animal that don't belong to 'em. Anyhow, not up on
that ridge range."

"Has Black Jack Meadows, or any of his boys,
worked for you *since* th' round-up layout was *first*
given out?" asked Corson, curiously.

"Yeah: Black Jack's not very much on size, but he's
shore handy with a forge. I had him put our wagon
in shape for th' spring work."

"Did he work for you *after* th' original assign-
ments were changed?" persisted the sheriff.

"No; he didn't; but everybody knowed about th'
change right quick. It warn't no secret."

"Yes. How did you work th' ridge?" asked the sheriff.

"Took it in sections, along th' bottom, first," answered the straw boss. "You throw worked cattle uphill an' they'll likely work back down. That means that you'll gather a lot of th' same critters over an' over ag'in, if you work from th' top of th' ridge down. We worked north along th' bottom, throwin' th' cattle behind us an' below us. Then we turned an' worked back over th' middle benches. Then we turned ag'in an' went back along th' top of th' ridge, throwin' back th' cattle on th' downhill side. Th' Bar W was workin' th' same way over on their own side of th' ridge."

"Then you made three sweeps, north an' south?" asked the sheriff.

"Yeah; an' we shore swept clean."

"An' now yo're all through between this creek an' th' ridge," muttered Corson without intending to put it into question form. He himself would have worked that ridge, bottom to top, in a straight line, taking it as it came; but he had nothing to do with the layout of the work at the BLR wagon.

"Yes, we're plumb through, over there, an' glad of it," replied the straw boss.

Corson nodded. He turned and looked at his companion, a steady, level look.

"Just between me an' you, Jerry, three ornery hombres loosened up at me at long range, damn' long range, back at th' old 'dobe ruins. They could shoot right good, too. They used glasses, too, because they saw every move I made. Yo're right shore that Slade ate dinner with you?"

"Yes, he did. You mean to tell me that you was shot at?"

"Yeah. From three different places at near th' same time. I figgered it two, three ways; an' then I kinda expected a fourth shot, from a plumb different direction."

"Yeah? You musta had a reason. My boys were all with th' cattle. Slade was settin' in camp when I rode in. I sent another rep. over to yore outfit as soon as I learned that Slade had cut his string. I'm goin' to tie a knot in his tail, first thing he knows. When I send a man out to another wagon, I expect him to stick with it till th' job's done. An' so he went sour right after Nueces found that cached herd, huh?"

"Yes," answered Corson, nodding; "but he shore wanted to run yore brand on 'em, on *all* of 'em. He wanted to do that right bad."

"Huh! He mighta been playin' to save his face; or he might not. We'll mebby find out which, later on; but him wantin' to put our brand on th' whole lot of 'em didn't make it look any too good for us, did it?"

"Yo're right; it didn't," admitted Corson; "but I've played poker too long to believe everythin' I hear an' see. It struck me that Slade was bluffin'. You can save me quite a job if you'll kinda keep an eye on him. I can't be everywhere at once, an' this thing seems to take a lot of ridin'. It's spread out considerable. An' besides, I got to get this horse back on th' ranch. I been ridin' him purty hard, an' his forefeet are gettin' a mite tender. I shod him for workin' cattle, an' then never got th' chance to do it."

"Go home by way of our headquarters," said the straw boss. "Tell th' boys there that I said for 'em to slap a pair of shoes onto him. It ain't very far outa yore way, an' you'll save fifty, sixty miles of barefoot ridin'."

"Might do that, but I ain't shore till I see how things break," said Corson. "I'm figgerin' on yankin' his shoes off an' turnin' him out on th' range. My roan is a better trail horse. You reckon it's time to eat?"

"Yeah; must be. Let's go back. Ain't no use of gettin' a good range cook all riled up for nothin'. What you think of this Association round-up idear?"

"I think it's th' proper idear," answered the sheriff.

"Yeah, it is; but there's one thing about it that I hate like I hate a heel-fly. It's a damn' shame to slap th' Association brand onto every maverick. That shore sticks in my craw."

CHAPTER VIII

THE hard press of work at the Baylor wagon was now over, and the riders showed it in various ways. No longer were the cattle coming so thick as to call for working the gathers in sections or holding a herd during the night. Up to now the stray herd had been a big one, but now it was growing no larger. It was grazing placidly on the bed ground, a swell rising up from the pasture floor, where the cattle were caressed by every movement of the wind. From now on the gathers would be made in the morning and the herds worked in the afternoons. The straw boss was holding nothing in the Baylor mark, since they were squarely on their own ranch, but turning them back on the range as soon as the branding irons were lifted. After a few days more the stray herd would begin to shrink rapidly as the various stray men went home with their drags.

The men rode in to the wagon hungry, in good spirits. They acted as if a tension had been removed, the tension of hard and persistent work, as, indeed, it had. From now on to the end of the round-up it would be more or less of a romp, with plenty of time for fun.

Signs of this became apparent when the Turkey Track rider loafed over to where the straw boss and the sheriff were idly talking. He nodded, dropped to his haunches, and pulled at a weed stem growing near his feet.

"I ain't seen nothin' in our mark for five days," he said, suggestively.

The straw boss nodded in turn. The statement was true. The wagon had worked well beyond the wanderings of any Turkey Track strays.

"You want to cut yore string an' drag?" he asked.

"Shore like to," answered the Turkey Track representative; "but not if you want me to stay."

"No reason a-tall for you to stay," said the straw boss, smiling. "Th' work's gettin' lighter every day. If we should come acrost any of yore critters we'll slap on yore brand an' drive 'em home with us, an' hold 'em for you. There ain't no use of th' Chain rider stayin' with us, neither. We ain't picked up one of his animals since we made th' second sweep along th' ridge. Both of you boys might as well go home, an' tell my reps. with yore wagons to do th' same. I hope both of you boys will be with us ag'in in th' fall."

"My boss shore will be glad to see me ag'in," said the stray man, with a grin. "He's just been waitin' for this here round-up to get over, so he can send some of us up th' trail after some registered cows he's bought. He's shore spendin' money; but he's gettin' th' stuff."

"Is French goin' in for registered stuff?" asked Corson.

"Little bit," answered Turkey Track. "He figgers on raisin' our own registered bulls."

"Good idear; cost him less, an' they'll be acclimated," said the straw boss. He turned to the sheriff. "You been doin' that for two, three years, ain't you?"

Corson nodded and smiled a little.

"Yes. I been raisin' registered bulls for Baylor without him knowin' it," he admitted, laughing gently, "against th' time when he'd have to cross his Herefords; an' then he went over west an' picked up his Durhams at a sheriff's sale."

The straw boss chuckled, looked thoughtfully at the stray man, and nodded.

"Cut yore string, an' get yore cattle together right after breakfast. It's too late to do anythin' now."

"Yeah. I'll do that in th' mornin'. Me an' th' Chain rep. will throw in together, an' split 'em near th' Alkali Holes."

"All right: that's yore own business," said the straw boss, and turned to Corson. "How old are them registered bulls you reckoned you was raisin' for us?"

"Two years," answered the sheriff.

"Be about right for us next year," grunted the straw boss. "We didn't pick up enough Durhams, over west, an' Baylor an' me have been talkin' about gettin' more of 'em. It's a tough enough breed, but even so, we'd rather have them that was born an' raised right here

in this part of th' country. I'll talk to th' old man
when we get back home."

"Come an' get it!" bawled the cook with leather
lungs, and was instantly obeyed.

After supper was over Corson listened to the conversation going on about him, particularly to what
Slade had to say, and to whom he talked. The man had
grown a little sullen when he had ridden in and found
the sheriff at the wagon in conversation with the
straw boss, and Corson had felt the rider's eyes on
him all during the meal. It was light yet, and would
not be dark for two hours. The straw boss had paid
Slade no more attention than he had to any other
man present; but after the extra cups of coffee were
disposed of and tobacco smoke began to rise into the
air, he turned suddenly and faced his representative
to the JC wagon.

"How come you cut yore string, Slade?" he demanded, coldly.

Slade's sullen eyes flicked to Corson and then back
to his boss.

"They got to ridin' me too damn' hard," he
growled.

"When did you leave their wagon?" persisted the
straw boss.

Slade told him, and the straw boss became thoughtful. After a moment he spoke again, crisply.

"What did you do with yore drag?"

"Turned it loose on our range," answered the rider.

"Oh, then you came home by th' south?"

"Yeah. I come up th' Kiowa an' through Brown Canyon," said Slade.

Corson's expressionless face remained expressionless at the calm enunciation of this most palpable lie. Slade had come home through Packers Gap, and if he had turned his little herd of stray cattle loose on Baylor range, then he must have been riding a bird instead of a horse. He had gotten rid of the cattle before the sheriff had seen him at the JM ranch. Had he turned his little stray herd loose on Baylor range, where he said he had, and then got back to the JM, it would have taken him at least one full day more than he had had at his disposal.

"You see any numbers of our cattle, over where you worked?" asked the straw boss, casually.

Slade shot a venomous look at the sheriff, thought swiftly, and decided to play safe and to tell what he held to be the truth, since it might have been already told by Corson.

"Yeah; forty-two of 'em in one bunch," he growled. "Right up on th' fringe of th' JC range, holed up as slick an' purty as you ever saw. Struck me as bein' damn' funny!" He was now looking Corson squarely in the eyes. "I wanted to slap our brand on 'em, but that damn' Nueces wouldn't hear of it."

"Meanin'?" gently asked the sheriff.

"I don't know just what it means!" retorted Slade, angrily. "But mebby you do."

"Yeah," answered the sheriff, smiling thinly. "Mebby I do."

"Anythin' to show that they belonged to us?" asked the straw boss.

"I knowed three of 'em right well!"

"That's good," grunted the straw boss. "An' they wouldn't let you burn 'em in our mark, huh?"

"No, they wouldn't! That horse-faced —— —— got right fond of Association rules, then an' there! They slapped th' CA Circle Star onto every last one of 'em. What th' hell: with me there they didn't dare do anythin' else!"

"Where'd you turn yore little bunch of strays loose?" asked the sheriff, suddenly, hoping for a misplay.

"None of yore damn' business!" snapped Slade, his face crinkling with anger. He had already told them that.

"Mebby yo're right, Slade," said the straw boss, calmly. "It mebby ain't none of his business, but shore as hell it's some of mine. Where'd you turn 'em loose?"

"I've told you that," growled the rider. "Just this side of Brown Canyon."

"You drove a herd of cows an' calves all th' way from our wagon, up th' Kiowa, through Brown Canyon, an' turned 'em loose there, in th' time you had?" asked Corson, crisply.

"Said so, didn't I?" snapped Slade, his eyes glowing with anger.

"You sayin' so don't mean a damn' thing to me!" retorted the sheriff.

"Yeah?"

"Yeah!" snapped Corson, and continued his inquisition. "An' then, after doin' all that, instead of ridin' on to yore own home ranch, less than five miles away, or of comin' on in to this wagon," persisted Corson, "you had time enough left to ride over to Packers Gap, ride down Lucas Arroyo, an' reach this wagon in time to eat dinner here today?"

"You been eatin' loco!" snapped Slade, slowly getting to his feet. "I ain't been over Packers Gap in weeks!"

Corson glanced swiftly at the straw boss and back to the angry puncher, watching him narrowly.

"Jerry," said the sheriff, very slowly. "Slade was ridin' a bay geldin' when he went down through Lucas Arroyo. There are four, five places, in there, where its shoes show up right plain in th' clay. Have one of th' boys cut that hoss out of th' cavvy, an' we'll take it back there, an' match them prints. I know what I'm talkin' about when it comes to tracks."

"What you mean?" shouted Slade, tense and set.

"Don't you know?" asked the sheriff, ironically. He, too, was set and tense.

"No, I don't know!" shouted Slade.

"All right, then: I'll tell you," said the sheriff, grimly. "I mean that no man livin', ridin' th' horse you was ridin', can drive a bunch of cows an' calves th' sixty miles you said you drove 'em, over that kinda range, turn 'em loose where you said you did, go down th' Carson road, up over th' Gap, down Lucas Arroyo, an' then hit this wagon when you did. I mean that those cattle were not turned loose near Brown Canyon. Where's yore remuda?"

"An' *that's* none of yore damn' business!" shouted Slade.

"But it's a hell of a lot of *my* business," said the straw boss, suddenly taking part in the conversation. "What'd you do with yore hosses?"

"Throwed 'em up onto our range!" snapped Slade. "I knowed that we was all through th' hard work, an' wouldn't need 'em out here."

"You pull their shoes before you turned 'em loose?" asked the straw boss, coldly.

"No!" snapped Slade. "I didn't have a tool on me, an' I didn't have th' time. I wanted to get to this wagon an' go to work."

"You was so damn' anxious to get here an' go to work that instead of comin' here, you went foolin' down th' Kiowa, an' over th' Gap?" asked the straw boss.

"I didn't do nothin' of th' kind!" retorted Slade. "I come on right straight here. You saw me ride in from th' ranch trail!"

"How'd that geldin's tracks get into th' clay in Lucas Arroyo?" asked the straw boss.

"They never got there a-tall!" yelled Slade.

"I saw him ridin down th' arroyo," said the sheriff, shortly.

"You know —— —— well you didn't!" cried the harassed puncher. "You goin' to stand for talk like that, boss?"

"Me?" inquired the straw boss, slowly. "*Me* stand for it? I got nothin' to do with it. Instead of talkin' to me, you better listen to what Corson has to say to you, because you might be able to get a job with him. Yo're all through here. Yo're fired."

"Yo're all through here, an' on this whole range, Slade," said the sheriff. "Me an' you'll go off an' find that little bunch of cattle that you turned loose near Brown Canyon, an' we'll hunt up th' hosses so you can pull them shoes. First thing in th' mornin'."

"I'll see you in hell first!" snapped the enraged puncher.

"Well, only time will tell about that," replied the sheriff. "First thing in th' mornin'," he repeated.

"With me an' some of th' boys," amended the straw boss, slowly.

"Yeah?" sneered Slade, glaring at his erstwhile boss. "You just said I'm all through here. I told you where I throwed th' strays, an' th' hosses. If you want 'em, then go get 'em; but *I'm* through!" He was tense, hair-trigger; desperate and at bay. He had had no

time to make up a better story, a story which would
stand scrutiny, not dreaming that he would be called
upon to explain his movements since leaving the JC
wagon.

He was thinking swiftly. Corson had followed him?
Yes: the only question was, how closely? Where had
he picked up his trail? He had turned the horses loose,
but he had no fear on that score: they were all geld-
ings, and had been born on the Baylor range. They
would return to it. They might even have returned by
now. As to the stray cut he had taken from the JC
stray herd, they were ordinary cattle, and once let
loose on the range could hardly be identified. If he had
to, he could lead the straw boss to the western end of
Brown Canyon, where cattle were thick, point out any
bunch of them, and claim them to be the ones in question. He had had three days for the total of his riding. All right: he'd stay with his story. If he had
driven the cattle over the shortest route, he could have
cut nearly twenty miles from the sheriff's estimate of
sixty.

"You'll find that stray cut where I said I left 'em,"
he asserted. "They're there because I put 'em there!
As to not havin' time to do all th' ridin' Corson says I
did, even if I rode where he said, I had time enough."

"You didn't if you drove them cattle up th' Kiowa
an' through Brown Canyon," said the straw boss.

"Huh! I didn't say how *far* up th' Kiowa I drove
'em, did I?" asked the puncher.

"No," admitted the straw boss: "you didn't. But you can say so now."

"I'm not sayin' anythin'!" snapped Slade. "An' you'll find th' remuda headin' for home."

"Just where did you turn them hosses loose?" asked the sheriff thoughtfully.

"Yo're so —— —— smart, I'm goin' to let you find that out for yoreself!"

"Just where did you turn them hosses loose?" asked the straw boss.

"You better ask somebody that's on yore payroll!" retorted Slade. "I would of told you that before, if you'd asked me right; but I ain't tellin' you now."

It was an important point. It would either make or break his story, and the sheriff, knowing this, pressed it.

"You'll take us there in th' mornin', Slade," he said, grimly. "I figger it'll tell us right close where you hit th' Kiowa."

"It'll tell you nothin' because I won't be taken there!" snapped the puncher.

"You'll take us there if we have to drag you at th' end of a rope!" snapped Corson, slowly getting to his feet. "We'll iron one of yore wrists to a wagon spoke tonight, so you'll be on hand in th' mornin'. You'll go if we have to drag you with a rope!" he repeated.

Slade paled a little. He did not like to hear about ropes. How much did this so-and-so sheriff know? He knew about Packers Gap and the ride down Lucas

Arroyo; and that meant that it was possible he knew that the Meadows boys rode with him. That was dangerous knowledge. The sheriff had the reputation, well earned, of being a first-class trailer. And then a new thought made him stiffen and threw him into a panic: if they searched for the remuda they would be searching ground that he did not dare let them search. He had to tell them the truth.

"All right," he said, with a sneer. "You fellers are so damn' smart that I'm goin' to show my hand. I knowed I was all through with this outfit when I left th' JC wagon. I'd made up my mind, then, to throw up th' job. That bein' so, what a fool I would have been to be bothered with that stray cut an' th' remuda. I pushed 'em both. As soon as I got well away from th' wagon, an' out of sight of it, I shoved up over Saddle Pass an' left 'em there. You'll find 'em all next round-up, unless they're worked over into another brand. I left 'em on th' JC range, an' not very far away from Bull Canyon. They'll be right handy for somebody to practise usin' a straight iron on."

Corson's eyes narrowed at this indirect imputation.

"We're not workin' over any brands into th' JC mark," he said; "an' if you've got any brains a-tall, you know that th' Baylor mark can't be worked over into anythin' else that would do anybody any good."

"No!" snapped Slade. This man Corson knew too much about what had been going on out on the ranges. His mouth had to be closed. "No!" he repeated, nastily; "but their next year's calves won't have any brand! What about that forty-two head that we found hid out in JC territory?"

"Meanin' that we're on th' rustle?" coldly demanded the sheriff and owner of the JC ranch.

"Reckon you know what I mean!" retorted Slade. "Somebody's throwin' a wide loop down here. An' who would gain anythin' by holin' up Baylor yearlin' mavericks on yore own range?"

"Make it plain, Slade," said the sheriff. "You might as well, because you've gone too far now to be backin' out."

"Plain?" jeered the puncher, slouching a little. "Ain't I done that?"

"Fill yore hand!" said the sheriff clearly but softly.

Slade's reply was motion, motion as swift as the striking head of a snake. The two heavy roars seemed to come together. Slade fell backward as Corson staggered, his gun falling from his hand. The sheriff tossed his own gun into his left hand, and recovered his balance, ready to shoot again if the need arose. Men were bending over the Baylor rider. One of them raised his head and looked slowly around.

"Hole through his shoulder," he said, and explained the fall. "He must have been a mite off balance."

"Put him in th' wagon an' take him down to Bentley," said the straw boss, coldly, as he strode toward the sheriff. "Get you bad, Corson?" he asked, a little anxiously.

"No. Just grazed my elbow. My arm's numb. Be all right in a few minutes. Touched th' funny bone, I reckon. I didn't want to kill him, Jerry," he said, in a low voice. "I want him to get well, an' stay loose. He's worth a lot more to me, that way."

"Where you figger he left that cut, an' them hosses?" asked the straw boss in tones so low that Corson barely heard them.

"Where he said he did, th' last time. Every animal carries th' BLR mark, an' it can't be changed. They're all right. None of 'em are worth a lead two-bit piece to a rustler. As a matter of fact, they'd just braid a rope for his hangin', an' he'd know it."

"Then why did you push him so hard?" asked the straw boss, curiously.

"Two or three reasons, Jerry," slowly answered the sheriff. "One of 'em was that I figgered that you an' Baylor would be a whole lot better off if Slade got through workin' for you. Th' other reasons are th' sheriff's business."

"Yo're dead shore he was over Packers Gap way?" persisted the straw boss. "Yo're right shore of them prints?"

Corson watched the work horses being hitched to the wagon. Slade already was inside the vehicle.

"Yes; but that ain't all, Jerry. I *saw* him, myself; an' I saw some other things. Yo're dead shore that you cleaned that ridge, an' cleaned it good?"

"Yeah; nothin' was overlooked, Corson. We'd been

a little lazy, up there, other round-ups; but this year I made up my mind that there wouldn't be a square yard of that whole slope that was overlooked. An', by G——, there wasn't!"

"All right: that's good," replied the sheriff. "That's a right big section for one man to comb, an' I'll have enough country to ride over without addin' that stretch to it."

The JC representative rode up and stopped.

"I'm goin' in with th' wagon, Bob, so that —— —— won't get away from us after he's doctored up."

Corson turned a surprised face to the rider.

"He ain't under arrest. Don't start workin' up no lather. Strip yore saddle off, an' take things easy."

"Ain't you figgerin' on makin' him take you to where he left them cattle an' turned loose his string?" asked the puncher in surprise.

"Don't need to do that now," answered the sheriff, and then he laughed as he saw his puncher's face fall. "There's an old sayin' about skinnin' cats. Strip off yore saddle."

CHAPTER IX

When one closes one's eyes and thinks of Western streams, the mental picture will most often show one type—steep, barren banks rising perpendicularly from ten to fifty feet, broken here and there by dry gullies, and twisting like a snake's course. The bottoms, in the summer months, are usually dry or, at best, a mere trickle of water running over and under a bed of sand and gravel from ten to twenty times the width of the stream.

If they are dry it is possible in many cases to dig down into the sand, wait for a few minutes, and then scoop up a few handfuls of roiled and unpleasant water. The surrounding country, usually being innocent of trees and other retainers of water, and being long, rolling slopes with nothing to check and hold a surface flow, turns these arid gashes into swift death traps when heavy rains fall higher up on the watersheds. The result very often is a wall of water roaring down these open pipes without warning. A cloudburst miles away will here work its greatest havoc. Many travelers have been overwhelmed, horses, wagons, and all, by a seething flood which lasted perhaps ten minutes. An hour later and the stream would be as dry as usual. All Western streams are not this kind; but because of the striking characteristics of this one type, it is the picture which most often will come to mind.

Crooked Creek was such a stream, and it was characteristic of nine-tenths of the streams in this section of the country. A man might ride along on its bottom for forty miles and never once show his head above the perpendicular banks. The Bentley trail followed along its east bank at varying distances from it and never once crossed it. This was in strong contrast to the trail along the Kiowa, which crossed the latter stream twenty-six times in forty-odd miles, and had been hated for this reason by every man who had ever taken a wagon along it. Sandy river bottoms are often treacherous. The Kiowa was the principal exception to the type of stream just described.

Corson left the Baylor wagon right after breakfast the following morning and rode back the way he had come until the shoulder of a ridge put him out of sight of the camp and the men out riding on circle. He had been shot at the day before, and he had not forgotten the incident. He was returning to the general vicinity of that unpleasant episode, but he was not going back by way of the trail. He was going to return by following along over the sunken bed of the creek, not only for the purpose of keeping out of sight, but also to pick up more quickly and easily the tracks of the distant marksmen.

Crooked Creek lay about a third of a mile west of

the old adobe trading post, and the shots must have come from points west of that. If the shooters had belonged to the country east of the creek, which he strongly suspected to be the case, then they must have crossed the creek at some place or other in order to get home. Nothing that walked on hoofs could cross that ribbon of sand and gravel without leaving some sign of its passing. And when he came to those signs he believed that they would lead him to or in the direction of the JM ranch, if he could follow them that far on the hard range soil.

The reasons for his belief have already been given, if they can be called reasons. In Western parlance "he had a feeling" that Black Jack Meadows and his boys had played the parts of riflemen on that occasion. It was just his luck, he bitterly reflected, to be opposed to the menfolk of her family; but there was no thought in his mind of abandoning the trail or of dodging the issues as they arose. A cattle thief was a cattle thief, and a sniper was a sniper, no matter whose father or brothers they might be.

He came to the precipitous bank of the creek and rode along it, looking for a way down. He could have reached the bottom by spectacular riding, but his first thought, in matters of this kind, was for the welfare of his horse. The way down was soon provided by a gully, and he gained the bottom easily, and instinctively thought of the trap he was in if heavy rain should fall on the upper end of the watershed. He thought of it, and put it out of his mind with the same ease with which a dweller of California might shelve thoughts of earthquakes. The odds were so great against a flood at any particular time that it became almost absurd.

He also thought of the trap he was in if one or all of the long-range riflemen of the day before should be lying in wait on the top of the bank in anticipation of this move on his part; but this, also, was a necessary risk; to ride along the plain would be as risky, and would advertise his presence and purpose as far as a man could see. He had to make a choice of going on, or of giving up the attempt; and he had already made it.

It was noon by the sun when he took advantage of another gully and rode up out of the stream bed. He had seen no tracks, and he had long since passed the vicinity of the adobe ruins, and Bentley, as well. He pushed eastward in the direction of the Old California Trail and reached it after a six-mile ride, which told him that he had been right in believing himself to have passed the town. Two hours later he rode into Bentley from the north and swung down in front of the so-called hotel. He had long since thrown away the stale food provided by the Bar W cook, and he was hungry, despite the fact that range riders are more or less accustomed to go without a noon meal. The hotel dining room was closed, but he found a restaurant run by a Mexican.

As he slowly chewed his food he was debating what to do next. It was too late in the day to ride on to the JC or the Bar W. He would drop in for a moment at the marshal's office and then return to the Baylor wagon and spend the night there. He would much rather roll up in his blankets out in the open than to sleep in a comfortable bed under a roof.

Apparently the marshal had not moved since the day before, for his legs were crossed on the chair, with the same careful allowance made for spur clearance. Just why the marshal should wear spurs in town, when he seldom did any riding, was nobody's business but his own, but the sheriff could not help asking himself the question. The answer was somewhat obvious: he might be too lazy to remove them.

"Set," grunted the town officer, and waved at a chair.

"No time to," replied Corson, impatiently. "Did th' doctor fix up Slade's shoulder all right?"

"Y-e-p," grunted the marshal. He shoved a calloused finger tip down into the pipe bowl and regarded his visitor through sleepy eyes.

"I allus heard you was a right good shot," he remarked, sadly.

"Yeah?"

"Y-e-p."

"Which just goes to show that you can't believe all you hear," said Corson, gravely.

"Lord, I knowed that forty, fifty year ago," replied the marshal.

"Uh-huh," grunted Corson.

"A man ain't worth nothin' to nobody when he's dead," stated the marshal sententiously.

"Well," replied the sheriff, smiling a little, "I don't reckon you have to copper that."

"It is sorta generally admitted," said the marshal, nodding wisely. He puffed thoughtfully for a few moments. "Nobody would reckon that he had a forty-five slug through his rifle shoulder, th' way he rode outa town."

"Yeah. What way did he ride outa town?" asked the sheriff, with a little curiosity.

"Pert, sassy, an' south."

Corson looked curiously at the speaker. South? That would be in the direction of the Baylor wagon and the Baylor ranch; and it also would be in the direction of the old trail up Lucas Arroyo and over the Gap.

"But he's all through with th' Baylor outfit," said the sheriff, slowly, and waited. He did not wait in vain.

"Officially, yes; practically, mebby not," said the marshal. "He rode off with Black Jack Meadows an' his boys."

Corson retraced a course of thought which had originated earlier in the day: if the hidden marksmen of the day before had been the menfolk of the Meadows family, then they would have had to cross

Crooked Creek to get over to their sharpshooting positions, and cross it again to leave them, and go home. He had found no signs of either crossing. He looked closely at his companion.

"You see Black Jack an' his boys after I left you yesterday?" he asked, carelessly.

"Y-e-p. They come back about an hour after you left. They'll shore get cross-eyed, watchin' my door so close."

Corson sighed with relief. Perhaps, after all, he would not have to tangle up with her family. The thought pleased him and made him glow a little. If Black Jack and his boys had been in Bentley an hour after he, himself, had left town, then they could not have been mixed up in the long-range shooting.

This thought was followed by one not so pleasant: he now had no idea whatever regarding the identity of the dry-gulchers. Somewhere on the range, or in this town, were three unknown and unsuspected men who wanted to shoot him. He might stand shoulder to shoulder with them at some bar, or even talk with them, without the slightest suspicion as to their intentions.

Why had they shot at a range so long as practically to assure missing him? They had shown their hands, in a way, without accomplishing anything but to put him on his guard, and from their point of view that could hardly be considered an accomplishment: it would be a mistake. But was it a mistake? Had they intended it as a gesture? Were they aroused by his riding and questioning after the discovery of the cached herd, and hoped to make him show less interest in their affairs? Were they strongly hinting for him to keep on the east side of Crooked Creek? They must know him too well for that: his reputation would tell them otherwise. And there was a thought: he would take a good look at the semi-arid country west of the creek, and he would do it the following day.

He remembered that the forefeet of his horse were getting steadily more tender: all right, he would have them shod, and not give himself any further chance to forget about it. Then he would buy some supplies, and give that Dry Arroyo country an inspection. It would not be necessary to ride back and forth across it, which would take days: all he had to do was to circle it, looking for tracks leading in or out of it; tracks of a number of cattle at once, herd tracks. Solitary tracks, here and there, would not tell him much, except that a few cattle were straying. He turned slowly and faced the door.

"My horse needs shoein'," he said, abruptly.

"Noticed he was a mite tender in th' fore hoofs," replied the marshal. "You got a long ride ahead of you."

"No," said the sheriff. "I've changed my mind, an' figger to stay in town overnight. Got a new job on my hands."

"Might be a good idear," grunted the marshal.

"Yes. I might learn a little somethin' from th' gamblin' you say is goin' on."

"Might," agreed the marshal, nodding. "You comin' back here after yore hoss is shod?" he asked, somewhat anxiously. He enjoyed having company, and he liked the sheriff.

"Reckon so," answered Corson, "after I drift around a little." He stepped through the door, mounted, and rode straight to the blacksmith shop, a score of yards distant.

The smith picked up one hoof after another, and slowly straightened his back.

"Won't have to bridge 'em," he grunted. "That's a fool way to shoe a hoss."

"Put light shoes on him," said Corson, ignoring the gratuitous comment. "I don't want to make him clumsy."

"Clumsy? Hell!" snorted the smith. "You fellers reckon all alike. You reckon a little more iron will make any difference in th' way *he* picks up?" He reached an arm behind him and groped for the handle of the bellows. Then he drove home his point. "He ain't no race hoss, is he?" he asked with heavy sarcasm.

"Race horse or no race horse, I want light shoes on him," said the sheriff, going toward a box and seating himself to watch the work.

The smith grunted something under his breath,

glanced at the brand, and then turned mildly curious eyes on his placid customer.

"Reckon you might be Sheriff Corson," he said.

"Yo're right."

"We don't see you over this way very much," stated the smith. The words held a challenge.

"Mebby not," grunted Corson. "I'm usually where I'm needed."

"Are, huh?" inquired the smith, stirring the fire with a shoe he had just put in. He laid the tongs across the anvil. "Are, huh?" he repeated, somewhat derisively.

"Yeah."

The silence lasted until the job was done. Then Corson got off the box and led the horse outside. The smith loafed to the door and leaned against the casing, idly jingling the silver coins the sheriff had just given him.

"An' so yo're usually where yo're needed?" he gently inquired, squinting speculatively at the mounting officer.

"Yes. Town affairs are no business of mine till I'm sent for," said the horseman, and swung away toward the hotel.

He stabled the horse, hung his riding gear on the place provided for it, strode around the building and entered the office.

"Fix me up for th' night?" he asked the frowsy clerk. "I just put my horse in th' stable."

The clerk gazed at him calmly, impersonally; and

then, something clicking in his mind, the gaze became pointedly personal. Black Jack Meadows was a friend of his, and he now recalled that the sheriff was in town. This stranger answered the description he had heard.

"Room an' bawth?" inquired the clerk, with what he believed was a heavy English accent, and intended to be insulting.

"Yes!" snapped Corson, well knowing that such a combination was not to be found in Bentley's one hotel.

"But we 'aven't any bawth," drawled the clerk. In his own peculiar way he was enjoying himself. "I'll give you Number Six," he said.

"Where is it?" asked the sheriff, thinking of location in reference to other parts of the building.

"Right here, under this roof," said the clerk.

"Just one more smart yip outa you," said the sheriff, pressing solidly against his own side of the counter, "an' I'll smear yore nose over both yore ears, an' let th' rest of it run down yore dirty shirt!"

The clerk stepped back, the insolence gone from his face as if wiped off with a sponge. He looked into a pair of blazing eyes levelly regarding him.

"Number Six is over th' kitchen," he hastily explained; "but I reckon it won't be comfortable this kinda weather. I'll give you Number Two, corner room in front."

Corson still gazed at him, and then slowly signed

the register, put the room key into a pocket and, turning abruptly on his heel, walked out of the building. When he stopped he was inside the marshal's office, and his eyes still blazed.

The marshal placidly continued his game of solitaire after a brief glance and nod. He was no engineer, but he believed that he knew steam pressure when he saw it.

"Just had some words with th' hotel clerk," finally said the visitor.

"Pimply little tumblebug," grunted the marshal, without looking up.

"An' th' blacksmith was hostile as soon as he saw th' brand," growled Corson. "What's th' matter with this town?"

"I told you that th' gamblin' has clum up to new heights," said the local officer.

"What th' hell's that got to do with me?" growled the sheriff. "I ain't aimin' to stop it! If that's anybody's job, it's yours!"

"That's right, you ain't," replied the marshal, carefully putting the six of hearts on the seven of spades, after wiping off the seven to see just what it was. "They're right fond of their games."

"But, damn it all!" exploded the sheriff. "I just said I ain't scotchin' th' gamblin'!"

"That's so: you just did," admitted the marshal. "But you don't want to fergit that fellers that has got used to playin' four-bits ante, an' five-dollar limit, don't hanker much to go back to no measly two-bit an' one-dollar game. They've been spoiled."

"Mebby," grunted Corson, doubtfully. "You reckon I oughta go out on th' corner an' make a speech, sayin' I ain't figgerin' to hobble no games of chance, honest or otherwise?"

His sarcasm was lost on the sleepy, lazy local peace officer.

"That wouldn't make a mite of difference," said the marshal, flatly.

"Meanin' they wouldn't believe me?"

"An' *that* wouldn't make no difference, neither; whether they believed you or not. That ain't the p'int." He reached out a card. "Black five on th' red six, an' red four on th' five," he muttered, making the plays.

"Then what you drivin' at?" persisted the sheriff.

"When I was a yearlin', down Dodge City way, I saw buffalo hunters spend a hundred dollars in a single night, night after night. I was one of 'em. Before I quit, most of 'em couldn't spend a dollar, all at once."

"You must have been there quite a spell," commented Corson, his wits on set triggers.

"Quite a spell," agreed the marshal. "Until after there weren't no more buffalo. An' then there warn't no more heavy spendin'." He sighed with regret. "Then th' big games got kinda scarce, except among th' cattlemen."

Corson was leaning forward on the chair, regarding the older man with a complimentary stare. The silence held for perhaps a minute, and then the sheriff slowly stood up, and without thought readjusted the two low-hung holsters to a nicer fit.

"I'm goin' up to th' general store," he said. "See you later."

"But I've done told you that it was two hundred an' twenty-five dollars, without no odd cents," complained the marshal, hastily putting the cards aside.

"I'm not thinkin' about that quarterly check," snapped the sheriff, and was gone.

The marshal watched him disappear through the door, and then thoughtfully rubbed the stubble on his chin.

"Huh!" he muttered. "There he is, all lathered up ag'in."

CHAPTER X

Corson's belated lunch had been a light one, calculated to hold him until suppertime, and it was past suppertime now. He glanced at the little pile of supplies in a corner of the room, checking them against the needs of his coming journey, stepped through the door and closed it behind him. He reached the hotel dining room just as the doors were closing, and did justice to the food which, to his surprise, was well cooked and tasty. When he reached the street the town was just beginning to come to life, and he moved slowly along toward the marshal's office.

Bentley's population seemingly had doubled since the sheriff had gone to the hotel, and men were still riding into town, keeping the deep dust stirred up. Horses stood at the tie rails outside the various buildings, and tinny pianos and scratchy fiddles added their quota to the total of the sounds along the main street. Loud talk, laughter, the scraping of booted feet on sanded floors, and an occasional Rebel yell gave notice to all and sundry that Bentley was waking up. Suddenly he bumped into a man who lurched through the door of the first gambling hall, and forthwith had an argument on his hands, but it was soon over.

"Why'n hell don't you watch where yo're goin'?'" hotly demanded the inebriate, spreading his legs as an aid to balance.

"My fault," chuckled Corson, grinning into the angry face. "I'm so plumb full of liquor that I don't know where I'm at."

The inebriate swayed gently and his anger died down. He slapped the sheriff on the back, and laughed, holding out his hand.

"So'm I," he said. "Put her thar, pardner!"

Corson gravely shook hands, gently tried to disengage his own, and found that he was expected to keep on shaking. He did so.

"Th' town's wakin' up," he said, pumping steadily.

"You shore must be a stranger," replied the inebriate, and chuckled with pride. "You jest wait, pardner; you jest wait awhile!" He loosened his grip so as to be able to use both hands in an all-embracing sweep of the horizon. "When she hums, she hums; an' when she roars, she roars! Wide open, she is: jest like *that!*" and again he waved his arms.

"You stayin' in town this evenin'?" asked the sheriff, with deep but simulated interest.

"Yeah; why?" asked the inebriate with instant suspicion.

"Then I'll see you ag'in," answered the sheriff, slapping a sloping shoulder. "An' we'll see what makes th' town go round."

"Keno, pardner," chuckled the inebriate, teetering

on his heels as his new acquaintance moved on. "But I've seen her go round faster'n she is now," he called, and then whooped loudly and staggered on.

"Hello, stranger!" cried a thin soprano voice from a window across the street. "In a hurry?" it challenged.

"No; but I'm dead broke," answered the sheriff, making the best practical answer to such a hail. It was one which never failed to forestall argument. There was no reply as he walked on.

Argument roared in the Last Chance, with a placating voice cutting into it. The latter, no doubt, belonged to the bartender, trying his best to avert a tragedy. A chorus roared raggedly from the next building, having to do with someone who wanted not to be buried on the l-o-n-e p-r-a-i-r-i-e. The words of the lugubrious song rang through Corson's mind as he kept on toward the marshal's office. It was cheap, maudlin sentiment, untrue to human nature, and composed by someone who cared more for rhyme than for common sense or artistry.

The marshal was seated outside the door, tipped back against the wall. He motioned toward the inside of the building and waited while his caller dragged out a chair. The night was fine, and not yet too cool to force a man indoors.

"Well?" asked the marshal, emptying his odorous pipe.

"Well," grunted the sheriff, seating himself and leaning back comfortably.

They spoke infrequently, being content to let time pass and the twilight to deepen in that silent companionship enjoyed by men. The brighter stars began to wink, and then others, until the sky was filled with them and belted by the silvery magnificence of the Milky Way. A gentle breeze stirred the night-hidden rubbish on the street; and the already noisy town grew noisier. Somewhere a horse squealed, and the muffled sound of the kick told that it had landed on hide and ribs as tough as its own. There came a shot, a yell, and a sudden burst of cursing.

The marshal dropped forward and stood up. He strode rapidly up the street toward the excitement, with Corson crowding his heels.

The general noise, for an instant hushed by the crash of the gun, took on new volume. A man lurched through a door and for a moment was plainly revealed by the lights from within. Blood was spreading over his shirt sleeve. Another man jumped through the door, his gun up even with his cheek, ready for the deadly chop. Before it could fall, the marshal leaped, a swinging fist preceding him. It landed flush, and the belligerent went down in a heap. As he struck the ground the wounded man leaped for him, both heels directed at the prostrate face.

The sheriff's right shoulder hunched suddenly and his arm shot out. The second belligerent, already in the air, was turned around by the blow, and dropped like a sack. In another moment the two men were disarmed and being ignominiously dragged by their collars toward the adobe jail. They revived on the way and finished the remainder of the journey on their own feet, protesting vehemently; and in a few moments found themselves locked up, to sober up and cool off during the rest of the night. The marshal and his visitor returned to their chairs and again tipped back against the wall. The language coming from the rear of the building was frank and uncomplimentary.

"She's startin' a little earlier than usual," said the town peace officer, stating a casual fact casually. "I'll mebby be full up by mornin'. Th' way things are goin' in this town, these days, we shore oughta enlarge th' jail. Puttin' 'em two deep ain't hardly fair to them that's underneath."

Corson smothered his laughter, and rolled a cigarette entirely by the sense of feeling. He was enjoying himself hugely.

"I like th' way you handled that," he said, after a moment. "After all, it wasn't anythin' more than a drunken brawl. They'll be good friends again by mornin'."

"Reg'lar thing," grunted his companion, placidly.

"Yes, I know. What I mean is, I'm glad you didn't shoot."

"Didn't have to," replied the marshal. "When I shoot, I shoot to kill; which means that this little rukus warn't no killing matter. Th' boys like me better for it, too. We get along right well, me an' th' boys. Knowin' me like they do, they know that they don't have to go for no gun to save their lives. Their hand ain't forced. Th' worst they get is a punch on th' jaw, an' a night in jail, which saves 'em a dollar. But they know that I'll shoot if I have to."

Corson stood up, lazily stretching.

"Reckon I'll move along an' look th' town over," he said, and held out his hand in the darkness. "I'll shake hands with you an' say so-long. I reckon that I'll be on my way in th' mornin' long before yo're out of th' blankets."

"So-long," grunted the marshal, shaking hands. "You got a fairly long ride ahead of you, but you could have waited till you got home before you had yore hoss shod in front."

"Not goin' home," replied the sheriff. "Not right away, anyhow."

"I kinda suspicioned that when you went to th' blacksmith," said the marshal. "Well, good luck."

"Same to you," responded the sheriff, grinning widely, and then strode away in the night, heading for the steadily increasing noise and the patches of yellow lamplight straggling through grimy windows. The town was, indeed, awake.

He pushed open the first swinging doors that he came to and entered the "Palace," the doors squeaking softly behind him. The long, narrow room was

crowded, the bar almost hidden by the line-up along it.
In the far, left-hand corner of the room a stud poker
game was under way, a limit game, it seemed, for
small stakes; but stud poker is like a modern, high-
powered rifle, making up for an apologetic caliber by
the pressure behind it. A three-card monte spread
came next, and was heavily patronized; and next to
that was a faro layout, with its dealer, its case-keeper,
and its eager devotees. A man had a better chance at
faro than at any other set game.

"An' what's yourn?" asked a husky, unpleasant
voice from the right-hand wall.

Corson slowly turned and glanced along the line-up,
his eyes flashing to a narrow space between two men,
and behind that, the ugly face of the bartender.

"Nothin', right now," he answered, and again
looked slowly and deliberately around the room.

He saw that three men at the faro table had pushed
back, pocketing their chips, to become carelessly
interested in himself. He smiled understandingly.
Other players eagerly took the vacated places before
the table and the game was not interrupted.

He had never seen these three men before. One of
them had shifty eyes; but the other two suffered from
the opposite complaint, and stared steadily and belligerently at him. That, decided the sheriff, was one
way to start a fight; and a good way, since it was a
silent challenge, and put the responsibility of direct
action upon the person stared at. In his capacity as a

peace officer it was his duty to show resentment slowly, if he could, and not to set the pace in rowdyism. His job was to stop brawls rather than to start them, but at times he found his patience sorely tried. He moved forward, heading for the stud-horse game, ignoring the three ex-farobank players. There would be plenty of time for the development of trouble, and it suited him to follow a lead rather than to make one. In this manner he might possibly learn the identity of the three sharpshooters of Crooked Creek.

The next man to deal gathered up the cards, looked the sheriff in the eye, sneered, shrugged his shoulders, and deftly shuffled. The play went on. Corson leaned against the wall, the end wall, near the corner, from where the whole room lay under his eyes. His left side was against the wall, his right free and unhampered. While he knew none of these men, there was no doubt that many knew him, or at least what he represented. He allowed himself to speculate a little.

It was not just a question of being a peace officer, he reflected, that lay back of this silent hostility. The marshal was a peace officer, and appeared to be well liked, taking him at his own word. It was, perhaps, purely a question of jurisdiction. That of the marshal was narrow, concerned only with what went on in the town itself; that of the sheriff was county-wide. Hostility, more often than not, is founded upon something definite. He let his thoughts run on in logical sequence, and again felt the vagueness, the tenuousness of the things which were engaging his official interest.

He heard a short, sharp laugh, and glanced at the three ex-farobank players, and found three pairs of eyes upon him; and then but two pairs, as the shifty-eyed person looked quickly away. Before anything could come from it, there was a stir along the bar, and a stud-horse player grunted with satisfaction. Other actors were about to step upon the stage.

"We'll have some action now," said the stud-horse player, looking at the swinging doors.

Four men had come in, the first a step ahead of the other three; and the three were shoulder to shoulder, figurative chips lying on their shoulders. They walked with a swagger that announced them to be somebody; and somebody was right: They were Black Jack Meadows's boys, and before them importantly strode their father. Men turned from the bar to nod friendly greetings, and the players at the various tables nodded, waved, or spoke. To an observant observer all this had a meaning.

Black Jack moved steadily on toward the stud-horse game, acknowledging the friendly and sometimes obsequious greetings. He glanced at Corson, still standing near the corner, and looked away again without showing more than casual interest. Black Jack was no mind reader. At the table a chair scraped as a player pushed back and stood up, waiting for Black Jack to take it. Taken it was, and Black Jack slowly seated himself, shoved his hands down into his pockets, and brought them up brimming with bright yellow coins. He pushed the money on the table in front of him and looked around the little circle.

"Same limit an' table stakes?" he mildly inquired, and was satisfied by the answering nods. The three ex-farobank players grinned and sat up a little straighter.

Corson was looking upon a metamorphosis: a caterpillar of poverty who had suddenly become a butterfly of affluence. Remittance man from the East, eh? A few scrub cattle on the high, ridge range, which were good for, in the words of the marshal, tobacco money? If that were so, then Black Jack's tobacco came high. The sheriff saw the deference surrounding the owner of a worthless brand, the three sons acting as a bodyguard standing solidly and silently behind their father. It was a piece of ridiculous, cheap theatricalism, and it was all he could do to keep from loosing a burst of laughter; but he kept it back, held his face expressionless and his eyes cold and blank.

There was a terse, muttered sentence at the studhorse table, and Corson saw Black Jack's eyes shift quickly to himself. The three sons stiffened a little, and had small interest, thereafter, in the rest of the room. For a long moment Black Jack studied the face of the man near the corner and then, making a one-handed gesture of contempt, gave his attention to the game; but his bodyguard had no thought for the game. Here and there throughout the room there were subdued sighs of relief or regret, and the play got under way again.

In the opinion of those in the room the sheriff had been in a damned tight place; and perhaps, even now, the past tense was not the proper one. In more than one mind was the thought that, no matter how poor the sheriff's judgment had been in visiting Bentley, and this one building in particular, there was nothing at all the matter with his nerve; and the men who thought in this way felt a sudden friendliness for the owner of the JC ranch. The majority of those present had no affiliations with Black Jack, and were just the ordinary, common run of customers, and they warmed toward the young man who stood alone near the corner, with his back, physically speaking, to the wall. He might not be without friends if it came to a test.

Corson studiously watched the stud-horse play for several deals, and then moved slowly toward the three-card monte spread, nodded in reply to the dealer's nod, and idly wandered on again. He loitered for a few moments near the faro table, pushed close enough to it to make two small bets, which he lost, and then walked slowly up the room and stopped before the bar. He found a vacant space and filled it.

"I'll have that drink now, with you," he said to the man behind the counter.

The bartender smiled broadly. Now that he knew

his customer's identity he was a little more friendly. Corson's reputation was well established.

"Got somethin' special," he confided, and reached under the bar. "Johnny Walker, straight from England. They made a mistake in my last order. Want to try it?"

Corson smiled and nodded. In contrast to the common run of the liquor obtainable in that part of the country, this was like a bouquet of flowers. He put down the glass and smiled again.

"That's shore liquor," he said. "You got a right lively little town. I'm glad I stayed over for th' night. What else is there to see?"

"Go down this side of th' street, an' back along th' other, an' you'll see it all. In town on business?" asked the bartender, with assumed carelessness. Ears strained to catch the answer.

"Yes," answered the sheriff. "I been servin' writs. It's all paper work, these days. I never was a great hand to kill a good hoss, so I'll lay over an' finish my ridin' tomorrow. Well, see you later, mebby."

"Have one with me before you go," invited the counter man.

"Reckon I will. I allus preferred rye, but that liquor's right fine. Here's good health, an' a long life."

"She goes both ways," said the counter man, downing his teaspoonful.

The sheriff pushed away from the bar, nodded to the line-up, and walked slowly toward the swinging doors, ignoring the rear of the room. Behind him was silence. The doors swung gently after him, gently squeaking. The tension in the room was high.

A lone voice, sounding loud in the quiet, stated a fact querulously:

"Them damn' hinges oughta be iled!"

CHAPTER XI

BLACK JACK MEADOWS'S eyes left the swinging doors and gazed abstractedly at the table in front of him; and then, as if making up his mind suddenly, he shifted in his chair, turned his head, and glanced at the three ex-farobank players. He jerked it sideways, in the direction of the swinging doors, and faced around again to watch the cards as they began to fall.

Outside the building, Corson moved a little closer to the side-wall window he had been looking through, careful to keep out of the rays of light streaming through it. He pressed against the wall and listened intently, finding that he could hear fairly well, until the general noise in the room resumed its regular level. Over his head heavy roof beams jutted out beyond the adobe wall, and just behind him stood a great freight wagon, its seat even with the top of his head.

One of the ex-farobank players stood up casually and stretched. He slowly glanced at the bar, around the room, and down at his companions, as if trying to make up his mind as to his next move. Two long, slow steps took him close to Black Jack's side, and he leaned over the player.

"You mean th' sheriff?" he asked in a sibilant whisper. At that instant there occurred one of those strange silences which sometimes happen in a noisy crowd. The whisper carried well throughout the room, and even out of the window. Whispers are tricky, their sibilance often betraying them. This one, stabbing like a blade through the sudden silence, made the speaker start.

"Shut yore damn' face!" snapped Black Jack furiously, his face growing blacker. "Do as yo're told, an' don't ask questions!"

"Shore; all right!" muttered the henchman, and moved hastily back to his friends. He looked down at them and tried to smile. "I was up 'most all night," he said. "So I'm buyin' a round an' turnin' in."

His companions arose eagerly and followed him to the bar, watching Black Jack out of the corners of their eyes. Their backs felt twitchy with Black Jack and his three boys behind them. They downed the liquor at a gulp, forgot to make it three rounds and all square, and swung toward the door. The leader yawned and stretched again, stretched with luxurious enthusiasm, to make good his pretense. The shifty-eyed man laughed at him. At this moment, outside the building, the sheriff stepped on the hub of a front wheel, then on the tire and then on the seat. His upraised hands gripped one of the roof beams, tightened under the sudden strain, and then loosened as his lean stomach rested on the timber. He jerked suddenly, twitched sideways, and in another moment he was on the roof, his bare head resting on the top of the wall.

The shifty-eyed man glanced at both of his companions, and then he looked back at the leader.

"Turn *in*, if you want to," he said. The art of dissimulation is a delicate one, and is more often bungled than not; overemphasis is fatal to it. "You look like you need to, but not *me*. *I*'m goin' down to *Pete's*. Where *you* goin'?" he asked the third man, loudly enough for his voice to register throughout the room and to make Black Jack suddenly squirm.

"With you, I reckon," came the grunted answer, and the doors swung shut behind them; but once outside, sleepiness, casualness, and indolence went out of them like gas out of a pricked balloon.

They stepped swiftly out of the little patch of illumination made by the lamps inside, and slid around the corner for a brief consultation. They well knew the danger of three men hunting one man in the dark, the ever-present hesitation caused by the fear of shooting each other, while the hunted could pull trigger, safe in the knowledge that he was not menacing an ally. This danger was especially true if the three men separated, and to do this job quickly and well, they had to separate.

Number One stated that he would take the other side of the street and the western part of the town, and he audibly hoped that they would be more successful this time than they had been in their long-range shooting out at the old adobe ruins.

Number Two was assigned the eastern half of the

town, while Number Three, the shifty-eyed, was to choose a vantage point covering the hotel entrance and, once there, was to lie low and do no moving around.

Number One passed away from the wagon wheel he had been leaning against and led the way from the premises, choosing to cross the street at a point remote from the Palace. They moved past the lamp-lighted windows, heading for the rear of the building, and then turned the corner and were lost to sight.

Corson pushed his head out past the wall and looked down at the wagon, and in another moment he was hanging from the roof beam, feeling with a foot for the seat. He found it, let his weight rest on it, and then got to the ground. He could have remained up on the roof in perfect safety until daylight, but after what he had just heard he preferred to let himself be found, providing he could direct the finding. Some of the mystery had been removed from that long-range shooting on the Iron Springs trail.

He turned abruptly, slowly crossed the street, and melted into the deeper darkness along the wall of the building which faced the Palace. This wall was a blank one. He dropped to his knees and then lay prone, at right angles to the adobe, his feet almost touching it. By merely turning his head his arc of vision was a full half-circle, and the rest of the circle was blanked by the wall. No one could move along that wall, from either end, or along the street at his right, without being seen by him. And then he realized, as he weighed the situation, that a man moving along behind the buildings on his side of the street might be able to pick him out against the faint light of the thorough-fare, where lighted windows lessened the darkness.

The thought itself took less time than the words which express it, and the action which it caused was prompt and swift. He arose, ran along the wall, and reached the corral behind it, where he dropped down, full length, against its front side. Every plainsman knows that a man lying prone against the earth can see much better at night than a man standing up; and everyone knows that movement will be detected where immobility will not.

Very few nights in that part of the cattle country were pitch black, for the stars were seldom masked by clouds; and starlight, to eyes grown accustomed to it, will reveal movements at quite some distance. What movement there would be, would by necessity be done by the hunters, and not by the hunted.

The sheriff smiled. All along he had been bothered by the vagueness which had lain like a blanket over the problems he was trying to solve; now it began to look as if the blanket would be lifted, or at least one corner of it turned back. And it was well to know the identities of the long-range snipers; but how they had crossed Crooked Creek without leaving signs of their movements was something to challenge him. Very likely they went farther down than he did before they crossed it; or farther up, past the point where he had entered it. That was of no moment now.

Youth, courage, and imagination put a premium upon action; and he, possessing all three, waited eagerly for the game to begin. Here was a situation where shooting from the waist, without sighting, might easily prove its value to the last possible measure. Darkness does not bother a pointing finger, if the target can be seen, although it may well hide not only the sights on a gun, but the barrel as well. The sheriff seldom used a belt gun in any other manner.

Number One, having drifted through the saloons, stores, and gambling halls on his allotted side of the street without finding the man he was seeking, drifted down to a specified place on the far end of the thoroughfare to hear from his companions; and one of these, having looked through the buildings on his own side of the street, loafed up to the appointed spot, spoke tersely to his friend, received a terse answer, and then, to his surprise, saw Number Three approaching. Number Three felt lonesome. He had, he said, questioned the hotel clerk and looked into the corral and stable behind the building. The sheriff had not turned in, or showed up, and his horse was in its stall, and well worth stealing, if it wasn't so risky.

"You keep yore eyes plumb onto that hotel," warned Number Two. "You missed him twice at long range," he reproved. "Now let's see what you can do, close up."

"Yeah?" inquired Number Three, with a sneer. "We was givin' him a hint, more'n anythin' else; though, of course, if we had got him, it would been a lot better. You both missed him, too, out there near th' old tradin' post, so you needn't put on no damn' airs."

"Which is only half as much as you did, seein' that you shot twice," countered Number One with unassailable logic. Twice one is two. He scratched his head, thinking deeply, which was simply a continuation of what he had been doing since he had left the light, laughter, and safety of the Palace. "He's wary, wary as a coyote. He's shore holed up som'ers, an' now we got to dig him out."

"Yeah?" asked Number Two with a rising voice. He was no digger. "You mean that we got to go pokin' around in th' dark, lookin' for a feller that's taken to cover, an' can shoot like th' hammers of hell?"

"Shore. He don't know that we're lookin' for him, does he?" answered Number Three with suspicious eagerness. His own assignment called for lying low, holed up, instead of moving around like a blithe idiot for a two-gun expert to practise on. He felt a sudden liking for the vicinity of the hotel.

"You *sound* downright set an' positive," countered Number Two with unconcealed suspicion.

"Shore I do, because I'm right. He don't know nothin' about us huntin' for him."

"Hell of a lot of huntin' you'll be doin'," said Number One.

"Now you hombres shut up, an' listen to me," said Number Two, earnestly. "I got an idear."

"So has a jackass, but it don't amount to nothin'," said Number One, politely.

"Shut up!" growled Number Two. "I've heard a lot about this Corson coyote. So've you. He's Injun-trained. I was plumb willin' to go after him, locate him in some saloon, wait for him to step through th' door, an' then drop him. This is different."

"A hell of a lot different," said Number Three with fervor.

"Shut up!" snapped Number Two. "You don't have to tell me that: I just told it to you. Now, then: where's Black Jack, with a tough job like this to be done? *Shut up!* I'm tellin' you, ain't I? All right, then. Black Jack's passin' th' time playin' stud-hoss, with his three gun-fightin' —— backin' him up. An' who are th' three gun-fighters? His boys. An' where are they? Watchin' their old man play stud-hoss. Here's th' pint: Black Jack can play his stud-hoss, an' his three boys watch him do it. Nope, that wasn't th' pint: not quite. It's comin' now: Now then—you want to know what *I'm* goin' to do? Why, just what yo're goin' to do if you've got th' sense of a cow tick. *I'm* goin' to get me a big drink, mebby two of 'em, an' then hunt my room, roll up in my blankets, an' go to sleep. That's what *I'm* goin' to do!"

"But you can't do it!" expostulated Number One. "We don't have to go pokin' round in th' dark an' run ag'in no slugs. We can watch th' hotel, front, side, an' back. He'll show up plain ag'in th' lights, an' it'll be plumb easy."

"Will it?" sneered Number Two.

"Shore it will!" said Number One with vast confidence.

"Will it?" again sneered Number Two. "Shore it will: *if* he shows up ag'in th' lights. But if he should get to go crawlin' around on his belly, out behind us, it would be us that would show up plain ag'in th' lights. I've been tryin' to tell you somethin'; he's *Injun*-trained. An' he's so damn' well trained that he's gone an' holed hisself up. An' why? Why does a man hole up? Because he reckons he oughta. An' when does he figger that way? When he don't like th' looks of things. Every one of them windows in th' Palace was wide open. He's got eyes an' he's got ears. Now I'm all set an' ready to call you hombres heroes; but to do that, *I*'ve got to be alive afterward, ain't I? I've got to *know* about it. *Some*body's got to, an' I'm damn' shore it won't be neither one of *you* fellers: *you*'ll be th' *heroes,* an' deader than hell. I'm gettin' them drinks an' I'm gettin' 'em now. There ain't no tellin' how soon he'll be crawlin' around like a damn' Apache, with a gun in his hand, an' a hos-tile *intent. Adiós!*"

"Well, I dunno," growled Number Three, his shifty eyes searching the darkness in vain. "I *know* he's Injun-trained: heard all about it. There ain't nobody here-abouts that can touch him readin' sign or trackin'. But if we quit, an' go home, what'll we say to Black Jack?"

"Use yore head!" snapped Number Two. "We'll say that we hunted to hell an' gone an' couldn't find him. Th' only place that we didn't look was in th' jail, an' I'm dead shore he ain't a-visitin' th' marshal. An' we *did* hunt; an' we *did*n't find him."

"Somebody shore tipped off th' play to him: I'll help you drink that liquor," said Number Three, his shifty eyes still shifting. His favorite targets were shoulder blades.

"Well, I won't help you do any drinkin'," said Number One, angrily. "I can't do all th' huntin' myself, but I shore can watch th' hotel!" He drew in his stomach spasmodically as a gun muzzle jammed against it. "What you doin'?" he grunted savagely.

"Just tellin' you to remember that th' two of us left you th' hotel end of it, while we went huntin' for him in th' darkness. You savvy that?" demanded Number Two.

"Yeah: you savvy that?" echoed Number Three, grimly.

"Shucks, yes! I don't blame you, but I want to get this hombre before he gets me. It'll be a show-down sooner or later, an' right now I'm figgerin' to run in a cold deck on him."

"All right: run it in," growled Number Two. "Shore wish you luck!"

"Yeah: wish you luck," grunted Number Three, and faded into the darkness, following closely on the heels of his companion.

Their friend watched them disappear, and slowly turned toward the hotel. There was a pile of boxes on the south side of it. They made good cover—in fact, the only cover close enough to the building to assure good shooting after dark.

"First one is far enough," said Number Three, pulling his companion toward the open, hospitable door of the nearest saloon.

"What'd that bar hog tell us th' last time we was in there?" demanded Number Two, holding back.

"That's right," growled his companion. "Told us to clean our slate or stay out. You got any money?"

"No; not enough. How about you?"

"Same as you. Well, we can go back where we started from, an' get our drinks: back to th' Palace."

"Yeah? An' what do you reckon Black Jack'll ask us?" demanded Number Two, with deep scorn.

"I don't know what he'll ask; but I shore know what I'll tell him; an' that is that we're gettin' a little drink before startin' out ag'in."

"All right: come on!" urged Number Two, starting toward the street.

"Not *that* way!" expostulated his companion hurriedly. "Th' street's too light!"

"Gawd, yes! Come on: we'll slip along th' back of th' buildin's, an' go in th' rear door."

"Wait a minute! This here Corson coyote ain't no fool, an' I'm bettin' he's layin' out behind that buildin', waitin' to see what busts. I'm takin' th' other side of th' street, behind them other buildin's."

"Then you'll have to cross th' street," expostulated Number Two with feeling.

"Well, what of it? That'll be all right, if he's layin' behind th' Palace."

"Look here!" said Number Two, hastily. "There's too damn' much guessin' in this to suit me." A brilliant thought registered in his brain. "Are you awful thirsty?"

"No: are you?"

"Not near as much as I thought I was. Let's go turn in, pronto."

"All right: come on."

They roomed in a building on the northwest side of the town, and they were anxious to gain its shelter. To walk along the side street leading to it would make them feel as prominent as a parade; and parades and prominence did not please them. They had a further choice: they could cut across lots, slipping from one building to the next, from one corral to another, after short periods of intensive looking and listening. They did not seem to realize that in this they would be trading a two-bit piece for a quarter; but on the other hand, they had to make some choice, take some course of action. They hoped, luckily, to choose the least of the evils. They wanted to get under cover, and as soon and as directly as was compatible with safety. Therefore, proceeding warily and slowly and furtively, either one of which would make them interest any person who might see them, they headed away from the ghostly light of the street and began to seek the protecting sides of the building. And they at once loomed up against that ghostly light-haze like a hilltop tree against a summer night's sky.

Everything might have been all right except for the marshal, who liked to make the rounds of the town several times after dark. It so happened that he was returning from the northwestern part of the town and that he, also, was taking a short cut. He saw the two figures outlined against the distant light-haze of the street, and their actions awakened suspicion in his yeasty mind. He struck straight for the corral behind the building next to the one which the sheriff had so recently favored, and he did so without thinking of a whitewashed adobe structure which stood some twenty paces behind him, and against which he was faintly silhouetted. Himself being on the stalk, he, too, was moving warily; and in the minds of Numbers Two and Three, he was someone to be avoided.

"Betcha that's him!" whispered Number Three, thinking of the sheriff. His sibilation of the letter "s" was like a whistle. "We got th' light behind us!" he warned, and ran swiftly toward the next corral, his companion threatening to step on his spurs. Then they stopped with a jerk as a dark figure mysteriously arose from the base of the corral wall. They jerked out their guns.

There came two vivid flashes from the corral wall, two spurting stabs of flame, and Number Two twisted sideways and bumped into his companion's gun-hand as he slid to the ground. Number Three's shot went skyward, and as he jerked his hand down to try again, another jet of fire leaped from the wall. Number Three fell forward, flat on his face.

From another direction there suddenly roared the voice of authority.

"What's this? Put up them guns!"

"Don't shoot!" called out the sheriff. "It's Corson!"

"All right," came the answer in a grunt as the vague figure of the marshal loomed up at the corner of the corral wall. "What's th' trouble?"

"Couple of fellers lookin' for me," explained the sheriff. "How they found out where I was, I don't know; but they headed straight for me on a run. When I stood up they went for their guns. They had more nerve than good sense. Let's take a look at 'em."

"All right," grunted the marshal, stepping forward. He bent down, struck a match, one opened hand between it and his eyes. "Denver Joe," he muttered. "You got him on th' side of th' head. He's a long way from bein' dead, worse luck. Now," he said, standing up and moving again, "let's see th' other coyote. He'll either be Squinty, or Long Bill." Again he dropped to his knees and again a match flared "Squinty. His chips are cashed in. Where's Long Bill? They usually went together."

"Layin' low, near th' hotel, waitin' to dry-gulch me when I showed up," answered the sheriff.

"That so?" asked the marshal, slowly. "How come they went gunnin' for you?"

"Black Jack Meadows' orders. I'll tell you about it later, after I locate Long Bill."

"That'll be easy," said the marshal, thoughtfully. "You head for th' hotel, but don't get close to it, or in no light. I'll tell a couple of th' boys to tote Denver Joe over to th' doctor's, an' a couple more to move Squinty. Then we'll see what Long Bill's got to say about it."

"There's a pile of boxes an' stuff near th' south wall of th' hotel," said Corson speculatively. "I got a good notion to rake it with my left-hand gun, an' see what busts out of 'em."

"You wait for me. I know what'll bust out of 'em," said the marshal. "Meanwhile, you get scarce. It's dark, out here; an' some of th' boys will be friendly to these fellers. Can't watch gun hands very well in this kinda light."

He walked toward the street, where a crowd had gathered, and he called out to establish his identity. Then he answered questions as he neared the thoroughfare. The crowd moved forward, passed him, and streamed to the scene of action.

The marshal kept on going, moving slowly and deliberately toward the hotel, his nickelplated badge shining in the lamplight of the open door. He went in and spoke a few words to the night clerk, and then turned and faced the side wall so that the lights of the room would clearly reveal him to the watcher outside. He had no wish to walk around the corner of the building, without warning, and be mistaken for the sheriff. After a moment he walked deliberately toward the door, through it, and loafed around the corner, whistling softly. When opposite the pile of boxes he stopped, carelessly hooked his thumbs to the arm holes of his vest, and smiled broadly.

"It'd be a good idear to come on out," he said, conversationally, addressing the boxes. "Sheriff Corson has just worked around on th' dark side of you, an' figgers to empty one gun at th' pile, keepin' th' other ready. There's been enough shootin' tonight. Squinty's dead, an' Denver Joe will be laid up for a few days. You come on out, Bill, with yore hands in plain sight, an' empty."

There was no answering voice, and the peace officer smiled grimly and leaned back against the wall, dropping his hands to his gun belts, where he hooked them to the leather by their thumbs. He spoke again, this time in a louder voice.

"I'm tellin' you once more to come on out, Bill," he said, and waited for an answer. It did not come. Then he raised his voice. "You might try a couple of shots, Corson, if yo're ready; but don't hit me. Take th' east end of th' pile."

There came a double roar from the south, and two spitting tongues of flame flared vividly into the darkness, and died swiftly. The pile of boxes heaved suddenly.

"Don't shoot!" shouted an angry voice. "I'm a-comin' out!"

"Don't shoot no more, sheriff," called the marshal loudly. "He's a-comin' out, with his hands empty."

Long Bill crawled out from the heaving pile, cleared it, and stood up. His right hand hung down against the holster, and he was glaring at the lazy man who was leaning against the wall.

The corner of the building was two jumps away and, once around it, Long Bill could get to his horse and ride off before anyone could stop him. Squinty had been killed, Denver Joe wounded; and he, Long Bill, had been a party in the attempt to kill the sheriff. A long prison term was staring him in the face. If he made a break for it the sheriff might get in one shot, but the light was poor, and Long Bill would be moving swiftly. He would try it, first dissembling to throw the marshal off his guard.

"Hell, marshal: I ain't done nothin'," he said. "There ain't no reason——" His hand jerked up and curled around the handles of his gun. The marshal slipped sideways, his own hand moving, sudden smoke enwrapping him. Then the peace officer again leaned back against the wall. Smoke churned and rolled along the ground in front of him. Long Bill stumbled, slumped, and lay quiet on the ground.

"Come on, sheriff," said the town officer as he pushed from the wall and waited for his friend to join him. He turned on his heel. "I knowed Long Bill wouldn't come to no good end." He gently scratched his head. "He toted a pearl-handled gun, silver-plated," he explained, with contempt. The terse sentence well could have served as Long Bill's epitaph.

Corson fell in step with him, and they turned the corner of the hotel side by side. Opposite the front door the marshal slowed and stopped, expecting his companion to say good-night and turn in; but the sheriff kept on walking. The marshal joined step again, nodding his head in gentle commendation. It was always well to strike while the iron was hot. He knew where they were going, and knew it without a word being said.

They entered the Palace side by side, the two little doors swinging to and fro behind them. The marshal stopped near the bar, facing the rear of the room, and felt for the rail with one groping foot. His face was placid and expressionless; but just let somebody's hand slip toward a gun——

Corson kept on down the room. He moved sideways

between two tables and followed along the north wall, and stopped to lean against it at exactly the place where he had leaned against it earlier in the evening. Black Jack's gun-fighting sons watched every move he made, and one of them spoke softly to his father.

Black Jack looked up quickly, the expression on his face betraying surprise, and saw the sheriff carelessly regarding him. While one might count a dozen the two men coldly studied each other in grave silence. Then Corson's cold face broke into a flinty smile.

"Huntin' in th' dark is right uncertain," he said, casually, as casually as he might have predicted the morrow's weather. "Right uncertain. Squinty's dead. Long Bill's dead. Denver Joe lost part of his face. There's plenty of light in here, an' I'm stayin' for about five minutes. That oughta give you plenty of time to make up yore mind. Then, if nothin' excitin' happens, I aim to walk over to th' hotel, an' turn in."

"What you want me to do?" barked Black Jack angrily. "Throw my arms around yore neck an' kiss you?"

"Anythin' you want to do," answered the sheriff, "except that." He glanced over Black Jack's head and smiled provocatively at the three-man bodyguard. "An' that goes for you hombres," he added.

There was a moment's silence, and then Black Jack's voice broke it. He was looking down at the cards on the table. "Where th' hell was we at? Who's bet is it?" he demanded.

Time slipped past. At the end of the stated five minutes the sheriff pushed from the wall, saw that the marshal was watching the three-man bodyguard, and turned on his heel. He moved slowly toward the door, nodded to the marshal and the man behind the counter, and let the double doors swing shut behind him. The marshal waited a few moments and then, pushing his hat a little to one side, smiled significantly at the discomfited bodyguard, turned his back on them, and left the building.

Alice Meadows stirred restlessly and slowly awakened. The darkness outside was turning gray. She heard movements and low voices in the next room, where her stepfather and stepbrothers were getting ready for bed.

She sighed and then clenched her hands as a little burst of anger seized her. If they would only stop this everlasting night riding! Nothing good could come of it, and it made her life no better than a dog's. Not that she worried much for their sakes: the bitterness of her own existence, shut off up here in the hills, without companions of her own sex, working for men who steadily grew to mean less to her—all this had killed any real affection which she once might have felt for them. She was nothing more nor less than a slavey, and they did not even have the decency to try to conceal it from her. All four of them had taken pains at odd times, as they said, to put her in her place. She could cook and mend and wash and scrub and iron, and even go out to gather her own firewood, without thanks or appreciation. It was rapidly becoming intolerable.

One voice raised above the others, and she found herself listening because she had nothing else to do. Many nights she had been awakened by the low rumble of indistinguishable conversation, but tonight the words were intelligible, due, perhaps, to sharpened tempers. Evidently something had gone wrong.

"He's got th' brains of a coyote, an' that means that he's damn' cunnin'," said Black Jack's voice, edged like a knife. "Them three fools shoulda got him tonight, but they bungled it like a lot of boys. An' they missed him at th' old 'dobe tradin' post, an' he was too smart to start trailin' 'em."

"We've got to get him," said Maurice, sharply.

"Of course we got to get him!" snapped his father. "There ain't no question about that now. Ridin' all over th' country like he is, turnin' up a fact here, an' a fact there, is somethin' that's got to be stopped. It can't go on!"

"No, it shore can't," came a sharp reply. It was Mortimer who was talking now. They called him Mort, for short, a grisly irony although an unconscious one on the part of the Meadows family, whose knowledge of French did not include even an occasional word. Mort was a name well suited to him, both in regard to the past and the present, but it was more particularly suited to him in regard to the future, because for him the future would prove to be but a brief span of time.

"We can trap him," said another voice, this one belonging to Matthew. In the naming of his sons, Black Jack had called in alliteration's artful aid, to borrow an apt phrase. There were Mortimer, Matthew, and Maurice. Mortimer had been a contribution of the mother, whose favorite reading matter might well have borne the name of Bertha M. Clay.

"Shore," said Mort, with confidence.

"I was talkin' with Slade a while back," continued Matt. "He said every man of that outfit is dangerous. He said, too, that th' sheriff is worse than any of his men, unless it might be that damn' horse-faced Nueces. An' after tellin' me all that, what happened to Slade? Why, he went for his gun, an' th' sheriff shot him. From what I heard, th' sheriff could just as well a-killed him, but didn't, for some reason known to hisself. All right: that makes it easier for us—Slade's fair itchin' to get him. All we got to do is let Slade alone, or edge him on a little, an' th' first thing we know, that ranch will be lookin' for a new owner. An' when that time comes we'll make a grand clean-up over there durin' th' excitement."

The voices became low and indistinct for a few moments, but she did hear the name "Franchère," and then the talk grew loud again.

"Wonder just how much that damn' Bentley marshal knows?" asked Mort, slowly.

"Hard to tell," answered his father. "He keeps his mouth tight shut an' don't meddle with things that don't concern him. As long as he keeps on doin' that, he'll find this climate healthy."

"But he shot Long Bill!" exclaimed Matt, angrily.

"What else could he do?" demanded the father. "Long Bill was a damn' fool, an' he shore had it comin' to him. Mebby th' marshal just saved us that job."

"That's all right, but him an' th' sheriff do quite some visitin'," objected Matt, referring to the marshal.

"An' that's all right," replied Black Jack. "They know each other, an' it's only natural for a man to hunt up somebody he knows when he goes to a strange town."

"There ain't no need to worry about that," said Maurice, reassuringly. "We're keepin' cases on th' marshal. There's a draw up on that little bench just outa town that commands th' marshal's favorite sittin' place. Not much of a range for a good rifle. A buffalo gun would make a joke of it. How soon are we goin' to get back to work, Pop?"

"Not till things are a lot better than they are right now, an' th' round-up wagons are off th' range. Not while th' sheriff is hangin' round this part of th' country, neither. An' after him there's that Nueces hombre. He's a deppety, an' he'll be th' next in line if he makes a play that we don't like. We got things goin' too well to let anybody or anythin' interfere with 'em."

"We've had some hard luck, too," growled Mort, thinking of cached cattle.

"That's somethin' you've got to expect, more or less," replied his father. "Come on, now, let's get to sleep. I'm near dead."

The voices ceased as the four men dropped off into slumber, but in the next room Alice was very wide awake. She found herself tense and holding her breath. Her temples throbbed from excitement, and her throat was tight and dry.

She had been right in her growing suspicions concerning the nocturnal activities of the Meadows men. She was certain now that they were engaged in some enterprise outside the law, some enterprise that was so desperate that it called for killing the sheriff, whoever he was. If they would kill the sheriff, then they might do the same thing to any stranger who made it a habit to ride up to the house.

She suddenly clenched her small fists, and anger surged through her; they might take from her the one thing she treasured, the wonderful thing that lay in the future of her life, like the sun behind the still dark eastern hills. Her mind played with the simile, and she slowly relaxed and smiled. She would have her sunrise if it lay within her power. She would have to warn him not to ride even through the arroyo, but if she did that, then she would be keeping him away from herself. Nevertheless she would warn him, the first chance she had.

She had listened every day for the sounds of his riding, but she had listened in vain. Then she smiled again; it had only been three days since he had been here. Three days: yes, but she never before had known how long a day could be.

There were no sounds of any kind coming from the next room, and she quietly slipped out of bed and hurriedly dressed, blushing a little from the thoughts in her mind. Then she closed the door softly behind her and stole into the kitchen to begin this day's drudgery. Oh, if the time would only come when she could leave this house, leave it forever! Almost no price would be too much to pay for that; and yet, if she did leave it, perhaps he would not know where to find her; and that would be too great a price to pay.

CHAPTER XII

BACK in Bentley, Corson had an early breakfast the morning after the shootings, and left the hotel immediately afterward, long before the night-loving population of the town was awake. He was equipped for three days in the open, and he headed straight west, crossed Crooked Creek by means of two contributing side gullies, and then turned to follow down it, along its west bank, for a dozen miles. There he left the creek to begin the great circle which would take him entirely around the suspected rough country beyond, country which lay outside the territory to be covered by the nine wagons assigned to his part of the range. It was an arid section so far as he knew, with scant feed and no water; but under the circumstances he could not afford to overlook it.

It was noon of the third day when he had completed the task and again approached Crooked Creek, miles above the point where he had left it after leaving Bentley three days before. He had seen many scattered signs of cattle, mostly signs of individual animals, but nothing which led him to believe that any worth-while number of them had either come out of or gone into the country he had circled, at any one time or place.

He passed Iron Springs and loped along the regular wagon road leading to Bentley, passed the creek where he had visited the Baylor wagon, and kept on without pausing. When he reached the old, ruined trading post he caught sight of the dust sign of the Baylor outfit, and about mid-afternoon he reached their wagon and found that they were about through working the day's gather. A mile beyond their camp was the entrance to Lucas Arroyo, and only a few miles beyond that was Bentley.

He stopped at the wagon, unsaddled, and watched his horse roll enthusiastically. Carrying his saddle and blankets to the wagon, he put them under it, out of the way. He exchanged a few words with the cook and, following that person's nod, swung around to look at a ludicrous sight not far from the camp.

Somebody's horse must have "crossed the rope" and given its rider a bad spill or a bad few minutes. Crossing the rope was a paramount sin in a cow horse. An animal trained to work cattle should keep its feet away from a taut lariat when cow, calf, or steer was in the loop at the far end. The cure for such a mistake was nothing more than bitter experience, and this particular cow horse had been getting large doses of that; and its air of hopeless dejection was so apparent that Corson had to laugh aloud.

The rider of the animal had driven a steer up close to the camp, to save himself from walking any distance. He had tied the loose end of his rope to the pommel, thrown the loop over the steer's short horns, pulled it tight, and then, dismounting, had stridden back to the wagon, leaving the two animals fastened together.

What they had done to each other in the ensuing gyrations was plenty, although not serious. Now they stood nose to nose in the tangle of rope, bruised, rope-burned, dejected, and about exhausted. Occasionally one or the other would hump himself furiously for a moment, and then subside to suffer dumbly and resignedly. When that rope was finally loosened, the tangle straightened out, and the steer turned loose, that chastened saddlehorse would have learned his bitter lesson so well that nothing on earth could ever successfully tempt him again to cross the rope. Not even when the loop was empty; not even a picket rope.

The cattle worked, the riders began to straggle into camp, leaving the slowly growing herd under the watchful eyes of two men. The Baylor wagon was now holding everything and would drive the entire gather back to the home range. What they rounded up now could be regarded as strays that had worked too far from the home range; and once on the home range, they would be turned loose after the strays of other brands had been cut out, and would not be molested again until the beef round-up in the fall. By this time the Baylor wagon carried no stray men, and the strays outside its own brand were practically nil. Now half the riders were going into town for a little fun after the high-pressure work of the last three weeks. They had earned it.

The straw boss swung down from his saddle and moved to the sheriff's side, nodding his welcome.

"Couple more days, an' we head for home, lock, stock, an' barrel," he said, grinning.

"You got a line on yore tallies?" bluntly asked the sheriff.

"No; not yet," answered the straw boss. "I don't know how many head our reps. brought home. When I get 'em figgered I'll let you know. You boys over east got through yet?"

"I don't know, Jerry," slowly answered the sheriff. "I haven't been over that way since I saw you. I've just come back from circlin' that Dry Arroyo country. Either there's a lot of fool coincidences goin' on down in this part of th' country, or there's th' damnedest puzzle a man ever had to struggle with."

"I ain't seen nothin' positive," said the straw boss. "Even that little bunch of cattle that used to hang around th' Broken Jug pasture could have drifted along without anybody helpin' 'em on."

"Yes, they could," admitted Corson, frowning. "Still, too many things have happened, Jerry. I don't know that I would worry much about a coincidence or two, but when I get a dozen things that don't look right, then I've got to do some lookin' around, an' thinkin'."

"Yeah. Reckon so," agreed the straw boss, rubbing his chin thoughtfully. "You've been all over th' range?"

"Yes."

"If anythin' big was goin' on, you'd have found signs of it," said the straw boss, slowly.

"I've just told you that I'm beginnin' to think I have found signs of it."

"I mean out-an'-out signs," explained the straw boss.

The sheriff had turned his head and was letting his gaze drift slowly along the rough slopes of the great ridge range east of him, the watershed between Crooked Creek and the Kiowa River; the vast ridge on which Packers Gap, Saddlehorn Pass, and the JM ranch were located. As he looked, his frown deepened and then suddenly disappeared: the man at his side had given assurance that the whole of the great ridge had been combed for cattle, and combed thoroughly.

The straw boss seemed to read his companion's thoughts, and nodded slowly and understandingly.

"We shore swept it clean, Corson," he said, reassuringly. "We worked every yard of it, an' we threw 'em over on th' downhill side."

"Yes, I know you did," grunted the sheriff, and then spoke of other things.

The remainder of the afternoon passed idly. Supper came and went. The straw boss had long since untangled the cow horse and the steer, turning them both loose after unsaddling the former. The horse was his own, and he now considered it cured of crossing the rope.

Twilight crept over the range, hiding its general ugliness and touching it here and there with a great magic. The ridge glowed like some vast, variegated flame in the beautiful tints of the afterglow. The cook's work was finished, and he lazily wandered over to the fire, joining his boss and guest. The riders of the first night trick had gone out to the herd, and the relieved pair rode in, picketed their horses, and sat down before the glowing embers.

Corson was silent, tormented by damnably persistent thoughts. Ever since the tragedies in Bentley, he had been hounded by them. He had suspected, earlier than that, the conditions of affairs which easily might arise. They had arisen, and with a vengeance: Black Jack Meadows and his boys were now definitely on the wrong side of the game, whatever the game might be. They were on the side he had to fight against.

He knew enough now to take the offensive against them, on one count, at least; but so far their play had only been against him, personally. It was a fact, known to him as such, that he had been hunted that night in town by Black Jack's orders. Pride and courage had insisted that he go back to the Palace after the killing of Long Bill; but he had gone there to play only a passive part, so far as initiative had been concerned. Had it been anyone but Black Jack or his boys, he would have made his accusation then and there and would have followed it up with action. As it was, he had been content to let Black Jack make the play and then ride with it to the bitter end; but Black Jack had not made it, perhaps believing that his own share in the night's development was not known to the sheriff; or that, perhaps, a better situation would later arise to do what he had failed to have done. Black Jack was her father; his sons, her brothers. Suddenly he swore out loud, swore bitterly; and then tried to grin as he saw his companions looking at him curiously.

"That Slade coyote," he said quickly, in an endeavor to cover his break. "Any of you boys seen him since?"

Negative answers were given in several ways, and the general conversation veered around and started up with a new subject to work upon. The minutes passed, and the night air was revealing a nip. One by one the men moved from the fire and became busy with blanket rolls. The fire died down and became a faint glow, a lambent dot in the middle of space.

Midnight passed. Another hour went by, and then a noisy bunch of riders came up the trail from town. They sang, they fired into the air, and they whooped. Some of the round-up pressure seemingly was still confined; but the following morning would find them dull and subdued. They rioted into camp, awakening everyone; and no one, finding excuse for them, made an objection. Most of the others would be doing the same thing on the following night. After a while the camp settled down again, the only interruptions to its silence being the shift riders going to and coming from the herd. Corson took advantage of the opportunity to rearrange his blankets, and then was instantly asleep again.

At breakfast the sheriff saw curious eyes regarding him, and knew that the Bentley tragedy was now known to the Baylor outfit. Nothing was said about it, however, until he had mounted, said his good-byes, and was riding off. Then the straw boss mounted, pushed up even with him, and rode at his side as far as the Bentley trail, saying nothing, his eyes on the already grazing herd moving from the bed ground. As they reached the trail, the straw boss raised his hand in a parting salute.

"You shoulda got Denver Joe," he said, quietly. "He's bad."

"That's one of those little coincidences that I was tellin' you about," replied the sheriff, smiling. "An' it's only Denver's good luck that I didn't get him; that an' th' dark."

"Uh-huh. I reckon mebby somethin' is wrong some-where," slowly admitted the straw boss. "It wasn't a personal disagreement?"

"No; not to my knowledge."

"Well, I reckon you'd a-knowed about it, if it was," said the straw boss, thoughtfully.

"Reckon so," admitted the sheriff. "Those were the three that shot at me at long range, down by th' old tradin' post. That was th' beginnin', an' there wasn't nothin' personal in *that*."

"Looks like you been doin' too much ridin' around," suggested the straw boss, experimentally.

"I've begun to reckon that way myself," replied the sheriff, with a smile.

"By Gawd!" said the straw boss, sitting erect in the saddle. "You need any help? I ain't got past th' trigger-pullin' age."

"Don't need any help, yet; there's nothin' to work on," said the sheriff. "I'm obliged for th' offer, though."

"Anythin' a-tall that we can do," said the straw boss. "All you got to do is holler."

Corson nodded, smiled, and turned to ride toward town, leaving the straw boss sitting a motionless horse squarely in the middle of the trail.

After a few moments the Baylor foreman shook his head gently and pressed his knees against the sides of his mount. The riders were leaving camp, following him. He turned, waved his hat in a circling gesture, and saw the men ride off to take up their positions for that day's circle. The press of work faced them and, after all, the sheriff's business was the sheriff's business. What made him sore was Slade turning his remuda loose with the shoes on them. It didn't amount to very much, but it was not workmanlike, and Slade was Slade. He was just no good. If he hung around the BLR range he would be looked after, which was a fact that nobody had any call to copper. Monkeying with a man's cattle and horses was dangerous business. That was that.

Corson rode into the sleeping town and swung down in front of the hotel. He knew that the marshal would not be stirring until considerably later in the morning, but this morning was to be an exception. The first man to come out of the dining room was, to the sheriff's surprise, the local peace officer. The marshal nodded to his brother officer, looked over the register on the desk, and grunted something. He turned around, shoved a fresh toothpick into his mouth, joined the waiting sheriff, and walked out to the street with him.

"Black Jack an' his whelps stayed over in town last night," he said. "They're asleep upstairs, right now. You want 'em?"

"No," answered Corson. "That's not th' play. Worst thing to happen, right now, would be to jail 'em. We'll give 'em more rope." A picture sprang into his mind. He could see the cow horse and the steer, hopelessly tangled. "Let 'em run, give 'em rope, an' mebby they'll get tangled up, nose to nose, with more trouble than they can handle. I'm lookin' to them for my leads."

"Gals shore do make a hell of a fuss on a range," grunted the marshal.

"Yeah? Well, that ain't no call for you to make a jackass outa yoreself!" snapped the sheriff. "Girls ain't got nothin' to do with it. You know why I want 'em loose: I just told you!"

"Y-e-p, you did," said the marshal, placidly. "You shouldn't go on th' prod so early in th' mornin'. It'll mebby spoil th' day. Besides, I don't blame you, not a mite. You shore got one hell of a mean job on yore hands; but don't you pull leather, son."

"Don't aim to," retorted Corson, sharply. "If I can get my puzzles solved, an' it works out that Black Jack Meadows an' his boys are mixed up in any deviltry, there ain't no woman on earth that can save 'em from gettin' what they deserve. But there ain't nothin' to stop me from quittin' my job th' very next minute, is there?"

"Don't see that there'd be any reason to quit it *then*," drawled the marshal, slowly. "What you want me to do with Denver Joe?"

"Put him under arrest an' hold him for th' fall term, on a charge of attempted murder!"

"I've already done it," said the marshal pleasantly. "That's why I'm up so damn' early. Did it before breakfast. I knowed that if you didn't want him, I did. I've had my eye on Denver for two, three months; but he was as slick as a greasy fryin' pan. Now he's where he belongs; an' I got three less to worry about, with him in jail an' his pardners dead."

Corson swung up into the saddle.

"See you again some day," he said, waving a hand.

"I got more ridin' to do; an' if it don't pan out better than th' last I did, I'll be guessin' even more than I am now: an' that's shore aplenty."

"You'll rope it, throw it, an' tie it; an' you'll put yore mark on it, if you just keep workin' at it," said the marshal, slowly stepping back. He cocked an eye upward, weighing something in his mind, and he was about to speak, but checked himself in time. He wondered if the sheriff knew of the step-relationship in the Meadows family. He had not been asked any questions, and what he had in mind would not help the county officer in his official duties, would not help him unravel the tangle. He compromised with himself. "I wouldn't do personal worryin', sheriff."

"I'm not!" snapped the man in the saddle, missing the marshal's thought by a mile or two and putting an entirely different and very unjust misinterpretation on the words. A cloud of dust marked where his horse had stood, and the marshal hurriedly stepped back a little farther to get out of it. A grin slowly came to his face, and he shook his head and chuckled.

The town was more than a mile behind him before Corson's temper simmered down enough to let him realize that he was not in a horse race, and he pulled the horse down to its regular trail lope. By God, he'd show them! He'd show them all! He'd show them that he'd get to the bottom of this mystery, Black Jack or no Black Jack, no matter where the lightning struck. No matter if he lost the most precious thing that had ever come into his life. If Black Jack and his boys were guilty of rustling, then Black Jack and his boys would pay for it, no matter what it might cost him.

Lucas Arroyo was opening up on his left, and he sent the horse along the lesser trail. Bench after bench was put behind him, and steadily the hills drew closer together. His mind was a torment of deduction and conjecture as it struggled to put into some sort of order the various factors of the problem before it; as it shifted the discrete pieces about into one pattern after another, and none of them complete. He was so preoccupied that he did not consciously hear the beat of the shod hoofs of his horse or the echoing clatter from the arroyo walls.

The little side draw lay ahead, and he slowed the horse, controlling his own almost breathless eagerness. The little trail up the draw steadily extended itself. The corral gate came into sight, and then the upper part of the adobe house and the top of the door. The door was closed. He slowed the horse still more, hoping against hope, until it moved at a snail's pace, but the door did not open. And then the shoulder of the arroyo pushed slowly toward him, and moved like a curtain across the front of the little adobe shack, wiping it from his sight as a sponge wipes figures from a slate.

The rider found himself slumped forward in the saddle. She was a Meadows, of course, daughter of Black Jack, and the sister of his sons. He stiffened and sat erect in a sudden burst of anger and defiance. A man was a fool ever to allow himself to be hurt like this, a blind, silly fool; and a man was a fool to consider anything but the job on hand. He had known now for several days that the time would certainly come when she would have to make her choice, but he had hoped, foolishly, that it would be deferred until the last, cruel instant. A man was also a fool to temporize. All right: she had made her choice, and he would have to abide by it—and God help Black Jack Meadows and his side-winder sons if he could connect them with rustling! And he would do that very thing if the connection existed.

The agonized bay leaped convulsively from the cutting roll of the spurs, pitched sideways, sunfished, and then buck-jumped stiff-leggedly. Corson fought it savagely, realized after a few moments that it was himself and not the horse who was at fault, and gradually pacified the animal. And from that time on, until he came to the first crossing of the Kiowa, he was unconscious of everything but his own angry, bitter thoughts.

The door had not opened. She had made her choice. A dull, apathetic, leaden-hearted horseman rode down the Kiowa trail, instinctively left it at the proper place without realizing it, and found himself nearing the little hamlet of Willow Springs. He thought of the Cheyenne and Steve's liquor; and savagely shook his head. Liquor never drowned anything but common sense, and what common sense he had would need to be as keen as was possible. And then after a while he was sitting on a motionless horse before the door of the JC bunkhouse, and steps were moving across the floor inside to see who had stopped before the door.

CHAPTER XIII

CORSON awakened early the following morning, despite his poor night's sleep, and prepared his own breakfast in the ranch-house kitchen, rather than to go down to the bunkhouse and eat a better one already prepared. He was not in any mood to listen to Shorty and the cook, each of whom could be unduly garrulous upon the slightest provocation; and there were times when provocation, slight or otherwise, was not needed. They were both good men, and loyal to him and the ranch, and he loved them like brothers, but there were times when even brothers could be infernal nuisances.

After breakfast he cleaned up the mess he had made in the kitchen and went down to the corral to see what Shorty had wrangled in from the range in the shape of horseflesh, and he felt a little guilty toward that squat person when he saw that his pet roan was in the enclosure. Shorty had easily guessed that there would be no working of cattle for his boss, and had driven in a road horse without a peer on the range. It took only a moment or two for Corson to drop the rope around the roan's neck and to lead him out of the enclosure; and only another moment to throw on the saddle. Before Shorty's laggard steps had carried him to the door of the bunkhouse, the sheriff was riding down the little trail along Willow Creek, heading for where he believed he should find the JC wagon. The creek never had gone dry in his remembrance, and flowed for twenty miles down its own bed and that of the Horsethief, which had a different reputation. There the waters of Willow Creek sank slowly out of sight in the bed of the other, and only a long, saline scab marked the scene of the infamy.

He passed the salt sink and soon reached the entrance to the arroyo which marked the southern edge of Horsethief Hills. The head of the arroyo opened out into a gently sloping upland pasture a mile or more in diameter, which was blessed by three small springs, two of them apparently everlasting; but their waters died out in sinks before reaching the main creek bed. At those springs he should find Nueces and the wagon.

The wagon was there as he had expected it would be, and the attenuated circle of riders was already working down the surrounding slopes toward the common center. This sweep touched the imaginary line which marked the edge of the territory being worked by the Bar W outfit, and from now on the wagon would work home toward the ranch. Four more days should end the spring round-up, so far as the JC was concerned, and the regular work of the ranch could be resumed.

The cook grinned a welcome, saw that something was wrong with the usually sunny disposition of his boss, and discreetly kept his mouth shut. A closed mouth is one of man's greatest possessions, and also one of his rarest. Half the troubles known to him have their origin in spoken words.

Corson scowled at the cook, slowly dismounted, walked to the wagon, and leaned against a wheel. He let his somber gaze range over the slopes of the basin, watching the cattle appear like miracles out of the draws and scanty thickets, popping into sight here and there like jacks-in-the-box. The cook, suspiciously intent on his duties, cleared his throat, and the JC owner looked quickly at him, scowled again, and glanced along the dusty circle, which was rapidly constricting as it worked down toward the camp.

"That Chain stray man with us yet?" suddenly asked the boss of the JC ranch.

"Yeah," grunted the cook, pulling some of the glowing coals away from his number one oven.

"Does th' damn' fool reckon Chain cows have wings, to get away over here?" demanded the rancher.

"We got eight or ten of 'em yesterday," replied the cook, smiling to himself.

"Huh!" grunted the rancher. "Who's th' new Baylor stray man with us?"

"He was Matt Joyce," answered the cook. "He cut his string an' pulled his drag yesterday."

"Huh!"

Silence fell. Golden silence, to the cook's way of thinking. He cocked an eye at number two oven and judiciously flirted four glowing embers from its top. Cooking has its niceties as well as watch-making, and cookie was a cook. Corson was about to ask what the hell difference those four embers would have made, but remembered that he was in no mood to talk to human beings, and kept his mouth shut. It's just as well that he felt that way, for range cooks are range cooks, and he would have been promptly answered; and then Nueces might have had to go off hunting a new cook, and with only four more days to go.

One line of dust on the rim of the basin straightened out its circling course and moved in a straight line down the slopes, headed directly for the wagon. It was being made by the straw boss himself; and he was riding as if the devil were after him. Corson picked out the distant movement and dust streak, thought for a moment, and then strode to his horse. The cook watched him ride off to meet the oncoming horseman and grinned.

"There'll shore be some wonderful language when Nueces tells him *that*," he said, confiding to number three oven. As a prognosticator the cook was not without merit, at least in this case.

The two horsemen slowed to a walk and then stopped, their animals almost head to head. Nueces' face was hard, and his expression stormy. He did not seem to be in good humor, and on that score both men were about equally matched.

"This —— —— new-fangled Cattlemen's Association have any rules about th' open season on cows?" he asked.

"What you mean?" barked the sheriff. He had the disposition of a rattlesnake this morning, if a rattlesnake has any at all.

"What I mean is that four of our cows have been shot!" snapped the straw boss. *"That's* what I mean!"

"What's th' Association got to do with that?" demanded the sheriff, his jaw muscles setting.

"I reckoned mebby they'd have some rules about it bein' all right in round-up time," answered the straw boss with heavy sarcasm. "This round-up was planned to be over with, for us, four or five days from now. Me an' th' boys reckon that's too long by just about two days. You watch us clean up th' rest of this range; an' *then* you watch us! —— —— th' cow-killin' skunks!"

"Where are th' dead cows?" demanded the sheriff, his purely personal troubles forced well into the background by this unexpected slap in the face.

"Up near th' rim," growled the straw boss. "Looks like they was shot two, three days ago."

He whirled his horse as Corson pushed ahead, and they breasted the slope at fair speed, both seething at pretty high pressure; but neither had a word to say until they had turned into a little draw and dismounted. The four animals had been shot through the heart.

"Were their calves hangin' round here when you got here?" asked Corson sharply.

"Yes," growled the straw boss. "They're all right. They're old enough for weanin', anyhow."

"I see you kept th' boys from millin' around an' messin' up the signs," said the sheriff, his gaze sweeping the ground immediately around the dead animals. While Nueces grunted affirmatively, the sheriff's eyes picked out a little nest of boulders farther up the slope on the right, and he regarded them suspiciously.

"Yeah; that's th' spot," grunted the straw boss. "Knelt on his right knee, an' took th' shells away with him." He scowled at the rocks. "He was right careful."

The sheriff dismounted, studied the ground, found no definite signs, and then went slowly up the slope to the boulders. It was as Nueces had said. The killer had knelt on his right knee, which fact proclaimed him to be right-handed, and had carefully picked up the empty cartridge shells.

Corson backed away, turned, and followed a very faint trail along the slope. It angled obliquely downward and led around a clump of brush and into a little draw. Here the killer had left his horse, and here, of course, he had returned to it, mounted, and ridden off. The sheriff dropped to his knees and intently studied the prints of the horseshoes. They had no distinguishing features. He stood up, following them with his eyes until they were lost to sight in the scanty vegetation farther down the slope.

"Any cattleman hereabouts would know that you

hadn't yet combed this section," he said, thoughtfully. "You can bet this feller spied out th' lay of th' land purty well before he went to work. An' he would know that you would comb it within a few days, after figgerin' out yore drift. Instead of killin' cattle on range that you'd already been over, where they wouldn't be discovered until th' beef round-up next fall, mebby—instead of playin' safe an' doin' that, he up an' killed 'em deliberate on range you would come to in a few days. That looks to me like he wanted 'em found. That right?"

"Right as hell!" snapped the straw boss, angrily.

"I've been pokin' around on th' other side of Crooked Creek," continued the sheriff, meaningly. "I've been askin' questions here an' there. I shot that Slade feller in th' Baylor camp, but didn't kill him. Shot him through th' shoulder. Remember that. Then I killed a feller named Squinty, an' shot away quite some of Denver Joe's face. I smoked Long Bill outa an ambush, an' th' Bentley marshal shot him when he made his play. Black Jack Meadows sent th' three of 'em out to get me in th' dark. Then I went back to Black Jack an' told him about it, an' gave him a chance to do some of his own shootin' hisself. He didn't try it, but he shore knowed just why I was there. So now they've sent a feller over here to shift th' war onto our own range. They didn't try to drive off th' calves. They just shot those cows so we'd find 'em. Only one man did it. Are all our reps. back with our wagon?"

"No. Tom is still with th' Bar W. Johnny is over with th' Turkey Track. Franchère came in th' night before last with th' Bar W's rep. from th' Chain wagon. They cut their drag here, an' th' Bar W rider took his on home with him. Jimmy brought home his string an' drag from th' BLR wagon a couple days ago. Th' only stray men workin' with our wagon are from th' Bar W, th' Chain, an' th' Turkey Track. So far as Turkey Track strays are concerned, their rep. could leave us now, but I asked him to stay on with us."

Corson grunted and nodded, his eyes on the dead animals.

The straw boss let his horse face show a grim smile, and he chuckled.

"From what you say it seems like you've been right busy. You say you didn't kill Slade?"

"No. Didn't have to, an' didn't want to," answered the sheriff. He thought for a moment, remembering what the Bentley marshal had said about Slade's physical condition. He had ridden out of town, sitting up straight in his saddle, and he had been cocky and defiant. Still, a man with a .45-caliber hole through his right shoulder would not want a rifle to kick it four times in a row; not for a while, anyhow. He looked at his companion.

"Let's cut out th' bullets," he suggested, thoughtfully.

They went down into the little draw and became

busy. In due time they had the four slugs, wiped them clean, and let them roll around in their hands.

"If these ain't Colt .45's then I'm a liar," said Nueces, squinting at them. He looked up at his companion. "They ain't nothin' else."

Corson nodded as he examined them again.

"Yo're right; that's what they are," he said, pocketing the slugs that his companion had handed him.

He looked around the draw again and then walked slowly down the slope, and in a moment he found what he strongly believed would be there. Bootprints were plain to be seen under the south edge of a stunted shrub. The prints up in the nest of boulders had been made to serve as a blind. They were fair rifle range away from the dead cows, and much too far for accurate shooting with a Colt; but these bootprints were so close to the dead animals that a good pistol shot could hardly have missed the marks. If the killer had fired from here, then the bullets would have ranged up into the animals, and this fitted the facts discovered by the dissection.

Why had the marksman tried to indicate that he had used a rifle? Why this elaborate attempt to hide the facts? The sheriff thought that he knew the answer to that. Those four shots had not been fired from a rifle held against a sore and shrinking shoulder. Slade was far cleverer than the marshal had given him credit for being, but he had not allowed for anyone digging out the bullets.

The sheriff was now so certain of his deductions that he did not believe it to be necessary to attempt the trailing of the killer's horse. This idea gave him another thought: perhaps these cows had been killed for the purpose of luring him to follow the signs and run into an ambush. In view of the conditions of the round-up, the Lord knew the dead animals had been left in plain sight and on ground certain to be swept of cattle in a day or so after the shooting. The invitation to follow the trail was entirely too pointed.

"Let's go back to th' wagon," said the sheriff, joining his companion and swinging into the saddle. "There's no need for you to try to crowd four easy days' work into two hard ones. Keep a-goin' just as you have planned. I know who shot th' cows, an' why. I'll just add it onto his score."

"I reckon I know who did it too," said Nueces, thoughtfully. "I'd say it was th' coyote you shot through th' shoulder. Slade."

"Yeah; he's th' coyote."

The cook looked up as the two riders dismounted near the wagon. He was pleasantly surprised. The temper of his boss was sweet again. Why the hell four dead cows should make their owner cheerful was something he could not understand. Not being well grounded in the theory of counter-irritants, and being without knowledge of this present situation which would allow him to apply that theory properly, the matter must, perforce, remain a mystery to him. He reached for the lard can and began to rub of its contents into the flour necessary to build up a biscuit batter, into which to dip the steaks when the time came. And as he worked, he whistled softly. In four more days his job would be over, and he would be free to indulge in a spree long deferred.

George Bludsoe rode in ahead of the others, nodded to Corson and Nueces, and hung around the tailboard of the wagon where the cook had sliced off the steaks.

"What you want?" demanded the boss of the ovens, suspicious eyes on the puncher.

"Little mite of tallow," answered Bludsoe, hopefully. He beamed as the cook grudgingly handed him two fair-sized pieces, took them and got his calf rope from his saddle. The formula for greasing a rawhide rope was tallow plus elbow grease and, having the first, George was not long in applying the other. Suddenly he paused in his work, struck by a happy thought: why hadn't he thought of it before? Up in that little basin on the slope were four dead cows! He turned his head and called to the straw boss.

"Hey, Nueces! Why can't I go up an' skin them cows? They'll make me four green hides to work on. If I'm goin' to make hackamores an' ropes this winter, I got to get me a supply of hide."

"You can, if you want to," replied the straw boss, "but I wouldn't wait much longer. They're beginnin' to grow ripe. Anyhow, you won't need 'em. There'll be plenty of chances for gettin' hides before winter gets here."

"What'll you do with 'em durin' th' next four days?" demanded the cook, ominously.

"Hang 'em on th' wheels of th' wagon, to drain, first," answered Bludsoe, a little dubiously.

"Hang 'em on yore gran'mother's chin!" snorted the cook. "You don't hang no hides on *this* wagon! Great Gawd!"

Nueces chuckled, glancing from the cook to the puncher.

"I just told you there'd be plenty of chances to get green hides before winter gets here," he said. "Them cows are too old, anyhow; an' you'll have to drain 'em, scrape 'em, peg 'em out on th' ground for th' boys to trip over, an' then pack 'em in to th' ranch. You will unless cook'll let you chuck 'em in th' wagon."

"You just watch anybody chuck any green hides in th' wagon," said the cook, belligerently.

"All right," replied Bludsoe, picking up the lariat. "I'll wait till later."

"Yo're damn' right you will!" muttered the cook, turning back to the work on hand.

Corson and the straw boss were seated on the ground, looking over the tally sheets, discussing the figures and what they might mean. Despite the mildness of the last winter and a range comparatively free from wolves, the figures were not as impressive as they might well have been. Corson stood up as the distant riders left the gather in the care of two men and raced for the wagon. In the forefront was the stray man from the Chain outfit, and the sheriff met him as he swung from the saddle, not far from the wagon. The man had stripped the riding gear and was idly watching the horse roll when he turned his head and saw the sheriff beside him.

"When you get home," said Corson, in a low voice, "you tell yore boss that if anythin' looks wrong with his calf tally, to send me word right away."

"Shore," assented the stray man, looking his companion in the eye. "There's a place over west of our range, outside our round-up assignment, on th' desert. Nice little pond of water down in a basin between th' hills. I've been wonderin' ever since we found them cached yearlin's. What you think about it?"

"Might be well if Rube sent somebody over there to look at it," replied the sheriff, slowly. "Look for cattle tracks an' other signs. If they find any, how fresh are they? I figger it's much too far east, accordin' to th' brands; but it might be used for a water place on a trail drive. That sounds loco, but it seems that anythin's possible."

"You figger they're drivin' 'em out that way?"

"I just told you I don't figger that a-tall. I said anythin' was possible," replied the sheriff.

"Y-e-o-o-w!" yelled a voice from the pickle barrel, holding aloft the two-pronged spear, otherwise known

as a fork, tied on a long handle. "First prize to th'
Turkey Track! Just lookit that hunk of cauliflower!"

"Match you for it!" shouted the Bar W man,
amidst a gale of laughter.

"Yeah?" snorted Turkey Track. "An' what do I get
if I win?" he demanded.

"You get th' cauliflower!"

"Man, I got that already. Go spear some yoreself!"

After dinner the sheriff, yielding to his growing
restlessness, abruptly arose. He nodded to the smiling
circle and went to his horse. In a moment he was making a thin line of dust toward the west, heading
straight for the tumbled hills and deep arroyos between him and the Bar W, and totally ignoring such
things as trails. It was five miles to the ranch buildings
the way he was going, while it was nearer fifteen by
the trail. The tracks made by the horse of the man
who had killed the four JC cows led southwestwardly,
toward Willow Springs. Corson was not following
them, although he was remembering them, and was
alert enough not to forget what they might mean to a
pursuer. He knew the identity of the killer, and for
the present that was enough.

When he reached the Bar W he found a scene of
great activity. Their round-up work was over, the
wagon standing under its shed, but another task made
the corral look like an anthill of effort. The outfit was
removing the shoes from more than two hundred

horses, preparatory to turning them loose on the range, there to roam in peace until the fall round-up should call them in again.

The sheriff had no more than dropped down the last slope before the foreman swung into his saddle and rode off to meet him. The two men met and stopped a quarter of a mile from the buildings and corrals.

"I'm allus prepared to give an' take on tally figgers," said the foreman, abruptly; "but th' figgers I'm talkin' about now are mostly take, an' no give. I'm guessin' we're short near two hundred head. All calves. Don't know nothin' about yearlin's. Won't know till fall. Does that mean anythin' to you?"

Corson swore, and nodded violently.

"It means a hell of a lot," he said. " 'Specially when you hook onto 'em th' two hundred that's makin' Nueces talk rabid, an' a few other things."

"By Gawd, somebody's swingin' a wide loop down here!" snapped the foreman.

"Loop?" echoed the sheriff. "Loop?" he repeated ironically. "Looks to me like he's swingin' two, three corrals! I'm beginnin' to figger they aim to make one grand clean-up an' then quit. You seen Slade in th' last two, three days?"

"Jack Slade?"

"Yeah. Worked for th' BLR. His stampin' ground is over Crooked Creek way. He'll be favorin' his right shoulder."

"I know who you mean," replied the foreman. "No, I ain't seen him. Why?"

"Not nothin' special. I was just curious. Our stray man's left you, I reckon."

"Yeah, pulled his drag th' first thing this mornin'. It'll cut down that missin' two hundred head of yourn to about one fifty. Not countin' th' cows, of course."

"Sorry I missed him," said the sheriff, "but I'm right glad about th' fifty head he's drivin'. Sorry I missed him because I'd like to have him stay here for a while. I might need a man to ride to th' ranch in a hurry, some day or night right soon," he explained.

"Hell, you got one, or two, or six," replied the foreman quickly. "You get any news that you want to send on to th' JC, you send it to me an' I'll see it's delivered like a bullet out of a gun."

"Thanks. That's good. Say, do I look loco?" demanded the sheriff.

"Not no more than usual," answered the foreman with a grin.

The sheriff sighed with relief.

"Then I'm holdin' my own; but if I ain't plumb crazy within a week or two, then it's only because of my well-known mental strength. Trait of th' family, mental strength. I can see a big herd of stolen cattle. Yearlin' steers and weaners. Th' fellers that are holdin' 'em are so damn' shore of themselves that they're holdin' th' weaners so they will grow up into beef. They can't be so very far away, because of drivin' off th' weaners. An' they can't be so very close because this whole range has just been combed so close that a coyote ain't been overlooked. There you have it: they can't be far, and they can't be close. There can't be no herd of stolen cattle, but there is. Yes, sir: if I ain't plumb locoed inside a couple of weeks, I'll be th' outstandin' marvel of th' age. Now let's ride on in."

"You do seem to be in a hell of a pickle," said the Bar W foreman, trying not to grin. "You want any help?" he asked as they started toward the ranch buildings.

"Not now," replied the sheriff. "There's a kinda personal slant to this thing that's like a burr under my saddle. If I do need help, I'll need a lot of it, an' mebby in a hurry. I'll be ridin' alone for a few days more, anyhow. After that, I don't know. It's one of them things that's right under yore nose, but when you reach out for it, it ain't there a-tall. God bless our family trait!"

CHAPTER XIV

CORSON dropped down the steep slope of Packers Gap, the sounds of the iron-shod hoofs filling the arroyo with ringing hammer blows. He slowed as he came to the shoulder of the wall at the entrance to the draw, and covered the next score yards at a walk; but the closed door did not open. Bewilderment and then slow anger wiped out the look of eagerness on his face, and then was, in turn, banished. He had no right to feel that way about her: she was a Meadows, and it was her right to remain loyal to her own blood.

He kept on down the arroyo, his mind far from the present moment, his present surroundings; but it was ripped back to matters close to hand, a mile farther down, by the spiteful crack of a rifle and a sharp tug at his sombrero. His instant roll took him from the saddle and against the safety side of a mass of fallen rock, while the roan clattered on for a few rods and then stopped to graze.

This was the second time he had escaped rifle fire, and neither time had he expected it. It was just luck, sheer luck, the luck of a fool, for only a fool would ride where he was and not keep his senses about him. Still a man might keep his senses about him and be on the alert and then not know of his danger until a shot was fired.

He wriggled forward to a more secure position and then flattened out on the ground and played dead. His rifle was in its scabbard on the saddle, and he had only his belt guns to oppose a weapon of far greater accuracy and range. He would have to make his man come to him. If he did not come of his own accord, to learn what it was vitally necessary for him to know, then he would have to maneuver the assassin into a vulnerable position. He did not dare leave cover or face the rifleman at a long range. All right: his training gave him promise that he could do this if necessary, if he took the needed time and care.

Half an hour passed, and then three quarters. There was no sound, no movement that his straining senses could catch. He lay flat on his back, his eyelids closed to mere slits, his left arm doubled under him, and long since numb. His other arm lay on the ground, flung out at right angles from his body, and its hand was far from the holstered weapon at his thigh. It lay under a stunted sagebush, a squat, cabbage-looking clump of dusty green, which hugged the earth jealously; and in that right hand was his left-hand gun, the empty holster pressed tightly between his body and a slab of stone, its emptiness hidden from any curious searching eye.

It took patience, Indian patience, to maintain this posture minute after minute, until more than forty-five of them had slowly trickled into the past; but the sheriff had that Indian patience, for he was, as others had stated, Indian-trained. The assassin must make certain that his shot had killed: it would be very disconcerting and rather dangerous to run unexpectedly into the man he thought he had murdered. He must be sure of his shot.

Early as the hour was, the sheriff's eyes began to ache from the still slanting rays of the sun, and this was one of the things he feared: the keenness of his sight must not be ruined by black sun spots filling the retinas. He closed the lids tightly, trusting in his hearing to give him a cue.

At last it came. The cutting rasp of sand between boot heel and rock. His lids opened to a mere slit, and he tried to breathe so gently and rapidly that the chest movement would not be noticeable at any distance. A pebble rolled and clicked to a stop. The assassin was doubtless clumsy from nervousness. He was not as good a man as his famous namesake. The sound came from straight ahead, from the other side of the sheriff's feet. He let his jaw sag open, and his tongue protrude a little, and tried to lie as limply as possible. He caught the shadow of a movement high in the air, a mere speck against the blue, where a puzzled vulture circled in long swoops without the movement of a wing.

A satisfied grunt almost startled him, although he thought himself to be prepared for anything. He was making a desperate play and thought himself fortified against the unexpected. A head, minus a hat, slowly, cautiously arose from behind a boulder, and then the neck and shoulders. It was Slade.

In order to fire another shot, if one were needed, the assassin would have either to raise the rifle above the intervening rock, or step out from behind it. The distance was, perhaps, six paces. To slant a rifle barrel at the proper downward angle, over the top of a rock so high, would be almost impossible for a man of his stature. He shrank from the thought of another gun kick against that sore shoulder, and drew a Colt. As its black, evil muzzle arose over the rock, there was a swift, almost spasmodic movement from the prone peace officer. The outflung right hand slid toward him, the wrist curling over into a short, swift arc, and the crashing roar of the big, black powder cartridge filled the arroyo with instant clamor. Slade's head dropped from sight as if his legs had been kicked out from under him. His spurred boots, now lying in plain sight of the peace officer, did not move. Corson arose, gun upraised and ready, and moved stiffly forward, his numbed left arm hanging inertly at his side. One glance was enough: Slade's ambushing and cattle-stealing days were over for all time.

To leave Slade here, covered over with rocks, or as he had fallen; or to take him in to Bentley, as he should do in his official capacity as sheriff; or to leave him on the trail, to be found by the first passing rider?

Which one of these three choices would ease his official conscience, without tipping off his hand? The location was the factor which chiefly bothered him: it must not be known, so early in the game, that this tragedy had occurred so close to the JM ranch, or even along the trail in Lucas Arroyo. Still there was a certain obligation he owed to Slade—now.

Corson hastened to his grazing horse, mounted, and sent it as swiftly as the ground would permit straight toward the place whence that first shot had rung out. After a short search he found Slade's horse, secured it without much trouble, and led it back to the boulder near the pile of rocks. By this time his left arm, through dint of rubbing, was normal again, and it was no great task for a man of Corson's strength to get Slade's body across the saddle of the led horse and to tie it there with Slade's own rope. Then he mounted and rode down the arroyo, leading the second horse, and his rifle resting across the pommel of his saddle; and as soon as he could, he sent the animals up the gently sloping outer benches due north in the direction of the Saddlehorn Pass wagon road.

He pushed on steadily, and when he neared the road he dismounted and went forward on foot until he could look down upon it. He could see nearly a mile of it, and there was no sign of anyone riding or driving along it. Hurrying back to the horses, he mounted and pushed on again at better speed and, finally, at the end of the long descent, found himself on the road. Heading down it at a walk, he plodded toward Crooked Creek; and where the main road swung to the north, he left it and followed the smaller branch trail straight across the rolling hills toward Bentley. And while he rode, he thought out the problem immediately confronting him and, taking his badge of office from a pocket, pinned it on his vest where it would show to the best advantage.

His appearance in Bentley caused quite a stir, but he paid no attention to it, and rode directly to the second building from the end on the west side of the main thoroughfare. Here he dismounted and went inside, and in a moment came out again, followed by the proprietor. It did not take them long to empty the saddle of the second horse, and then Corson led the animal around to the hotel stable. A few moments later he rode down to the marshal's office. He found that person leaning against the door, his eyes on the undertaking establishment.

"Come up to th' Palace," invited the sheriff, "an' I'll buy you a drink." He tossed the reins over the head of the horse and swung down from the saddle. "Save up yore questions, an' ask 'em in there. I got a reason," continued the sheriff, hardly giving his companion time to speak.

"I see you've changed hosses," observed the marshal as he pushed from the door. He was looking at the JC roan with admiring eyes. "You want to sell him?"

"Not unless you can tell me where I can buy a better one," answered the sheriff, smiling. "I don't believe you can do that."

"Reckon not; if I could, I wouldn't want to buy th' roan," replied the marshal, shifting his sagging belt to a more comfortable fit and joining step with his companion.

Heads turned to watch the two peace officers walk up the street, and when they entered the Palace, a fair-sized and very curious crowd followed in after them.

Corson stopped against the bar, waved his hand toward the marshal, and their wants were made known.

"Who was it you brought in, just now?" asked the latter, mildly curious.

"Jack Slade," answered the sheriff.

"Huh!" grunted the marshal. "What did he up an' do?"

"He tried to dry-gulch me," replied the sheriff. "Shot four of my cows, an' left a plain trail. It was a little too plain for me to get careless." He took off his big hat and pointed to the holes in both sides of the crown. "But at that, he near got me. He had first shot an' missed. I tricked him, an' he tried again; but this time I beat him on th' trigger. I threw him on his horse an' brought him down Saddlehorn Pass road."

The crowd was murmuring, and the marshal nodded encouragingly.

"That makes three times," continued the sheriff, "in

th' last couple weeks that somebody's tried to dry-gulch me. Th' first an' second times it was Squinty, Denver Joe, an' Long Bill. After a while folks will either take more pains in their shootin' or let me alone. They want to pay more attention to windage."

"Fill 'em ag'in," said the marshal, nodding to the open-mouthed man behind the counter. Then he turned to face his companion.

"I heard Slade was honin' to get square for that shoulder you gave him," he said. "You figger he was throwin' a wide loop?"

"Looked that way," answered the sheriff, frankly. "There's a little rustlin' goin' on, of course. It's scattered here an' there, over a big section of th' range. There most generally is more or less cattle-stealin' on a range as big as this. Some of them fellers knowed that I was doin' a lot of ridin'. I must have got close to 'em, some time. Slade was careless, an' I practically accused him of stealin' cattle. That was at th' Baylor wagon. He went for his gun an' I shot him through th' shoulder. There wasn't no need of shootin' him anywhere else. Then he itched to get square, an' fixed up a trap for me. It was his hard luck that it didn't work out right."

"Y-e-p; it was," said the marshal, slowly.

"Have one on me," said the bartender, pushing out the bottle. He let his placid gaze rest on the marshal, but there were calculating glints in his eyes.

"How's Denver Joe gettin' along?" This was a very vital question to some people. Denver Joe might turn state's evidence and tell what he knew. His erstwhile companions were not enthusiastic for his recovery.

"All right, I reckon," replied the marshal. "He's healin' up in good shape; but it ain't that gunshot wound that's botherin' Denver. He's lookin' twenty years right plumb in th' face." He put down the glass and drew the back of a hand across his lips. "He's worryin', Denver is; an' I don't blame him for it."

"Yeah," said the bartender, thoughtfully. "He oughta be!"

"Well," said the sheriff, turning from the bar, "th' round-up's over, an' th' whole range was never swept so clean before. It was swept so clean that we found every cached head, an' every man-made weaner. No place was overlooked." He dug out tobacco and papers and began to roll a cigarette. "After today's shootin' match, I reckon that rustlin' will be outa style in this part of th' country for quite a spell. I'll have time to take a little interest in my own affairs, an' I'm shore goin' home to help th' boys take th' shoes off th' cavvy. We've got a lot of broncs to break, an' if there's one thing I like, it's makin' broomtails into shavetails."

He looked casually around the room, his gaze taking in the marshal, the bartender, and the crowd, and his smile and nod were meant for all of them.

"See you all in th' fall, mebby," he said, and the swinging doors swung gently and squeakily behind him.

The marshal, nodding to the crowd, strode after his friend and, catching up with him, fell into step. They walked slowly back to where the JC horse stood before the marshal's office.

"I shore do like that roan hoss," said the latter enviously as his companion picked up the reins and placed one hand on the saddlehorn. "I see you got him shod all round."

"Yes," replied Corson, swinging up from the ground. "He's my pet ridin' horse. I don't work cattle with him. Well, I'll see you again, an' long before fall. *Adiós.*"

"Wait a minute," said the marshal hastily, as he looked up the dusty street. "Wait a minute! Here comes th' pe-rade." The term was so apt that it made him chuckle.

Corson turned his head and saw Black Jack Meadows riding up the street toward the Palace, and behind him rode his three sons, shoulder to shoulder. They would have made a hit in opéra bouffe without the addition of a word or action. They dismounted, fastened their horses to the tie rail, and disappeared into the building.

"You named it then," admitted the sheriff, with a wide grin. "Damn' if they ain't funny. Huh! Come to think of it, I reckon I'll wait a few minutes an' see what Black Jack does after he learns that I've killed Slade. Mebby th' pe-rade will head this way."

"No such luck," growled the marshal, unconsciously rubbing the walnut at his thigh. "Th' hull four of 'em might go ag'in me or you alone; but not th' two of us. Dry-gulchin' is more in their line." His eyes suddenly narrowed from speculation. "You say you got Slade on Saddlehorn Pass road?"

"That's th' way I said I come into town," answered the sheriff, with a grin.

"Well, you don't have to ride back that way," grunted the marshal, glancing meaningly at the Palace. "But it *is* th' shortest way home." He scratched his head gently and smiled.

The pleased expression on the sheriff's face was wiped off by a frown, and he muttered something under his breath.

"Saddlehorn Pass is shore good enough for me," he growled, sullenly. "If I take it, go down through Jackson Canyon to th' Kiowa, an' then strike across th' ridge, I can get back to th' ranch before dark. An' *that's* where I'm goin'."

"Yeah?" drawled the marshal, squinting upward. "What ranch?"

"Th' JC!" snapped Corson, the frown growing.

"Well, I shore figgered it begun with a J," drawled the marshal. He studied the scowling countenance above him. "There ain't no chance of bein' dry-gulched now." He turned his head and looked significantly at the Palace.

Corson's reply was to gather up the slack in the reins, press his knees against the saddle, wheel, and ride off, at right angles to the trail which led to Carson. He was starting east toward the Saddlehorn Pass road. He turned, looked back, raised a hand in a parting gesture, and then, facing about again, sent the horse into a lope. He cut the road at a point below where he had left it an hour or so before, and let the horse drop into a walk up the long, gentle slope. As he rode he fidgeted, becoming steadily more restless and ill-at-ease.

To follow the road over the divide and then go down through Jackson Canyon, he would have to turn and ride south a mile or more at the other end of the canyon: if he turned south now and went by way of the Gap it would not add more than two miles to his total riding. Two miles. A mere flea bite to a man on a good horse; but he hated to give in after he had so definitely settled the matter. She had made her choice. Oh, well: he would give her one more chance, not admitting to himself that it was he who was really receiving the benefit of the chance.

He turned to the right, left the road, followed along a bench, and not long thereafter he was on the Packers Gap trail, riding hand in hand with hope. The mouth of the draw went slowly past, but the door did not open. He could just see the top of it from the

Gap trail, but by standing up in the stirrups he could see a little more. No: he had been right the first time —the door was closed.

All right! She would wait a long time before he rode this way again, a long, long time. He was through: definitely, determinedly through. Women could all go to hell, along with the whole Meadows family; and he would begin to send the latter there at the first opportunity. He thought of the marshal's pe-rade, and thrilled to a quick anger: give him but half a chance and he would turn that pe-rade into a funeral procession!

Because of mental turmoil he forgot his intention to ford the Kiowa and strike straight across the ridge. The horse naturally enough followed the trail, and almost before he was aware of it Corson found himself nearing the trail fork at the Bar W. He had ridden along one side of the triangle, and in order to get to his own ranch he would have to follow the other, and longer, side. Well, as long as he was here, he would drop in at the Bar W bunkhouse and speak with the foreman. That person, hearing hoofbeats, was standing in the door as the sheriff rode up.

"Howd'y, Corson."

"Howd'y," replied the horseman. "Reckoned I'd drop in for a couple of minutes. How are things?"

"Quite some better than we thought," answered the foreman. "When our reps. got home from all th' wagons, with their bunches of strays, our tally was a whole lot better. Wouldn't be surprised if you found yourn th' same."

"Yo're thinkin' of calves," said the sheriff.

"Yeah: calves. As I said, I'm allus ready to give an' take a little on tally figures. These are some short of what I expected; but they seem to be close enough."

"Too bad we got to wait till fall to get th' figgers on th' older cattle," growled the sheriff. "What I'm mostly interested in is yearlin' steers, yearlin's an' over."

"Yeah," agreed the foreman. "I don't reckon there's much deviltry goin' on," he added.

"No?" inquired the sheriff, visualizing the double handful of gold coins lying before Black Jack Meadows on the stud-horse table.

"Well, there might be a little, here an' there, mebby," conceded the foreman.

"Shore hope yo're right," grunted the sheriff, shortly. He waved his hand, turned the horse, and headed up Coppermine Canyon toward Willow Springs and the JC.

If he only could put his finger on it! It was there, and he knew it; and he knew that it was not just "here and there," or scattered, disconnected effort. The conviction was so strong in him that it almost struck into his bones. He was certain that there was systematic rustling going on, and on a large scale. He was as certain of it as he was of his own name.

It had not been necessary to drive off the calves.

once they had been weaned, before the Association was formed. They could be left on their own ranges to grow up into unmarked yearlings. They could be left unmarked on a gamble that many of them would be overlooked in the heretofore more or less careless round-ups. Sleepering was an art as old as cattle-stealing, being, as it was, a part of it. When opportunity offered they could be branded in other marks, a few at a time; and, a few at a time, be drifted off to that other range.

The last phrase made him frown. There was the absurdity. What other range was there? Every mile of country had been thoroughly combed. Up to now, up to this last round-up, rustlers generally could depend upon finding a sufficient number of mavericks—unmarked yearlings, or over—to meet their needs, providing that their needs were modest; but from now on, knowing the thoroughness of the clean-up, they would be forced to wean calves away from their marked mothers, and either to brand them in their own marks, or to sequester them, if their operations were to continue. But where could they sequester them? Damn it all, it made his head ache! Here was another closed door, only this one had been slammed in his face. No matter where he turned, he found a closed door. And this unfortunate phrase, returning to his mind, started him all over again in a trend of thought which did him no good.

He rode into town and stopped before the Cheyenne.

Steve's welcoming smile greeted him, and he replied to it with a frown. Several men were at the bar, among them Franchère, the JC stray man who had been with the Chain wagon. Franchère looked a little sullen as his employer's gaze picked him out, but he managed a grin and nodded.

"Yore drag from th' Chain amount to anythin'?" demanded the sheriff.

"Yeah," answered the puncher, the grin becoming real, and somewhat derisive. "Fifty-odd calves, with their ma's."

"Any of th' other reps. come in?" persisted the sheriff, his frown growing.

"Yeah," answered Franchère, with deliberate slowness. "Johnny came in from th' Turkey Track." He stopped, purposefully withholding the rest of the information.

"Well?" growled Corson, impatiently. "How many calves did *he* bring with him?"

"Thirty-odd."

Could the Bar W foreman be right, after all? No; he'd be damned if he could! Calf facts to the contrary notwithstanding, there were rustling operations going on. Well, he might as well learn the rest of the calf story.

"Jimmy home from th' Baylor ranch?" he asked.

"Yeah, an' got th' shoes pulled from his remuda."

Corson's face grew deeper in color, and he spread his feet and glared at the exasperating puncher through level, unwavering eyes; and quickly, without more verbal prompting, Franchère told the rest of it.

"He brought twenty head—calves, of course."

Corson swiftly added the figures. They cut down the numbers given by Nueces and made a newly estimated calf loss of only sixty head. Sixty calves less than the expected number, a number obtained by rule-of-thumb figuring. Sixty calves! On a ranch as large as the JC it was ridiculous to find positive indications of thieving in so small a margin. They had figured that about eighty-four per cent of the mature cows would calve; all right, suppose that only eighty-three per cent had been fruitful? Eighty-four was a little high, anyhow. That estimated sixty difference would be accounted for right there. He swore, swung on his heel, and strode from the room, forgetting all about the drink he had ridden in to obtain.

Another door had slammed shut against him. He had Franchère's word for that. Franchère: huh! He was acting queer. Shucks, the puncher was all right; he was just enjoying a little joke at the expense of his boss. And then he remembered the puncher's actions down at the Chain wagon; the belated grin, the furtive glances. He had not acted natural. The picture came back to his mind. He was not so certain, now, about Franchère. He would keep an eye on the man. Damned if he was going to be made a monkey of by every man on the range! Then he grinned ruefully and felt a little ashamed of himself: if this kept up, he would

have the disposition of a cactus. Huh! Huh, a cactus
didn't get into a lather over a woman. A cactus had
its points. At that unintentional pun he had to chuckle;
for once he was right, for a cactus had little else but
points, and damned mean ones, too.

The lights gleamed pleasantly in the bunkhouse, and
a deal of noise came therefrom. Shorty's harmonica
and the cook's accordion were going full tilt, vying
with each other in the matter of volume. A figure
passed before the window. It looked like Shorty, walking while he played. Shorty never could sit still when
he played the damned thing. Off on a knoll a coyote
howled, being inspired to vocal effort by the music.
Shorty passed the window again, keeping step with the
music.

The noise, trebly loud in a confined space, effectively
drowned the sounds of the roan's hoofs, and Corson
pulled up just outside the door, swung from the saddle,
and took a step forward. He could see into the strongly
lighted room without being seen in turn. The accordion
was working like an elastic, and Shorty's cupped hands
partly concealed an ecstatic countenance with bulging
cheeks. Music! Who the hell wanted to listen to any
music? Corson could picture the outfit at the wagon,
getting ready to roll up in blankets. He could see the
glowing ashes of the fire, hear the night horses moving
about at the end of their picket ropes, industriously
searching and cropping. He could see the lanky straw

boss, feel his presence. To hell with the bunkhouse! It was no place for him. He swung back into the saddle and rode off without his visit being suspected by the two men inside.

The wagon was where he had expected to find it. The dying embers of the little, economical fire winked at him, and an occasional breeze fanned them to glowing life, revealing the blanketed cocoons lying about it on the ground. As he drew near, one cocoon, a long one, stirred and the sleeper sat up. None of the others had responsibility and, therefore, slept on like tired children. The alert straw boss peered into the sheltering darkness of the night.

"Who th' hell told you to cut out for town?" he demanded in a low but angry voice.

" 'Lo, Nueces," came the soft answer as the horseman stopped at the wagon.

"Huh! 'Lo, Bob," grunted the straw boss. "I guessed wrong. Anythin' th' matter?"

"Yeah! Too damn' much music in th' bunkhouse, an' I kept on ridin'." The saddle came off and was placed under the wagon. In a moment the sheriff had picketed the roan and was sitting down at the foreman's side.

"You been in town?" asked the straw boss.

"Yeah," answered Corson. "Dropped in to get a drink, an' then forgot all about it."

"Gawd, man!" marveled the straw boss. "Yo're shore slippin'! Don't you tell that to Shorty, or he'll worry hisself sick about you. Forgettin' to take a drink shore would be a terrible sign, to his way of thinkin'. See anybody you knew?"

"Shore," grunted Corson, finding his companion's presence to be like a healing ointment. The old horse-faced coyote was a man from the soles of his boots to the top of his big hat. Man, *all* man: about six feet six of it. No higher praise can be bestowed, and we are not forgetting medals of honor.

"You see Franchère?" asked the foreman of the JC. The trace of anger had returned to his voice.

"Yeah," answered Corson, expectantly.

"Drunk or sober?"

"Sober, when I left. Why?"

"Did he have anythin' to say about why he sneaked off to town when he knowed that he had th' first night shift with th' herd?" demanded the straw boss, the anger flicking up a little.

"No," answered the sheriff, and the dying fire was so low that it did not reveal his sudden smile of relief; *that* had been the reason for the puncher's peculiar attitude.

"No?" gently inquired Nueces, echoing the negative. He frowned. "Huh! When we all get back to th' ranch, an' get th' shoes off th' cavvy, we start right in bustin' broncs. Franchère will take his cut last; an' what th' rest of th' boys will leave for him to bust in won't be good news for anybody. I'll take up th' slack on him, all right; an' if he don't like it, me an' him shore will have plenty of words. Shore as hell, we will."

Corson was the owner and the boss of the JC ranch, but this matter and all matters of this kind were outside of his jurisdiction. What the foreman felt called upon to say to the members of the outfit was that person's own, peculiar business. Memory flashed him that little picture again, the picture of Franchère at the Chain wagon, and he was about to mention it, but thought twice, and dismissed the puncher from his mind.

"Checked up on th' calf tally?" he asked, instead.

"Yeah," answered Nueces, grinning in the dark. "I know right close how many we're goin' to get in th' next couple of days. When we're all through we'll be four, five dozen under th' estimate; but I never yet seen an estimate that was right."

"No, nor I," growled Corson. He savagely jerked at a weed growing near his feet.

"That don't change th' lay of th' cards none, Bob," said the straw boss, reading some of his companion's thoughts. He read them because he had the same kind.

"No?" asked the sheriff.

"It just means that we've cleaned damn' close, an' that nobody had time to drive 'em off after they was force-weaned."

"Looks that way from what we found," grunted the sheriff, nodding.

"Yeah. You keep right on ridin', Bob. This ain't

th' first time that folks have figgered you out to be a damn' fool an' then wished they hadn't. Keep right on ridin', just like you are. An' it won't be long now before you'll have a little playmate to keep you company any time you get lonesome. Th' round-up's just about over, an' Shorty can run things at th' ranch. You savvy me? An' yore little playmate will be another damn' fool, like yoreself; an', like yoreself, he shore will like th' stingin' stink of burned powder. Waugh!" he grunted in an altered voice, pretending to be an Indian. "I have spoken."

Corson's hand reached out in the dark and gripped the bony shoulder. His fingers closed like pincers as he stood up. Then, without a word, he strode toward his saddle, to get his blanket roll and become another cocoon on the dark, cool ground. When he came back again he found Nueces stretched out full length on the earth, a gently breathing, silent figure. Corson rolled up beside his straw boss. This was the way for a man to sleep. His mind flashed him the picture of the JC ranch house. It was dark and silent and lonely, for all its gleaming white paint. Never before had he thought of it in just that way, but he had to admit that it *was* lonely.

CHAPTER XV

CORSON rolled out of his blankets as the sun cleared the high horizon, and found that he was the last man to get up. The tantalizing odor of coffee was doing things to his olfactory nerves, and he discovered that he was very hungry. The cook's standard range meal confronted him, but somehow a man's appetite was not blunted by steak three times a day, not as it was prepared as this artist cooked it; not when sleeping in the open and riding hard from early morn to night were the hones and strops that keened the edge of a man's hunger. And steak was proper food to stick to a rider's ribs. The cook found his variety in the other dishes, and no one complained. The JC wagon was a little more generous than the usual run in its use of canned vegetables and fruits. It was a good outfit to work for.

Corson ate in silence, his mind reaching out over miles of country, scrutinizing it again and again, as he had done so many times before. Cattle were material things, occupying space. They had to eat, and in country such as this that meant a great deal of space. To a man accustomed to the turf pastures of the East, that space was surprising. A herd of any size would require miles for its feeding. Figuring twenty-five acres to a cow, for year-round feeding, the average range would not support more than twenty-six animals to the section. A section is, of course, a square mile.

This kind of figuring meant an assumption, of course, that a herd was being considered; a herd segregated from the other animals on the range. A more elementary and much simpler way would be to let the cattle run on their own, proper ranges, and to rustle them as needed; but this, in turn, meant smaller operations, stealing on a lesser scale. Somehow Corson's mind persistently considered the puzzle from the viewpoint of a herd, of segregated cattle. But this was absurd, on the face of it: the whole range had been too well swept by the round-up crews for this to be possible; yet his thoughts ran that way. That had been the basis for his facetious remark to the Bar W foreman that strength of mind was a characteristic of the Corson family.

He carried his dishes to the wreck pan, and then, sitting on the ground with his back against a rear wheel of the wagon, rolled a cigarette and watched the men catch their circle horses in the flimsy rope corral. They were soon saddled up and riding off toward the appointed line. The straw boss, standing beside his saddled horse, watched them leave and then, turning, strode over to his employer's side.

"Got you buffaloed, huh?" he asked with a smile as he looked down at the sheriff.

"Yes," grunted Corson, tipping his head back and grinning up at his horse-faced friend.

"If all th' wagons cleaned up as good as we did, there wasn't no place overlooked," said Nueces, thoughtfully, stating a simple fact simply. "Mebby one or two of 'em wasn't so careful."

"From what I hear, they swept as clean as we did." The sheriff chuckled. "You'd be surprised if you knew how many old mavericks, reg'lar old moss-headed outlaws, were turned up in this drag. I saw some that were twenty years old, if a day: reg'lar old moss-heads."

"Yeah?" grunted the straw boss, and grinned. "We found a few ourselves, over in th' brakes, that didn't do our former round-up reputations no real good," he admitted. "You suspicionin' any particular part of th' range?"

"Yeah."

"You know how it was worked by th' wagon?"

"Yes. It's a ridge range, and it was swept in three parallel belts," answered the sheriff.

"From th' top down?" asked the straw boss, quickly.

"No. From th' bottom up," answered Corson. "They threw th' worked cattle on th' downhill side."

"Huh!" muttered Nueces. "Any particular brand runnin' on it?" he persisted, gently scratching his head.

"Two. BLR an' th' JM."

"Hell!" said the straw boss, suddenly grinning. "Th' JM ain't got more'n two, three cows, an' they're scrubs." He chuckled. "I don't know how they fill their bellies on th' JM."

"Quarterly remittances from th' East," explained Corson.

"Yeah? Still livin' off th' bottle, huh?"

"Bottle?" asked the sheriff. "What you mean?"

"Still pullin' at th' nursin' bottle," grunted the straw boss, with contempt. "They ain't got guts enough to wrestle out their own livin' for themselves."

"Black Jack's quite a hand at stud-hoss," said Corson.

"That so?" quickly asked the straw boss, his face lighting up. "Where at does he hang out?"

"Bentley. Don't you get too excited, you old horse-thief: he makes a good livin' out of playin' stud-hoss, or at least it looks that way."

The swift change of expression on the face of the straw boss bespoke a certain restrained admiration. Any man who made a good living playing stud-horse regularly—well, he certainly was no infant.

"Reckon that takes him off'n th' bottle," he grudgingly admitted. "I don't wonder he ain't pesterin' his-self, associatin' with no cows." He again scratched his head and nodded understandingly. "Lookin' after th' cattle is what his boys are good for."

"They don't stay with th' cattle," corrected the sheriff. "They're too busy totin' walnut, playin' body-guard for their old man."

"Huh!" snorted the straw boss, with deep contempt. "Then that puts him back on th' bottle. What's *he* need a bodyguard for?"

"I don't know, but I shore aim to find out," replied the sheriff, slowly, thoughtfully. "That was one of th' things that didn't smell right, to me. There wasn't no sense to it, unless there was a hell of a lot. There's one thing shore, Nueces: a man that's pickin' up a cow here an' a cow there don't need no three-man body-guard; but if he was mixin' in with quite a bunch of fellers, then mebby—aw, hell!"

Nueces studied his boss in grave silence. He himself was nobody's fool, and he knew by experience that the sheriff was squarely in the same category. One little sound not quite right will catch an engineer's ear in a roar of sound. One overemphasized gesture or word, one little action out of place or character, has the same challenge to observant men. The great curse of acting is overacting. Nueces' mind was working swiftly, bridging gaps, taking short cuts. He knew how his companion's thoughts were running. Here was what some might regard as an inconsequential statement, which appealed to him with the force of visual, definite proof. In race-track parlance it might have been called a hunch; but it had a much better and deeper warrant than that. He thought it might be a good idea to winnow out some of the possibilities.

"Heavy winner, Black Jack?" asked the straw boss, his eyes narrowing from intensive thought.

"Don't know," answered the sheriff; "but he does tote quite a lot of hard money—yellow money."

The possibility was still a possibility.

"Huh! Does he play square?" persisted the straw boss, his thoughts now leaving the preservation of wealth and considering the need for a bodyguard from another direction. And he knew that he was talking to a master hand at poker.

"Far as I could see, an' I watched him right close."

"Was he winnin' while you watched him?" persisted Nueces, his eyes glinting with interest.

"Yes; right consistently."

"An' you say you watched him close?"

Corson nodded, smiling to himself at what a true bloodhound this foreman was.

"Huh! A lucky stud-hoss player with a three-man bodyguard!" snorted the straw boss. "It's loco!"

"Shore," admitted the sheriff; "but I'm figgerin' that there's a good reason for th' bodyguard just th' same."

"If there is, it's a reason that'll hang him!" snapped Nueces. "You reckon folks have begun figgerin' that yo're plumb loco?" he asked, eagerly, his thoughts again running obliquely.

"Don't know," answered the sheriff; "but mebby some of them are, over on th' Bar W."

"Hope so!" exclaimed Nueces, grinning broadly. "That's allus near a dead-shore sign that yo're on th' right hoss an' on th' right trail. I see yo're ridin' th' roan."

"Yes. There's no chance now for me to try out my hand with th' cattle."

"Well, we'll shore have a lot of broncs to bust," said the straw boss, with a grin. His mind flashed back to the other matter, and he spoke without preamble, knowing that preamble was not needed when he was talking with the sheriff.

"That ridge is a mighty good place for hidin' cattle," he said, abruptly. "But if th' Baylor wagon cleaned it, an' said they did, then it was cleaned good. That Jerry is a top hand in a round-up."

"Yes. Of course, if anybody's on th' rustle they could let 'em run, an' pick 'em up when they wanted to; but from now on they'll be faced with branded cattle."

"Yeah; from *now on*," replied Nueces. "It takes a lot of country to graze a herd of any size."

"They wouldn't have to graze 'em all year round," said Corson. "They could rest th' range half a year or more."

"Yeah, that's so. You figgerin' a herd?"

"I'm admittin' that I'm crazy," replied the sheriff.

"That's a good sign!" snorted the straw boss. "In two, three days I won't have nothin' to do but go crazy with you." His grin threatened the safety of his ears.

"Let th' broomtails wait awhile," said Corson, slowly. "We can break 'em later. Put th' boys to ridin' range, mostly after dark, in pairs. You know th' strategic points."

"All right," replied the straw boss. "Shall we take time to pull th' shoes off th' cavvy?"

"Yes. That won't take time enough to be considered."

"Anythin' more on yore mind before I join th' boys on circle?" asked Nueces.

"No. Crowd this work a little. Clean it up right soon, figger th' total tally, an' start th' range ridin'. I've arranged with th' Bar W to get word through to th' ranch, if an' when th' time comes."

"We'll be waitin' for it," growled Nueces.

"Well, now I've got some more ridin' to do," said Corson, getting up and moving toward the roan, already saddled.

"I reckon you shore can do lots of it, on that hoss," said the straw boss, gazing admiringly at the handsome, mettlesome animal. "He's got th' purtiest action on th' range."

Corson nodded and swung into the saddle. He watched his straw boss ride off toward the waiting circle riders, and then, raising his hand in a parting salutation to the cook, rode from the wagon.

The mind is a peculiar sort of switchboard. Originating there, thoughts make their own connections, and die there; but they leave a trace of their passing.

Other thoughts try to break in, perhaps unsuccessfully at first, but if they hammer persistently enough they may get through. Sometimes the opposite is true, and they slip through. Sometimes there appears to be no reason for the connections plugged in; but there is always a thread of continuity, except in those messages originating from objective stimuli. Even in dreams, when Reason is asleep at its post and the board running wild, the fantastic connections may have this thread. All this to state that Corson's mind was not engaged in the problem of rustling, or even in matters pertaining to the Meadows family in any of its persons, and to show that his mental state was a natural one.

He was keeping time in his thoughts to the alluring and restful tempo of the hoofs of his horse. The ever-repeated tattoo and the rhythmic accent were soothing and, at times, almost soporific. Perhaps it was the casual remark of the straw boss about the roan's action which was responsible for the mental circuit; but for whatever reason, the sheriff was considering nothing else. He rode between constricting rock walls, and the hoofbeats came thundering back at him; and then he stiffened suddenly as the new and pertinent connection was plugged in. The new line had vainly sought for this connection, sought it for days, and now it was made. Memory was getting its message through.

Although bombarded by the regular beat of the roan, shod on all four hoofs, with its own insistent and characteristic accent, he did not hear it; he was listening to other beats, to another horse; to the peculiar, double accent of a cutting-out horse, shod only on its rear hoofs; listening to a beat so distinctive as to have and to merit a meaning of its own. It had the merit, and now he suddenly realized that it also had its meaning; that to one pair of listening ears it was filled with meaning, was, indeed, a definite mark of identity.

What a fool he had been to overlook so obvious a thing, more especially when it had hammered at him through his ears mile after mile, day after day! Unable to see clearly over the half-mile, almost, which lay between the door of the adobe ranch house and the trail in Lucas Arroyo, a trail which would allow her to see no more than a rider's hat, she had known of his approach only by the tossed echoes of the hoof-beats of his horse. And what horse had that been, to whose hoofbeats had that door opened? The bay, the cutting-out horse, with its bare forehoofs and its iron-shod rear ones; the bay, whose hoofs gave it a signature all of its own! It was the only horse, to his knowledge, shod in that fashion for miles around. With him the shoeing had been an experiment. What a fool he had been!

The surprised roan leaped forward into its best speed. Horsethief Creek was behind and Willow Creek ahead. Now it was alongside, and the bend in the trail was ahead, now even, and now behind. Part way up the long, gentle slope of Horsethief Gap squatted the buildings of the JC ranch, the white-painted ranch house standing out like a beacon. The roan was too proud to slow down on the upward climb, but held its swift pace unflinchingly, although punished by it. Its rider finally came to his senses and smiled at the instant obedience of the horse, which dropped into the long, easy lope that was its normal traveling gait.

The roan was a little surprised and somewhat disgusted. After the way it had run, it expected and deserved to stop at the corral; but it went on past this enclosure and on up the slope. Its rider turned it suddenly to the left and shook out his rope.

The grazing bay raised its head inquiringly, its suspicions became certainty, and it forthwith trotted up the slope. The roan moved a little faster, the noose sailed out and dropped over the bay's head, and the instant the braided rawhide touched its skin, the bay stopped. It knew ropes, did the bay, and knew them well.

Corson dismounted, rubbed the nose of the intelligent animal, and then substituted hackamore for lariat. It was not long before the roan was free to trot off to drink and to graze, and the bay carried its rider toward the JC bunkhouse.

Shorty loafed to the door, oozed through it, and leaned against the outside wall. He considered his approaching employer and grinned a welcome as Corson rode up.

"You goin' out to chouse up th' cattle for th' boys?"

he asked, impertinently. He well knew that his companion was as good a hand with cattle as any man on the range.

"Goin' to climb down from here an' pull yore nose," said the horseman, grinning. He was in rare good humor now, and restless with a keen impatience. The new thought still had to be put to the test.

"Yeah?" inquired Shorty, straightening up. "Better wait till I call th' cook."

"Reckon you need some help?"

"Reckon somebody oughta hold me from behind, so you can do it," answered Shorty, his grin growing.

"Do what?" asked Corson, his mind on other things.

"Pull m'nose."

"It's too damn' long now," said Corson, insultingly. "You come on down to th' blacksmith shop, an' watch me take th' shoes off this horse's forefeet."

"I can't learn nothin' from you," retorted Shorty.

"Then you are goin' out to work with th' boys." He cocked an eye upward and then pushed away from the wall and headed for the blacksmith shop. When he got there he found his boss already at work on the shoes, and he moved a little faster.

"Gimme that tool," he said, holding out his hand. "I can pull off three shoes while yo're scratchin' yore head. Gimme it."

"I only want to take off two," replied Corson. He shoved Shorty back and bent down again. He straightened the clinched nails and reached for the nippers.

The shoe came loose and fell with a clink on top of its mate. Corson picked them both up and hung them on a peg in the wall. Then he turned and looked at his cheerful companion.

"Got somethin' to tell you," he said. "Keep yore big mouth shut, from now on. Nueces knows th' whole thing, or as much as I do. Until th' boys ride in with th' wagon, you stick right close to this ranch, here. Now then, you listen to me."

Shorty listened, and his more or less bored expression vanished until, at last, it showed a frank and enthusiastic delight. When the last word had been said, and Corson had led the bay outside and swung up into the saddle, the puncher's face was beaming.

He stood quietly and watched his boss ride away, straight for the great ridge along Coppermine Canyon, in a line with Jackson Canyon beyond. Shorty scratched his scalp: Corson could leave Jackson Canyon at its head and take his choice of the Gap trail or the Saddlehorn Pass wagon road. Both led to Bentley, but the road was better.

He glanced at the green hides draining on the corral wall, hides which he was going to work on until they were fit for cutting the strands so cunningly worked into hackamores and lariats by Bludsoe; but he did not really see them. His thoughts were elsewhere. He swung on his heel and walked rapidly back to the bunkhouse, finding the lazy cook lazily draped on the long washbench. That worthy was idly watching the sheriff lope down the slope toward Willow Creek, and he now put his thoughts into words.

"Shore is a damn' easy life, sheriffin'," he said, looking up at his squat friend. "Nothin' a-tall but paper work these days."

"Yeah?" inquired Shorty, an eyebrow moving upward. "Tell me where I'll find me some gun rags, you —— —— fool!"

CHAPTER XVI

BY THE wagon road it was sixteen miles to the mouth of Jackson Canyon; by rounding the butte just west of the JC ranch houses, crossing Coppermine Canyon, climbing the high ridge behind it, and then following down an unnamed canyon on the far side, the distance was cut down by a third. In his impatience to cover ground and keep to straight lines, the sheriff did not stop to realize that he would save but little actual time; but at the present moment directness was a fetish. The agile bay was better at this sort of going than the roan, and broke through its rider's preoccupation to awaken admiration for its goat-like abilities.

The road through Jackson Canyon was a fair one, and the bay swept up its almost gentle slope, crossed the Carson road, and then followed along the old trail to the Gap. For miles the peculiar beat of its hoofs had hammered at its rider, keening him to tension and expectancy. When the Gap finally lay behind, and the test of the soundness of his reasoning drew near, the Corson calmness was a reputation undeserved in this case, at least. He fairly squirmed in the saddle and grudged the slowness of his progress, which was not at all slow.

The arroyo suddenly deepened as the trail pitched down, and the clamor of the hoofs was like hammer blows. The shoulder of the side draw lay just ahead, and then he had passed it. Now came the moment. Standing up in the stirrups, he eagerly looked up the draw and saw the upper edge of the door. It was open. He sighed with relief, dropped back into the saddle, and sent the willing bay up the little JM home trail. He was surprised to find himself trembling a little.

She was standing in the doorway, watching him through every yard of his progress, fighting to retain her composure, to maintain her bitter decision; to balance that decision against the hurt it would give to him. Against her better judgment, against her expressed wish to the contrary, she had allowed him to do what she had forbidden; she had yielded this concession; but in the far graver matter she would be adamant, unshakable. She would not go to the man she loved as the daughter of a thief, as the sister of thieves.

The bay whirled against the edge of the porch, and its rider leaped halfway across the little platform before his boots touched it. She started to raise a hand, but she was too late. After a long moment she freed herself, and gently pushed him away, to hold him off and look at him.

"Dear boy, what are we going to do?" she asked him, her brown eyes moist.

"I can tell you, Alice! I *have* told you, but you asked me not to tell you that again. Tell me, dear: is there anything in all th' world that matters so much to us as this? I can solve this puzzle, and all other puzzles that bother us, if you will only let me."

"I know that you think so, boy. It is not you who are helpless, but myself. I should not have opened the door, but surely I am entitled to just a little happiness; surely I am entitled to see you once in a while, to speak with you. And even in that I am unfair to you. Right now there is no one on the ranch but you and me; but there is no telling when the others may return. And the time will surely come, unless I keep this door tight closed, when they *will* return; and then I may have reason to hate myself for the rest of my life. What can we do?"

"Do you want me to tell you that, Alice?" he blurted eagerly.

She shook her head swiftly, emphatically; and, oh, how it hurt her!

"No, dear: you have told me. It's something for me to treasure, to hide away deep in my heart; something to give me courage through the long, dark nights, and the dull, bleak days. I'm weak, dear: day by day, hour after hour I've listened for the hoofbeats of your horse; hoping that you would do what I've asked you not to do."

"I was a fool! A blind, blind fool! I didn't realize until this mornin' that it was th' bay's hoofs you listened for; th' half-shod bay! I had to do some hard ridin', an' its forefeet were gettin' tender. I had him shod all round. I rode home this way, a few days later, an' was disappointed because th' door didn't open. Then I was a bigger, blinder fool than ever. I turned th' bay out on th' range, shod as it was, an' rode th' roan. I passed here again. Then a third time. Th' door did not open. Then, this mornin' I realized what I had done, why th' door stayed shut. I rode in to th' ranch, swapped th' roan for th' bay, an' ripped th' shoes off his forefeet. An' I call myself a tracker, a trailer, a plainsman!" He stopped and caught his breath at the expression on her face, and moved forward hotly, eagerly; but she held him off.

"I'm glad, dear," she said in a voice so low he barely heard her. "I'm *glad!* Boy, I feared that you— that you had forgotten me."

She merited punishment for that statement, and she received it; but it was the kind of punishment that she could thrive on for the rest of her days. Again she freed herself and pushed him away.

"What *can* we do, dear; what can we *do?*" she again asked, hopelessly, and this time the tears were plain to be seen. "It isn't fair to you, no matter *what* I do. I'm helpless. If I tell you to stay away, if I keep the door closed, it is not fair to you; if I let you come, it is even more unfair. It is even worse than that: it is very, very dangerous."

"You love me, Alice?"

"Must you ask me that? Don't you know?"

"Yes! But I want to hear you say it!"

"I should not say it. I should deny it if I was honest and fair with you; but I can't hurt you, boy. You know I love you."

"Then come away, an' marry me!"

"No. I can't. I can't marry, ever. I won't! Oh, please, dear! Please don't urge me, don't torture me. I can't stand much more. Please don't, if you love me."

He was not as strongly intrenched in his stronghold of love as he well might have been: the day would come, and soon, he feared, when he would be obliged to shoot it out with this woman's father, this woman's brothers. But close as that day might be, inexorable as he knew it was, he would hold it off, up here, in this matter, as long as he could. He would not recognize it until he was squarely face to face with it; he would close his eyes and pretend that it was not so. But it was so, damnably so. It was so true and so close that he involuntarily stepped back to look quickly about the ranch.

The bay was squarely in his way, and he spoke to it. The knowing animal moved forward a few steps and stopped, like a curtain drawn aside. Corson examined the corral and the blacksmith shack with searching eyes, one hand instinctively resting on the butt of a gun. In all this mental welter, this emotional chaos, he knew that he was acting like a fool; and he forthwith proved it by leading the bay off to one side, out of possible gunfire, and dropped the reins down before its eyes. The horse was well trained, and by this simple act became as firmly anchored as if picketed. Corson turned slowly and walked back to the porch, his face set and grim and determined.

"What are you going to do, Bob?" she asked him, a note of fear and alarm in her voice.

"I'm goin' to camp on th' edge of this porch, an' get acquainted with th' menfolk of th' family when they come back. I'm right tired of playin' stranger!"

"Dear, do you want me to tell you never to come here again? Don't you want me to open the door—sometimes?"

"What you mean?"

"You can't stay here. You can't meet the men. You *must* ride on. Once in a while, when it is safe, I'll let you see me for a few minutes. But now you *must* ride on."

The argument climbed swiftly, and Sheriff Corson soon learned that the less logic a woman employs in matters of this kind, the more certain she is to win out. It was so in this case. He could have demolished her logic with better; he could have if his own entrenchments were not wide open and damnably vulnerable; why in hell hadn't Black Jack and his worthless cubs stayed honest, or at least limited their dishonesty to cheating at cards? But logic or no logic, he found that he had no weapons shaped to combat her appeals and her tears successfully. He was whipped, and he knew it. He must do nothing that would keep that door forever closed. He was whipped from the front, the rear, and the flanks.

He reluctantly got to his feet, strode savagely to the bay, and led it back to the porch. There seemed to be but one thing for him to do: to do as he had been told. It was a new experience for him, and one which he did not relish: but he did it.

And then he suddenly realized what a fool he had been. Playing the fool seemed to be his strong point these days. How could he remain to meet Black Jack and his sons, here on this ranch? That would mean shooting. What a fine and noble lover he would be to shoot down her father and brothers before her very eyes! The thought frightened him. It almost made him sick. He glanced quickly and apprehensively around the draw, now as eager to get away as he had been determined to stay. Great God! Was there no way out of this mess? He must never meet her menfolk here!

"Yo're right, dear," he said, moving quickly toward her. "I couldn't bear to think of th' door always bein' closed against me. In th' past few days I've learned how *that* hurts." He held her close. "Listen for th' bay an' its bare forefeet. That's a mistake I'll not make again."

"Good-bye, dear: you *must* go. I'll listen, boy, day and night. And even if the door stays shut, you'll know that I am listening, that I hear, and that I'm glad. Good-bye!"

Before he could reply, he was looking at the rough, heavy planks, and he heard the latch drop into place. In a daze he went through certain orderly, instinctive motions without being fully conscious of them. And then the great arroyo was opening up before him, and not much later he could see the distant, wide valley of Crooked Creek. The mental turmoil gradually subsided, and one thought emerged for a moment, to stand out clear and challengingly: his oath of office had been taken seriously, with his eyes open and without mental reservations, and it left him no choice of action running counter to it. Then another thought popped into his mind: he had heard somebody say, or had read, that the course of true love did not run smoothly. The damned fool hadn't known what he was talking about: it didn't run at all—it was all blown to hell and gone.

CHAPTER XVII

BENTLEY drew near, and then Corson passed the first building. A few moments later he stopped before the marshal's office and heard his name called before he stepped into the sight of the man inside. He smiled grimly and again reminded himself that he had been a fool.

"Knowed who you was, shore pop, this time," said the marshal. "See you swapped back to th' bay."

"Heard it, you mean," retorted Corson with feeling as he dropped into a chair. "You also heard that I've got it shod for workin' cattle again."

"Y-e-p. Came nigh to mentionin' that, th' other day," drawled the town officer. "But you had a long ride ahead of you, an' you was all sweat an' lather. 'Twasn't none of my business."

"I shore wish you'd made it yore business!" snapped the sheriff.

"Been shot at ag'in?" placidly asked the marshal.

"No. But I wish you'd made it yore business, just th' same," reiterated the sheriff.

"Well, sometimes that works out all right, but I've found out, generally an' in th' long run, that mindin' another man's business is a right shore way of gettin' into trouble. It's somethin' like bustin' outlaw **broncs** in these here fool Fourth of July exhibitions: a hell of a lot of sweat, trouble, an' bruises, without no sense to it. But I *am* goin' to drop my rope over th' head of one idear, this time, an' then hand it over to you to hold or run down, as you like: there ain't no hoss around here that sounds like that bay, shod like it is. Take a man holed up som'ers on th' lookout, an' he'd know who you was mebby before you come into sight. There ain't no use of givin' nobody any edge like that. How's th' new kind of round-up workin' out, over yore way?"

"Slick as a greased rope; but somewhere on th' range it left an awful hole," answered the sheriff.

"You got any idear where th' hole is?"

"Yes," answered the sheriff. "It's th' only place left, an' that's impossible."

"I woulda figgered it was impossible to take rabbits out of an empty hat, till I saw it done, right before my eyes."

"Bein' th' only place left, I got to take a look at it; an' I know all about th' bay's hoofs. Neither of these things are what's puttin' saddle sores on me. If you want to marry a woman, you can't very well do it after shootin' her father an' brothers, can you?"

"That would kinda com-plicate things," drawled the marshal, thoughtfully. Lights danced in his eyes. He pulled slowly at the dead pipe. "But it can be done."

"Yeah?" said Corson derisively.

"Y-e-p. Wimmin are strange creatures. If they're plumb in love with a man, there ain't nothin' you can say is impossible for 'em to do. As a class. If you hunt around, an' pick an' choose, you'll find one, anyhow, that'll do anythin' on God's gray earth, no matter what it is. There ain't no Hoyle on wimmin in love. There's one thing, among others, that you gotta look out for. That's th' maternal instinct. It's rabid an' it's blind. That's why I'm out in this part of th' country: I got plenty tired of bein' wrong *all* th' time. Son, you just can't figger 'em." He puffed again at the odorous pipe, and felt slowly for a match. "I just wouldn't turn in no badge yet awhile."

"I'm not goin' to!" hotly replied the sheriff. "I won't do that till th' job's all done; an' th' job's shore goin' to be done if I can do it!"

"That's th' kinda spirit that gets you places, even into matrimony," said the marshal, and again his eyes twinkled. "You'll find th' middle of that seat just as comfortable as th' edge."

Corson hastily pushed back on the chair, and drummed his fingers on it, staring out through the open door, his thoughts racing this way and that, and then eddying into little moments of stagnation. It was in one of these stagnant periods when he suddenly realized that he had eaten no noonday meal, and that he was hungry. He glanced at the shadow of the tie rail, looked at his watch, and learned to his surprise that it was past four o'clock. He had covered more than forty miles since leaving the JC wagon, and he had spent quite some time at the JM. During most of the time the bay had chosen its own gait, but the bay was an honest horse. The day had just sneaked past.

"You see anybody from th' JM in town today?" he asked, rolling a cigarette.

"No; an' I've made my rounds. There's quite a few of th' boys missin' from their reg'lar hangouts."

"Which gave you that idear about th' bay's hoof-beats?" challenged the sheriff.

"Y-e-p. Partly." The marshal refilled the pipe and looked up. "We've had a buryin' since you was here."

"Yes? Who?"

"Denver Joe," placidly answered the marshal while he languidly struck a match.

"Denver Joe?" exclaimed the sheriff in surprise. "Why, he wasn't hurt *that* bad. Blood-poisonin'?"

"Lead-poisonin'," grunted the marshal, his pipe finally going to suit him.

"Yeah?"

"Y-e-p."

"How'd it happen? He was in jail!"

"Y-e-p. He was. I don't know just how it did happen, or who done it, me bein' home in bed at th' time; but from th' signs I'd say that somebody called him up to th' bars an' shot his head near off. Close up, it was. Terrible mess to clean up."

"By Gawd!" muttered Corson, swiftly leaning forward. "He was facin' twenty years in th' pen. That was a terrible thought for a man who's spent all his life in th' open. They were afraid he'd talk!"

"Y-e-p. I figger it that way. If he'd turned state's evidence, he'd a-got off easy, mebby. Anyhow, it wouldn't a-been no twenty years. They wasn't takin' no chances. *That's* why I spoke about th' bay's shoes. If they'd shoot down a pardner, like that, they wouldn't do much worryin' about a sheriff. They've showed that, anyhow. Son, you put th' shoes back on them forefeet. You can carry a pair of pincers in yore saddle roll, in case you want to rip 'em off ag'in."

"Denver's passin' don't tell me anythin' new about that part of it," replied Corson. "They were workin' on me before they went to work on him."

"I just about said as much," grunted the marshal. He glanced idly through the door. "Th' games are shrinkin'. Money seems to be gettin' scarce. Then, on th' heels of that, a few of our well-knowed citizens fog it outa town, an' don't come back, which makes my job easier for me. If it works out like it's done before, they'll come back in about ten days or two weeks, with money to burn. What you think?"

"I think that I'm startin' out, tomorrow, to search that place I spoke about; an' th' bay'll be shod all around ag'in. Is there anybody in town you can trust?"

"Two, three. What you want?"

"A messenger."

"Y-e-p. A halfbreed Injun. Everybody picks on him

but me. It's got so he's a kinda one-man dog. I never
saw no use of makin' unnecessary enemies. What you
want him to do?"

"Ride over to th' JC wagon an' give a message to
my straw boss."

"Where's th' wagon?"

Corson sketched the place and explained the route
to be followed.

The marshal nodded understandingly, and then
reached over and put a hand on his companion's knee.

"That's th' way, son," he said slowly. "Don't you
turn in no badge, not never while yo're sheriff. This
county needs a man like you. No woman on earth can
blame a man for shootin' a —— —— cattle thief
to save his own life. I'll see that Injun, right after
dark." He scratched his head. "You ain't told me
what to say to him."

The sheriff gave the necessary information in less
than one minute, realizing that the less the messenger
had to repeat, the more accurate he would be; and
then the anxious expression on his face was translated
into words.

"Can't you send him before dark?" he demanded.

"Nope."

"Can't you find him before then?" persisted Corson, impatiently.

"Y-e-p."

"Well, then, why not do it, an' get him started?"

"Ain't wise," replied the marshal. He drew a hand

across the stubble on his chin, and regarded his companion thoughtfully. "Son," he said, slowly, "I'm goin' to tell you one thing, an' show you another. I'll do th' showin' first. You notice you ain't found me settin' outside, ag'in that wall?"

"Why, yes," answered the sheriff, quickly and curiously.

The marshal stood up, walked to a peg driven into the wall, and took down a battered pair of army glasses. Handing them to his companion, he drew the latter to a place halfway across the room, and a little to the rear.

"You see that kinda eyebrow of brush an' grass, up there just below that piñon on th' hill farther back? There's three patches of cactus just below it an' a little to th' right."

"Yeah, I got it," muttered the sheriff, peering steadily through the lenses.

"Hold right onto it," said the marshal. "That's th' nigh edge of a little wash. Hold th' glasses right onto it, an' tell me what you see."

Corson obeyed, and studied the so-called eyebrow intently for some moments, and then he stiffened a little. He caught the motion of a few twigs, and then to his surprise found himself looking into the face of a man. He could not see it clearly enough to learn the identity of the owner, but well enough to know that it was a face.

"Good Lord!" he growled. "They've got you watched!"

"Y-e-p. Drove me into th' house, away from my favorite settin' place —— —— 'em! How far away would you say it was?" asked the marshal, professionally.

"About four hundred yards," estimated the sheriff, also professionally.

"A leetle mite over," said the marshal studiously. "I'd hold for about th' middle of th' crown of his hat, or where that would be if he was bareheaded. You reckon that's right?"

"Yes! Th' middle of th' crown."

"You ever see a Sharps Special Buffalo gun," asked the marshal, "with th' twenty grain overload?"

"Yes. I've got one, out on my saddle. They're heavy, an' clumsy as a saddle weapon, but they make up for it when a feller needs a rifle."

"Y-e-p. They shore do," agreed the marshal, smiling grimly. "You ever see one with a telescope onto th' barrel?"

"No; but I know they're used," admitted Corson. "Why?"

"A man can do awful close shootin' with an outfit like that."

"He shore can, if he's got eyes in his head, an' a steady hand."

"Don't need a steady hand so much if he's got a good rest," said the marshal. "An th' more of th' barrel that lays on th' rest, th' better he can shoot."

"Yes, of course," said the sheriff, impatiently.

"There's a feller in this town that's right handy fixin' guns an' clocks an' things. Right handy, he is. Good workman. I happened to drop in there, one day recent, an' saw him hidin' a telescope rifle in a hurry. It was a Sharps. I'd figger it took th' hundred-twenty grain load, from th' ca'tridge I saw layin' on th' bench. Somebody thought a lot of that gun. It had set triggers. I'll see that Injun after dark, or he'll mebby ride right through th' gates of th' Happy Huntin' Ground before he reaches th' Saddlehorn Pass road." The marshal took the glasses and carefully hung them up again.

"Who do you figger is layin' up there?" asked Corson, assuming his official character. A situation like this came squarely within his province, and he'd be damned if he'd stand for bushwhacking.

"Ain't shore, but I got my suspicions," answered the marshal with a certain grim satisfaction. He seemed to be in very good humor. "There's one man that's missin' from town durin' th' daylight, that's here every night. An' he never rides into town twice th' same way."

"I'll not stand for ambushin', or attempted ambushin'," said the sheriff, stepping toward the door. "You put them glasses on that eyebrow in about an hour, an' you'll shore as hell see somethin' worth lookin' at!"

"Where you goin'? What you aimin' to do?" asked the marshal in quick alarm.

"Up there," answered Corson grimly.

"You stay away from there, sheriff!" begged the older man. "After tonight I won't be in a mite of danger."

"What you mean?" asked Corson, turning abruptly.

"I mean that after tonight his gun won't be near as good as he reckons on," answered the marshal. "I've noticed that when he comes into town every evenin' there ain't no gun in his saddle scabbard. That's all *I* need to know."

"Yeah?" asked the sheriff, curiously.

"Y-e-p. Man an' boy, I've been right well trained for movin' around on th' ground an' takin' care of myself. If I give him th' first shot, with me in plain, fair sight, an' he misses, then nobody can hardly blame me, or wonder what he's doin' up there. When he pulls that trigger, he up an' puts hisself on record for bein' an ambushin' skunk; an' if I get him before he can get in a second shot, then that's just kinda good luck for me. Huh?"

"Yes; but what if he don't miss you, that first shot?" asked Corson, impatiently. "With set triggers an' a telescope at that range?"

"That's my job, seein' that he misses me," answered the marshal, placidly. "It's a gamble on a cold deck. If he don't examine th' deck, then I win; if he does, I'll mebby lose." His old, leathery face was set and grim, and the sheriff knew that his mind was made up.

"All right, then: we'll let it go that way. It's yore play," assented the sheriff. "Now then, what was you goin' to tell me?"

"Not nothin' that has anythin' to do with stealin' cattle, or th' job you've got. It's kinda personal information. I just want to tell you that Alice Meadows is only a step-child, an' her gun-totin' brothers are only step-brothers. There ain't no blood relationship a-tall. I've seen th' gal, some weeks back, an' talked with her, kinda idle; an' I've heard others talk, Black Jack bein' among 'em. I'd go so far as to state, emphatic, that she ain't happy. Reckon that's all I had to tell you."

Corson was staring at the speaker in amazement, but the older man was now looking out of the door, in the direction of the eyebrow, and chuckling. The expression on his face was sardonic.

"I knowed he was up there th' very first day," he said, complacently. "He did too blame' much fixin' up. Likely there was a cactus that he didn't have th' guts to lay on, like I did once. He had to fuss with this bush, an' tinker with that one, gettin' everythin' all fixed up to suit him. Ho-ho-ho!"

He looked at his companion, found that no attention was being paid to him, and continued, unruffled by this lack of courtesy.

"Over there, in th' corner behind you, is another

Sharps special rifle that I can use at four hundred, makin' due allowances for shootin' uphill. An' *I* got a telescope that fits onto th' barrel. It's got set triggers, too. Cost me a heap of money, it did; but it shore made me a heap.

"I ain't had much to do lately, durin' daylight, but just to set here figgerin' range, an' estimatin' windage. Over in th' other corner, covered up, is an old buffalo huntin' tripod, 'though I reckon there won't be no time to set it up. There ain't nothin' th' matter with th' door casin' for a rest, an' it's right there in place all th' time. One puff of smoke in my direction from that eyebrow, an' there'll mebby be a dead skunk up there. I'll show that cuss how I used to make a hundred dollars a day, down round Dodge City an' th' Panhandle, shootin' buffalers for my skinners to skin; an' I didn't have no telescope then. He shore picked out a side-winder to play with when he settled on me."

Corson hardly heard him. Alice Meadows no blood kin to the Meadows men! A stepdaughter and a stepsister! The situation was still bad enough, but tremendously improved. He started toward the front door, hardly knowing what he was doing, and found the marshal's tight grip on his arm. He stopped, wonderingly.

"You've been shot at three times, or more," said the town officer. "When you go through that door, you jump through it, savvy? *Jump* through it, an' land right up close ag'in th' bay's shoulder. An' then you walk away, still ag'in th' bay's shoulder. I ain't had time to fix up that snake's gun, yet! You an' me have been holdin' quite a lot of pow-wows, an' that —— —— is gettin' th' trigger itch."

The sheriff nodded and obeyed, still thinking of relationships. He landed against the bay's shoulder and led it up the street, keeping under its cover. When he had passed the first building he swung into the saddle and soon dismounted at the hotel stable. Alice Meadows was no blood kin to Black Jack and his whelps!

Mort Meadows watched the coming and the departure of the sheriff with a frown on his face, and let his hand rest on the great rifle for a moment. Four hundred yards, and the 'scope brought the target right up close and big and plain. He knew the rifle, and he knew the range, and he had not forgotten that he would have to shoot downhill. He had been tempted to try it on the sheriff when the latter had ridden up, but on this point he had had his orders. The sheriff rode abroad and would be taken care of when his riding brought him too close for comfort, if not before. The marshal almost never left town.

Mort glanced at the sun and wished that it were time to leave. The old moss-head down below had done nothing, as yet, so far as was known, to turn him into a target. True, he and the sheriff had held several meetings, but that was natural enough, seeing that they were friends.

At last the watcher squirmed back from the sun-baked ridge and drew the rifle carefully toward him. Holding the gun carefully to keep the telescope from striking anything, he slid down the bank. Reaching the bottom, he stood up, flexed his muscles, and threw the gun across an arm. He followed up the wash toward its head until he came to a branch, a feeder, into which he turned. He had to crawl now, to avoid being seen from town.

At a small pile of rocks he stopped, picked up the canvas gun cover lying near them, and pulled it over the rifle. Then he placed the gun in a pocket especially made for it among the rocks, and covered it over with loose stones. In another few moments he was back in the main wash and walking swiftly to get to his horse. The animal was cached fifty yards or more below the lookout spot, and by going down the draw, could be kept out of sight of the town and trail below, and then cut back toward the road coming down from Saddlehorn Pass. Once near that road, there were several choices of routes into town.

Down in the town, the marshal stepped out of his side door for a glance at the sun. In half an hour the watcher was due to appear in town. That meant that he was halfway there now. The old man walked swiftly to the stable in the rear of the jail, saddled his little-used horse, and rode northward up the trail.

toward Carson. At the end of a mile he swung to
the right, left the trail at right angles, and struck up
over the rise toward the Pass road. Mort Meadows
was dismounting before the Palace at the same time
that the marshal was doing the same thing up in the
wash Mort had just left.

The old man followed the plain tracks of the
watcher's booted feet, came to the lookout place, and
went on past it, still following the plain trail. He himself was walking in his socks, and he watched where
he placed his feet. The bootprints led him to the
branch wash, and into it; and then he, too, dropped
down and began to crawl. It was so absurdly easy that
it made him chuckle. Nowadays they intrusted dangerous missions to babes in arms.

The curious little pile of rocks now faced him, and
the bootprints went no farther. Therefore Mort's
little journey had ended right here. He studied the
looks and arrangement of the upper stones so that
he could replace them in such a manner as to avoid
arousing suspicion. To arouse suspicion would be to
put his life into jeopardy. Then he carefully removed
the stones, one by one. The gun case was slowly revealed, and he studied it and the way it was closed
and fastened.

The old man drew the rifle out until its breech was
exposed, and then he lowered the block and drew out
the cartridge. It was a Sharps straight, .45-120-550,
chambered for a special cartridge of tremendous

power. The cartridge was also the same that his own gun handled. This simplified matters.

He had come prepared to find a different caliber, or at least a different load. There now was no need of using the tools he had brought with him. All that he had to do was to remove the cartridge that he found in the gun and replace it with the one he had brought along on just this chance. This pleased him, for he could not do as neat and good a job up here as he had been able to do down in his stable, where he had been able to make use of a vise. He juggled the huge cartridge in his hand and smiled grimly at it: there was a touch of poetic justice in the thought that the cartridge which was meant for him would be the one to kill Mort Meadows.

Replacing everything as he had found it, he made his way back to the horse, rode back the way he had come, and entered town where he had left it. If anybody had noticed him ride off and back they would think, possibly, that it was about time for him to exercise his horse.

He put the tools back on the narrow bench and walked lazily back toward the office. Up in the branch draw, beyond the eyebrow, there was a special Sharps rifle loaded with a cartridge that had considerably less powder in it than loading specifications required; and this difference in load, in fine, hair-line shooting, was enough to cause a miss, especially at four hundred yards. He would be glad to give Mort a chance to declare himself, to make his intentions known, and to grant him the very doubtful advantage of the first shot. If Mort was imaginative enough to change cartridges, then Mort would not need another shot, if his hand was steady and his estimate sound.

CHAPTER XVIII

ALICE MEADOWS stirred restlessly, opened her eyes, and struggled to orient herself. The dream had been a distressing one, and for a moment she did not know where she was. The room was pitch black, and the murmur of voices came to her faintly and indistinctly. Gradually she recognized the tones and knew that she was in her own room. She had no idea of what hour it was, and neither had she heard the men when they came in. She was wide awake now, and coherent and connected thoughts began to pass through her mind. The men were home again, after an absence of three days and nights. The window in the next room went up with a squeaky protest, and the voices became distinct.

". . . had another talk today," said Mort's voice in a growl. "I'm gettin' right suspicious about that damn' old fool. He knows more than he lets on, an' I'm willin' to bet that he's tellin' that damn' sheriff everythin' he hears. It's purty near time we got rid of him, an' I'm all set an' ready to do it, too."

"Th' sheriff don't know a thing that amounts to anythin'," said Matt, contemptuously. "He rides around, pokin' his itchin' nose into other people's business, but he ain't found out nothin' that we've got to worry about. An' if he does, we won't miss him th' fourth time."

"We wouldn't a-missed him before if we hadn't been careless," growled Maurice, angrily. "An' Slade! Slade, th' gunman, th' tough hombre! Huh! If he'd just waited till his shoulder got well, so he wouldn't flinch when he fired, he'd be alive today, an' th' sheriff dead."

"Matt's wrong, dead wrong," stated Black Jack, flatly. "Corson knows a lot more than he's let on. His wagon will be through in a few days, an' he can turn his outfit loose. They're a tough gang. We got to get th' cattle branded an' out of th' country before then. If I reckoned that Mort was right about th' marshal, I'd give th' word. That long-nosed old coyote picks up a lot of loose talk in town, an' he can put two an' two together. Him an' Corson are right thick. Why shouldn't they be? They're friends an' brother officers, ain't they?"

"Tell you one thing, Pop," said Matt's voice, argumentatively and determinedly. "When we get this present bunch away, we're shore goin' to sit back an' play honest for a while. We got to let things simmer down."

"Or else get Corson!" snapped Mort. "He's th' burr under our saddle. We made a damn' clever play, an' so far it's worked out all right; but we got to look out for him. An' when we get him, it's got to be over in his own part of th' country, as far away from here as possible. He's pizen dangerous."

"Hell!" snorted Matt. "We'll get him where we can. We can allus pack him away an' dump him where we want him to be found. Th' main thing is to get him before he can stop us an' mebby kill some of us. He's a bad hombre."

"If he'd only give us a little more time," said Black Jack, "we could be all through here an' be ready to leave th' damn' country. About two more drives an' th' job would be done. There ain't no use of leavin' here, where we've got everythin' set an' lined up, till we get all we need. This range was just made for us, an' I'll be damned if I'll leave it till I've made my pile. Two more drives an' then we'll pull out; an' nothin' from heaven or hell is goin' to stop me from makin' them drives. If Corson gets in th' way, he'll just get hisself killed. Can't we make a play over west that'll take his mind off of this part of th' country?"

"Hell," growled Maurice, disgustedly. "We've made plays over there, an' all they did was to head him this way."

"Oh, he'll get in th' way, all right," laughed Mort, viciously. "Him an' that damn' marshal are doin' a lot of powwowin'. I come right near pullin' trigger on that old fool today. Since Denver was killed he's been stayin' inside his office; but he'll be driftin' back to his favorite place."

"It might be a good thing if you did whang him," said Black Jack thoughtfully. "It'll not only stop his mouth, but it'll make other folks mind their business an' start 'em thinkin' in other directions. Besides, he killed Long Bill, didn't he?"

"Give me th' word, an' I'll drill him," said Mort, eagerly. "I got that range figgered down to a hair, an' that 'scope is th' sweetest thing I ever saw. His chest just busts right up at me on th' cross-hairs."

"You shoot any time you figger you oughta," said Black Jack. "That's up to you. But you remember this: after you shoot, you be damn' shore to ride north. You savvy that? You ride north! An' don't you try to circle back ag'in until yo're dead shore that you ain't bein' followed, not if it takes you a month. We'll mebby have troubles enough of our own, without you addin' to 'em. There'll be hell to pay an' no pitch hot when you kill him."

"Don't you worry none about me!" laughed Mort, boastfully. "I been tellin' you right along that both of them fellers were in our way. I'll get th' marshal, all right; let's see if you fellers can get th' sheriff. An' Pop's right about th' drives: we got to make two more before we're ready to leave this country. We'll never find another layout as good."

"All right," growled the father. "We've had enough talk for tonight. Let's go to sleep: God knows I need some."

The talking ceased. Alice found her heart beating

like a thing gone mad. The little room seemed to suf-focate her, but she did not dare move, did not dare get up and open her door. She had heard too much to risk making a sound. It seemed to be days rather than hours before the darkness lessened, before the side of the draw near her window began to reveal its de-tails in a ghostly, gray light.

While she lay there, waiting for the proper time to arise, her mind raced over the problems which were hers to solve. After what she had just heard, she could no longer remain under this roof. Thieves were bad enough, but assassins——! Bob Corson was the sheriff! He had been shot at four times, and some of them by the men in the next room, if she had heard aright. Oh, it was impossible; yet, it was true. She could hardly be expected to question the truth of their own admissions. And now they were going to shoot down the marshal, and without giving him a chance to fight back. They were going to kill her splendid rider. Perhaps, but not if she could do anything about it, and she felt that she could do considerable.

The room grew light, and she slipped out of bed, hurriedly dressing. She would catch one of the horses in the corral, saddle up, and be in town before her menfolk learned of her absence. Where she would go after that, she did not know, and did not care very much. The deadly apathy of hopelessness was settling down upon her. There was one thing she must do, and that was to get to Bentley and warn the marshal, and have him warn Bob Corson, and give him the facts as she knew them.

The kitchen somehow looked strange and unreal, notwithstanding the hours she had spent in it, the long, dreary hours. And on this morning, of course, the fire was slow to start. She had told them that the chimney needed cleaning out. She turned from the stove at a sudden thought: she was only wasting her time here: she could eat in Bentley. Let them fool with a foul chimney and get their own breakfasts themselves.

The thought sent her swiftly toward the door, and her hand was on the latch, when another thought stopped her in her tracks. If she fled now, they would know it, know it too soon, and also know that she must have overheard some of their conversation. They would be forewarned. Which was the better course? Slowly the answer came to her, the right answer. She must be here when they rode away, just as she always had been here. She must be the same, outwardly, as she always had been. Nothing must be unusual, no word or action must be different. Could she do it? It was not a question of whether she could or not: she must. If she let them leave first, it might be two or three days before they would return, before they would know that she had gone.

To say that time dragged would be to greatly understate the facts. Time barely moved, and each grudging minute was added torture to her. The sun

was halfway to the meridian before she heard a
stirring behind the closed door. More torturing minutes passed, and then Black Jack—she could no longer
think of him as her father—stepped into the sitting
room, rubbing heavy eyes with the backs of his hands.

He yawned and dropped heavily into a chair, groping on the floor for his boots. Again he yawned and
glanced carelessly out through the open kitchen door.
This sudden sizzling which assailed his eager ears
was a pleasant sound, and the smell of the cooking
bacon made his mouth water.

"Smells good, Alice," he said, standing up. He
loafed to the connecting door and leaned against the
casing. "Wake you up last night?"

"I seldom hear any of you come in, after I've gone
to sleep," she answered, trying to keep her voice
natural. She beat up the batter expertly and dropped
a spoonful on the smoking skillet.

"We try not to bother you," he said, yawning again.
"Seems like I'll never get caught up on my sleep," he
growled, and then brightened suddenly; "but th' time
is shore comin' when I will get caught up, when we all
can take life easy. God knows it'll be time."

"But you've said that so many times before," she
replied, smiling. If the blood would only quit pound-
ing in her head!

"Yeah, I know," he admitted, easily: "but this time
I'm talkin' good medicine. We'll be kissin' this damn'

country good-bye before you know it. Just got a few things more to do, an' then we start. An' we leave all this stuff right where it lays."

A few more things to do! Yes: kill Bob Corson and the old marshal, and steal two more herds! Just a few more things like theft and murder.

"By the time you pour your coffee I'll be ready with a flapjack," she said, steadily, casually; and turned the cake deftly and without a tremble. Not only was she the daughter of a thief and the sister of thieves, but now the terms included murder. After she had reached town and given the warnings, she would just ride off in any direction at all. It did not matter where she went or what happened to her: Bob Corson would never see her again.

"That shore smells good," said Matt's booming voice as its owner stepped through the connecting door. "An' mebby I ain't ready to eat! Alice, yo're a wonder."

"Pour your own coffee and sit down," she ordered with a laugh. Her dear brother Matthew, scheming right now how he could safely put a bullet into the heart of the man she loved! "This cake is your father's; you're next."

"Serves me right for bein' second," he chuckled, and reached for the sugar bowl. He looked up at his father. "What are we goin' to do today, Pop?"

"Nothin'," grunted the older man, reaching for the

blackstrap. "There ain't nothin' to do with our few head. Might as well go to town an' see th' boys."

"That suits me," said Matt, his eyes on the smoking skillet. "Let it brown more for me, Sis."

"All right," she replied, smiling to herself at the futility of this last little conversational gem spoken for her benefit. They spoke about riding to town, and then lacked the wit to carry out their pretense, riding off toward the head of the draw instead of down it toward the arroyo trail. She looked up to see Mort enter the room and heard Maurice close behind him. They were talking and laughing as easily as if their consciences were clean. A sudden feeling of revulsion swept over her: she could cheerfully poison them all!

The ordeal finally came to an end and she began, mechanically, to clear up the dishes and put things in order. She saw them get their horses and saddle up. This time they rode off down the draw toward the arroyo trail, and she found herself listening to the noise of the hoofs. Soon after they had dropped out of her sight most of the noise abruptly ceased, but one set of hoofs died out slowly, and then came back to her in the echo she had learned to listen for.

Three of them had turned to the right and were riding up the trail toward the Gap; the other, down it, toward Bentley. This, of course, would be Mort, on his way to keep watch over the marshal. She would give him half an hour's start before she followed.

This question of time bothered her. She wanted to get to town as soon as she could, to reduce the marshal's danger by as many minutes as possible; but she did not wish to get within sight of Mort. An hour would be better. She glanced again at the cheap alarm clock and nodded. She would wait an hour.

CHAPTER XIX

DOWN in Bentley the marshal had made his more or less perfunctory morning rounds and was seated inside the office, his thoughts on the innocent-looking eyebrow up on the slope across the road. He was wondering whether or not the sharpshooter had changed the cartridge in his gun, when he heard the steps of a horse coming down the street. Many horses passed that way, and he had no particular interest in this one until it stopped before his door. He looked up curiously. It was not Corson. He had known that since the sounds had first become audible—unless the forefeet had been shod.

He shifted a little on the chair to face the door squarely, and waited. And then he was standing up, looking with surprise at the woman who stepped into the room. The brightness of the sun outside on the gray white street threw her into silhouette, and the dim light of the room made it difficult for him at once to see who she was. She did not leave him in doubt.

"Perhaps you remember me, marshal," she said in a tight, strange voice as she slowly took the chair that he was quick to offer her. "I'm Alice Meadows."

"Yes, ma'am. I shore do remember you," he replied, studying her rather closely. Seated as she now was, with the brighter light on her face, he was no longer handicapped in the matter of vision.

"I'm riding—I'm riding off to visit some friends," she continued, hesitantly, with embarrassment. Her face flushed suddenly, and strengthened the marshal's peculiar ideas that truth did not abide in a woman. He was justified in this, somewhat, since that had been his own personal experience; and, besides, Alice Meadows did not lie easily.

"Yes, ma'am," he said, and waited patiently.

She did not know just how to proceed. As she had ridden toward town it had seemed a simple thing; but then she had been considering generalities. Face to face with the task, she found it difficult, and it was made more so because of her emotions upsetting her balance. Her face was set and drawn, and her eyes were desperate.

"Yes, ma'am," prompted the marshal, calmly studying her. "Yo're goin' to visit friends. On hossback?"

"Yes, on horseback!" she replied quickly, too quickly. It was an exclamation which was not necessary. Again she flushed, and her eyes grew more desperate.

The marshal was reflecting that from what he knew and had heard about the Meadows family, it had no acquaintances within horseback-riding range. If Alice Meadows was going to visit friends, then she would have to take the train, down at Carson, and ride many hours on it. An oblique thought impinged upon his consciousness: Mort Meadows, up there behind the eyebrow, must be doing some rough-and-tumble conjecturing about now. Then another thought broke through: perhaps he wasn't; perhaps this was part of a carefully thought out plan. He became even more alert.

"Is that what you rode in to tell me?" he asked her, watching her face through half-closed lids. He did not like the paleness of it between flushes, the drawn look, or the expression in her eyes. Had Mort changed the cartridge in that rifle?

"No, I just—just mentioned that," she said, her words so low that he had a little difficulty in hearing them.

"Yes, ma'am," he said, encouragingly, watching the nervous twisting and untwisting of her slender fingers.

"I came in to—I have a message for—I just came in to tell you that—that———" she said, and became suddenly mute. Her tongue refused to function.

"You have a message for me?" he asked curiously, mentally up in arms. Did Black Jack think he was a damned fool?

"Yes, for you and—and the—the———" again she faltered and stopped. She was rapidly going to pieces.

If it was a cooked-up message from Black Jack, then it would very likely concern the sheriff. Damn any blackguard that sent in a woman to tell his lies, to bait his traps!

"Sheriff?" he prompted, sitting erect in his chair. Her part in it was innocent, he decided, intuitively; and then he became a little anxious: she was threatening to lose control over herself, and he now believed that whatever resolution she had made, it was a desperate one. Going to visit friends on horseback!

"I—I've come to warn you—to tell you that—that ——" Her voice died out. Her throat was dry, and she swallowed laboriously to moisten it. That, he knew, was caused by fear. This was a matter that would call for all his wits.

"Miss Alice, you just take things easy; but you shore got th' wrong chair," he said, stepping forward quickly. Perhaps Black Jack had no hand in this unexpected visit, and there was Mort up on the slope with a rifle trained on that door. Before she could get up or even understand his purpose, he had dragged her, chair and all, a full pace backward toward the side wall, and farther from the open door. He was ready to risk his own hide on that doctored cartridge, but not hers: Mort might have slid in a fresh one of his own.

"Wrong chair?" she asked with surprise. "I don't see what that——"

"No, ma'am; you wouldn't," interrupted the marshal, smiling reassuringly and moving away from her. He talked as he moved, hoping to calm her, to get her thoughts into healthier channels, to give her time to get better control over herself.

"You see, th' boys are kinda wild, here in town," he continued. "There ain't never no tellin' just where a bullet is goin' to go. Of course, they're just playful, but you ain't got no idear, a-tall, how reckless some of 'em are. A bullet might come right smack through that there door any minute *now,* except that th' light in here is kinda dim."

Her hands were clenched, and she was staring at the door as if fascinated by it. Somewhere up on that peaceful hillside slope Mort Meadows was lying, with his rifle trained on this building. She shuddered a little and turned her head quickly to look at her companion, and caught him assuming his poker face.

"Why, you mean——" she asked, her fingers twining again.

"Yes, ma'am," he interrupted, calmly, kindly. Black Jack had nothing to do with this visit.

"You're not guessing?" she persisted, her voice strained and unnatural.

"Not much," he said, the smile growing.

"Then you *know?*"

"Yes, ma'am. I know quite a lot," he assured her, a certain grimness changing the pleasantness of the smile. The crinkles at the corners of his eyes deepened.

"You got any particular place in mind where yo're goin'?" he suddenly asked, flinging the question at her and watching closely for its effect. He counted a little on the abrupt change of subject.

"Oh, yes! Yes, of course I have!" she answered, but her eyes evaded him, and again the flush became noticeable.

This was one woman who did not make a practice of lying, he thought. She was having such a hard time of it that he felt sorry for her.

"Hum! Y-e-p. Of course you have," he said. "As an officer of th' law, I'll have to ask you to tell me just where that is, where I can find you if I need to," he stated, keeping his face grave and serious. He felt no pride, somehow, in this trickery; but it was necessary.

"Where it is—where I am going? I must tell you that?" she asked, incredulously. Her face had paled again and was set.

"Yes, ma'am; or not leave town."

"But I can't stay here! I can't stay here!" she exclaimed, almost in a panic. Her eyes were wide from fear.

"Well, you could stay on th' JM," he suggested with offhand carelessness, but he was missing nothing that her face might tell him.

"I can't stay there! I can't go back; but I must leave here and I must go somewhere!" Her panic was growing, and he felt sorry for her. "I can't go back there, now. I just can't stand it any longer!"

"You won't have to," he quickly assured her, now quite certain of at least one thing, and strongly suspecting others. "Have you any particular place in mind?" he demanded. His gaze locked with hers, and she shook her head without realizing it.

"Yes, of course," she answered, desperately. "Of course!"

He nodded understandingly, and his smile became gentle and friendly, a warm smile, inviting confidence. He was quite certain of his footing now.

"Well, ma'am, you can go. There ain't no reason why you can't. All you have to do is tell me just where yo're goin', an' promise me to stay there till you hear from me." At something in her look he shook his head reprovingly.

"Now, look here, Miss Alice: suppose you just listen to me. I'm old enough to be yore father. Yo're in a pile of trouble, an' it ain't no fault of yore own. Just a minute, now! You listen to me. Yo're in trouble, but you ain't goin' to stay in it very long. You said you came in to tell me somethin'?"

"Yes; but I don't know just how to begin."

"Y-e-p. Reckoned so. I don't want you to tell it to me. I don't want you to tell me anythin' that you might be sorry for later on. Yes, yes: but you just let me do th' talkin' for a few minutes, because *I'*m goin' to tell *you* a few things, a few things that you mebby rode in to tell me; an' then you won't have to say 'em a-tall. An' then I'm goin' to take you outa town an' leave you where you'll be safe an' well taken care of. Yo're to stay right there till I come after you or send

a messenger for you. You promise that you'll stay
there, like I just said, if I help you to get outa th'
trouble that yo're in, right now?"

"Oh, I don't know," she said, her fingers twisting
desperately. She could never see Bob Corson again,
did not dare to, for she knew that she could not hold
out against him in the long run. "I was just going to
—just going to go—oh, I don't know what!"

"Yes; that's just about what I reckoned," said the
marshal, his smile like a beam of sunlight. He was
now definitely arrayed on her side, her side and Bob's,
horse, foot, and artillery. "An' that's just what I'm
figgerin' to stop. But you wouldn't go to do that if it
wasn't necessary, would you?"

"Why, no; certainly not: but it is necessary. There's
nothing else to be done."

"Looks like it, mebby; but if we find that it ain't,
then you won't have no reason to go, will you?" he
persisted. He wished he could put his finger on the
mainspring of her actions.

"No, I guess not; not if we find that it isn't."

"Then there ain't no doubt about that," he said,
nodding. "This is a kinda game. It's a game I know,
an' you don't. Suppose you let me play th' cards, an'
you watch how they run an' fall. You don't know how
to play 'em, but I do. It's kinda right in my line. Now
you give me th' promise I asked you, an' then I'll tell
you what I was goin' to."

She nodded miserably, her eyes on his; and then a
faint gleam of hope eased the tenseness of her expression. She felt a growing confidence in this old man.

"Yes, I'll promise that," she said in a low voice.

"Why, we're gettin' along right fine," he said with
enthusiasm. "There ain't no real reason for you to
get all upset an' panicky; not none a-tall: not now.
Not with me an' Bob Corson settin' into this game."

At the mention of the sheriff's name her eyes
opened wide and a look of fear flashed into them.

"Now you just take things easy," he said, sooth-
ingly. "Take things right easy. There ain't no reason
for you to get scared. Not none a-tall."

"Oh, I don't know. I don't know. It's so——"

"So easy," he interrupted. "Now suppose we
straighten everythin' all out, so you'll keep that promise an' won't get all upset."

"Can we?"

"Yes, Miss Alice, we can. There ain't no question
about it. You want me to tell you what I was goin'
to?" he asked, patiently, and smiled again as she
nodded.

"All right; but first, Black Jack's yore stepfather,
ain't he?"

She nodded.

"An' them boys are yore stepbrothers, ain't they?"

Again she nodded.

"An' there ain't no real blood relationship between
you an' th' rest of th' Meadows family, is there?" he

persisted, driving the thought home. This was the crux of his argument, and he had to drive it home, to establish it firmly in her mind. After that, everything would be easy.

"No, there's none at all," she answered, her wide, questioning eyes trying to read his inscrutable old face.

He nodded at her reply.

"Thought so. Well, that makes thinks kinda easy for me; an' for you, Alice. 'Specially for you, an' Bob Corson. We don't want to forget Bob: he's th' hub of *this* wheel. One of th' wheels. If anybody was to ask me, I'd shore say that yo're th' hub of th' other wheel; an' there ain't no reason why them two wheels can't turn in th' right direction. That right?"

"I—I don't understand you," she said, but her expression was becoming less tense, and hope was gleaming faintly in her eyes.

"Why, th' cattle-stealin' wheel sorta turns around Corson—or it will, right soon. That won't make no difference to you, not now; not after you've slipped yore hobbles an' left th' JM. You didn't have nothin' to do with that, an' now you've cut loose from everythin' connected with it, an' showed that you have."

"Yes; but I'm the daughter of a thief, and— murderer," she protested in a whisper, and her face paled again.

"You ain't nothin' of th' kind," replied the marshal, flatly. Here was the mainspring he had been searching for. "If you was to tell that to Bob Corson, he'd just laugh at you. There ain't no reason for you to ride off an' disappear. Not none a-tall, an' there never was. If you did that, then th' other wheel couldn't turn, an' that wheel's th' best one. It wouldn't have no hub. Don't you get them two wheels mixed up. You keep 'em separate, each on its own axle."

She was shaking her head slowly while he spoke, and now he shook an old, gnarled finger at her, much as he would admonish a child.

"Don't you shake yore head like that," he said. "What Black Jack an' his boys have done, or are goin' to do, can't be laid at yore door. What Bob Corson, an' mebby me, does, ain't got nothin' a-tall to do with you or your kin. After th' trouble's all over, then I figger you an' Bob oughta give each other an even break. Nothin' else would be fair, would it?"

Her head was still shaking, slowly but persistently, and her answer was so low that he could not hear it, but he knew what it was, and smiled reprovingly.

"I've been doin' a lot of talkin'," he said, apologetically, "which is somethin' that I ain't a great hand at; but when I've got to talk, I can hold my own. I ain't got around to what I want to say, even yet. But I'll get there, right now."

"But I must tell you what I came in to say," she said, hurriedly. It would be much easier now.

"Don't you say a word!" he exclaimed, cutting her

short. "Not a word, till you've heard me, anyhow. Black Jack an' his boys are mixed up in cattle-stealin'. Some of us figger that they're th' leaders in it. It looks that way, anyhow. Bob Corson found out quite a lot of things that didn't look right. They all pointed one way, like th' dust of separate wagons on a trail. Then, when he was ridin' up Crooked Creek trail three or four hombres took some long-range shots at him. You didn't have nothin' to do with that, did you?"

He chuckled at her quick indignation, and wagged his finger at her again.

"'Course not," he said. "Not nothin' a-tall. All right. Then Bob an' Slade had words, at th' Baylor wagon, an' Slade's draw was a mite too slow, or he shot too quick. Bob coulda killed him, but let him off with a hole in his shoulder. You didn't have nothin' to do with that, did you?"

This time, instead of being indignant, she smiled a little.

"Thought so," he chuckled, as if he had just made the discovery. "There's a lot more, Alice. One night, a little later, three men tried to trail Bob right here in this town, tried to dry-gulch him in th' dark. It didn't work out th' way they figgered. An' you shore didn't have nothin' to do with that. Bob killed one an' wounded another, which didn't touch you no place. This last trouble took place in my jurisdiction, an' it was my job to finish it up. I did. Long Bill figgered that he had a lop-sided break in his favor, an' went for his gun. I killed him. Had to. He was actin' for Black Jack, too. When I shot Long Bill I wasn't no enemy of yourn, was I? An' Long Bill wasn't nothin' to you, was he? An' when Bob killed Squinty, he didn't do *you* no harm, did he?"

A little laugh broke from her, and she shook her head emphatically.

"Thought so," continued the marshal, complacently. He was driving home his points very well, he thought. "That was self-defense an' a matter of duty. Once in a long while duty an' pleasure ride th' same hoss. All three of them ambushin' snakes were workin' for Black Jack; but Black Jack's stepdaughter didn't have nothin' to do with it, did she?"

Again she shook her head. She was rapidly getting into a better frame of mind.

"Slade was workin' for Black Jack. He went over to Corson's home range, killed some cows, an' left a plain trail. It was so plain that Corson was too smart to foller it; but Slade figgered he would ride through Packers Gap—got to suspectin' that at th' Baylor wagon, where they had their first run-in—an' Bob did ride through it. Slade put a bullet through Bob's hat, an' got a slug through hisself in return. This one didn't go through no shoulder. It was dangerous to waste any more lead on him. Slade's dead, an' mebby buried, by this time. You follerin' what I'm sayin'?"

Alice nodded, her eyes opened wide from surprise.

The marshal seemed to know all that she did, and more, even to small details. Then, of course, Bob Corson knew as much, or perhaps even more. It was rather anticlimax so far as she was concerned. It made her feel rather flat, and this served to steady her.

"All right," continued the old man, placidly and with a measure of relish. "Corson an' me have been powwowin' kinda steady, accordin' to looks. Somebody got to figgerin', mebby, that I knowed more'n I let on, me movin' around town like I do, pickin' up a word here an' a word there. Corson was ridin' around th' whole country outside of town, also pickin' up a thing here an' a thing there. Then we looked like we was puttin' our heads together. An' remember that I got one of th' three skunks that was gunnin' for him that night. Somebody figgered that our powwowin' meant trouble. They couldn't let it go on. So what did they up an' do?"

Alice was about to speak, breathlessly eager to, but her companion's swiftly upraised hand stopped her.

"You let me tell you, instead of you tellin' me," said the marshal, quickly. "What did they do? Why, they put a sharpshooter up on that little hill, outside, with a Sharps special buffalo gun an' a telescope sight. At that distance he can see th' buttons on my vest, or what's left of 'em. First time I showed my hand real plain would be th' last of me. We'll see about that, however. I ain't no infant."

Alice was sitting with her hands clasped tightly to-

gether, staring at the speaker in a sort of fascinated
interest. She followed his glance and saw the great
rifle standing in the corner, and the glint of brass on
the telescope, where the black enamel had been worn
off.

"That's what I——" she began, in a very low voice,
but he again swiftly stopped her.

"Don't say it!" he almost snapped. "I'm tellin' you
all this so you'll know that you don't have to say
it, an' won't say it. If you do, later on you'll mebby
get to blamin' yoreself for th' deaths of folks that
ain't no kin of yourn. Mort Meadows is layin' up on
that hill with a buffalo gun, an' I reckon he's got th'
range figgered to a hair. Shootin' from a long rest,
with most of th' barrel touchin' it, an' with a telescope, an' a gun like that, he shouldn't miss no target
as big as I am; but I'm gamblin' that he will miss it.
I quit cuttin' my teeth years ago, an' I cut 'em on
ca'tridge shells!"

Alice was nodding gently, and her fingers and her
hands were still, lying quietly in her lap. Her expression showed a great relief.

"Well, let's go on an' get it over with," continued
her companion. "There ain't much more to say; not
near as much to say as there is to do. Black Jack an'
his boys have got to kill Bob Corson, an' Bob will
take a sight of killin', lemme tell you! They got to, or
throw in their cards an' get out of th' country. Looks
like things have been goin' right well for them, an'

now they're figgerin' to play out th' hand. Corson knows it. He mebby knows more'n I do; anyhow, he oughta."

She was a little pale now, and her hands were tense.

"Don't you do no worryin' about Bob Corson," he said, watching her closely. "An' th' folks that oughta be worryin' ain't no kin of yourn. You just let me take you off to a place where you can stay an' be safe an' think things over for yoreself. When th' time is right I'll come after you, or send somebody in my place. You've made me a promise. You figger on keepin' it, now?"

"Yes. I'll keep it," she answered, her eyes wide and moist and filled with hope. Her terrifying problem was terrifying no longer, and it had almost ceased to be a problem from any angle, thanks to this lean, tanned, and not overclean old man.

"You got any place in mind?" he asked, considering her wishes, now that they would work no harm.

"Is there a Turkey ranch?" she asked, and flushed deeply.

He studied her for a moment, and smiled suddenly.

"Yes. Turkey Track. Owen French owns it, but it's a right long ride from here," he said. "You'd get all tired out an' mebby crippled up, settin' a saddle so long."

"Does the distance really make much difference?" she asked, watching her hands.

"Not to me," he answered. "But it's a long way for

you, a mighty long way. We can't make it before late tonight." He thought for a moment. "Mebby it'll be nearer mornin'."

"Well, then, we can't go there," she said, trying to hide her disappointment. She would have liked to go where Bob had suggested. "That would take you away from town too long."

"Then we start for th' Turkey Track," he retorted, "an' we start right soon. But before we do start, let me take a look at th' weather; it might be stormy."

He stood up and moved toward the door, feeling that Alice Meadows's visit would be the weight which would spring the trap. His left hand reached out and gripped the great rifle; and then, still holding it, he moved his body squarely into the doorway and stopped there.

The expectant interval seemed to be a very long one, and many thoughts passed through his head. Most prominent among them was whether or not Mort Meadows had changed the cartridge in the gun. The interval really could have been spanned by a slow count of ten. It takes time to steady on a target and get set. There came a heavy, black powder roar from up on the hillside. A puff of dust, directly in line between the eyebrow and the marshal, sprang from the sand full fifty yards short, and the heavy bullet whined high above the marshal's head.

The old man moved like a striking snake. He jerked the heavy weapon through the door, threw it to his shoulder as he moved sideways, and for a moment his outstretched left hand held it steady and solid, clamped tightly against the door casing. The roar of it filled the room and the street and crashed back from the hillside; but the barrel did not drop at once. The old man's eye was peering through the telescope at the wavering cloud of smoke above the eyebrow. Then, briskly nodding, he stood the gun back against the wall and turned to his visitor.

"Weather's all right," he said. He motioned her forward. "I'll saddle my hoss in a shake, an' be with you right quick. We'll relay at th' Bar W."

"Was that—was *that*——" she whispered, a hand pressing against a breast. She could not finish the question without pausing, and she did not have to finish it.

"That was a pert young snake with murder in his heart," said the marshal, grimly. "I said it would be better if I told you things, 'stead of you tellin' 'em to me. Let's get movin': we got a mighty long way to go."

CHAPTER XX

THE Gap lay at an altitude of about forty-eight hundred feet. Sixteen miles southwest of it was the highest part of the ridge, four hundred feet higher, and in places all of eight miles across. Running up the middle of the north slope of this higher plateau was an arroyo, which slanted down to the north for about six miles; and then, turning abruptly, ran due west and pitched down into the wide valley of Crooked Creek. From no point in the lower valley could its upper section be seen, and neither could it be seen from any other direction where roads and trails lay. In width the arroyo varied from a few hundred yards at its upper end to more than a mile along its middle reaches.

The lower half, which pointed west, was deep, constricted, and had a steep grade; the arroyo here became a canyon. It opened out upon the Crooked Creek trail about two thirds of the way between Iron Springs and the old, 'dobe trading post; and directly across the trail and the creek arose a tumbled mass of rock, isolated spires, and small buttes, backed by a mesa. The canyons and arroyos in this wild country made a veritable maze, and of them it was said that a man could meet himself half a dozen times in a two-hours' ride.

The Crooked Creek trail was well traveled. At one time it had been part of the California Trail. In season, herds of cattle moved leisurely down it from the ranges lying to the south and southwest. The road itself was a narrow ribbon ground out by wheeled vehicles; but it lay on a wider, if fainter, ribbon that had been beaten by the hoofs of many cattle in the years that had gone. With care, a stolen herd could be driven out of the canyon, judiciously led on to the trail, and then judiciously edged off it, and become swallowed up by the rough country across the creek without leaving too plain signs of its passing. After that it could move in secrecy and security. One herd already had gone this way, irrevocably lost to its proper owners.

The morning following the death of Mort Meadows found three important things going on at distant points, but simultaneously.

Corson, having scoured in vain over the end of the ridge north of the Gap, had slept in his blankets under the stars and awakened to a new and important day.

Nueces, with Shorty, Burns, and Bludsoe, the cream of the JC fighting men, had covered the arroyos and draws on the Crooked Creek side, and spent the night in the old 'dobe post. They ate a hurried breakfast and saddled up, and now Nueces was bidding the others good-bye and leaving them to ride over the

Gap trail and to join his boss at the appointed place. The remaining three would continue their scouting.

Southwest of them Jerry, the Baylor foreman, having left his wagon to pick up its own odds and ends, had taken three men with him and ridden in to spend the night at the ranch. He was now leading his companions toward the Broken Jug trail, to search for the cattle he had spoken about to the sheriff.

Corson passed Shell Canyon and, following up the little draw on the right of the road, stopped when out of sight of the thoroughfare and waited for Nueces to join him. On the far side of the great ridge, and about eight miles away as the crow flies, was the JM ranch. He also was less than half a mile, as the crow flies, from that high, masked arroyo which was the very heart of the JM cattle business. It lay up on the top of the plateau, unsuspected by those who rode or drove along the main wagon road below it.

Corson was early. Nueces was not due to show up for an hour or more, if he had gotten away at the regular time. Unknown to the sheriff, the horse-faced deputy had gained an earlier start. Corson had nothing to do but just sit there and wait. Time would pass too slowly, and he was keyed up for action. He looked up at the escarpment hemming him in on three sides, idly scrutinizing it. When Nueces joined him they would return to the road, follow up Jerry's pet Broken Jug trail, and gain the top of the plateau from there. This little-used trail marked the southern end of the ridge and would lead them to heights from which to look down upon the great backbone.

Time dragged, and the waiting became unbearable. Movement, action was what he needed, if just for the sake of doing something. Again he studied the escarpment. At no place within sight could a man ride up, but there were any number of places where it could be climbed by a man on foot. Perhaps it would be an hour before Nueces would arrive, and that is a long time to be idle. He dismounted, left the horse where his friend could easily see it, and went ahead on foot.

The draw forked, and he chose the left or main stem. It ended abruptly against the lower escarpment, which here was about twenty-five feet high, and rich in hand- and footholds. Next came a steep slope for another half hundred feet, and then the second escarpment, this one nearly a hundred feet high. When he had pulled himself over the last rim rock and looked around, he found himself on a secondary plateau, above which the main ridge arose at quite some distance away.

He could now see the wagon road north and south of him. A horseman was coming down it from the direction of the Gap trail. It might be Nueces. All right: if it were, he had time to look around him. The trail up the Broken Jug lay almost under his feet, to the south. He traced it until it led around a shoulder; and he did not know it, but half a mile beyond that shoulder, Jerry was leading his three companions to search the little basin of which he had spoken so much.

Corson turned and walked to his right, toward a sharp angle of the rock wall. He reached it, started to round it, and instantly dropped to a knee. Faint clouds of dust were climbing up out of a depression perhaps a quarter of a mile away. They were not dust devils—of that he was certain. Moving wagons or bunches of cattle would more properly account for them. Seeing that this was cattle range, the answer was obvious.

But the answer automatically asked another question: why should a number of small bunches of cattle be moving in concert and so steadily? The only answer which suited this question made his face go hard. Right here, then, in the very heart of the open range, surrounded by ranches, roads, trails, and grazing grounds, was that impossible herd of cattle, of which he had been so certain. All the separate puzzle pieces shifted easily and fitted into this completed pattern. But how had it been managed?

The Baylor straw boss had combed every rod of this ridge. Because of the escarpments on the Kiowa side, the Bar W could not sweep that part of the watershed; and Jerry had met that line and covered that portion with his own riders. And yet he, and all of them, had overlooked a stolen herd!

Jerry had done nothing of the sort. If the herd had been here he would have found it. Where was it?

What had happened? Corson let his mind run back.

The Baylor outfit had taken the ridge in three parallel lines, throwing the worked cattle behind them on the downhill side. What had that to do with it? Throwing the cattle behind them on the downhill side: huh. There seemed to be no answer there.

They had worked the ridge in three parallel sweeps. Anyone who knew this could prophesy their movements for days ahead. And anyone could know it by just watching how they went about the work. What would such knowledge profit him? Three parallel sweeps, and throwing the worked cattle—*hah!* One and one make two, just as well as two and two make four. The answer popped into his mind automatically. A human is overly disposed to search for the difficult, overlooking the easy and almost obvious. He had been guilty of this fault himself.

All anyone had to do was to watch his chance, shift the stolen stuff from above, throw it below the round-up crew's next sweep, and scatter it well. If the cattle had been up here, there would have been plenty of time and opportunity for that. After several days the Baylor crew swept back again, along the middle benches. They would ignore scattered cattle well below them. Then the crew turned and went back again, this time along the top of the ridge, overflowing it to the escarpment at the Bar W's line.

As soon as the outfit was a few days farther along, the scattered cattle could be rounded up, bunched, and driven up to this little basin, where they would be safe from discovery on ground that had just been worked over; and from here the thieves could derisively watch the round-up operations going on down on the flatter range below them. It would be like playing tag with people who did not know they were in a game, or that there was any game at all; so absurdly simple that the more a man thought over the puzzle, in the abstract, the less likely he would be to hit upon it. All this thinking had taken but a flash of time.

Corson moved cautiously forward. The job was at hand even sooner than he had expected. He dropped to the ground and crawled toward a mass of rocks and boulders from where he could get a better view of the basin. Exact knowledge was what he wanted now.

The whole scene lay before him, and he could trace the arroyo far down the slope. He thought he knew where it cut into the main valley along the creek. He had noticed the canyon in his riding, noticed it idly, giving it no measure of its real importance.

The cattle numbered about three hundred. Six men were at work, driving in small bunches toward the main herd. To be branded, they would have to be thrown and tied. They were just lighting the fire for the irons. The work would go on slowly, since this was open-range branding of grown animals. They had rounded up and held the heavier beef, for most of it looked to be two and three years old. There were no corrals or chutes to help the work along. They could not risk the discovery of such material and permanent affairs.

Corson watched one of the riders who came closer to him than any of the others, and stiffened from surprise. It looked like Franchère, one of his own punchers. Yes: it was Franchère. The last time he had seen that puncher had been in the Cheyenne, back in Willow Springs. Apparently Franchère had cut his string that day. Franchère worked his bunch back toward the herd. Black Jack Meadows left the gather and rode toward the fire, where Matt was busy with it. Matt stood up and moved toward his horse, and then came unexpected action.

A three-year-old steer broke from the herd, dodged the nearest rider, and started on a lumbering run up the hill toward the sheriff. Running is not a natural gait with cattle, for they never run if they can walk; but when a range steer wants to get somewhere quickly, he can cover ground with surprising celerity; and before Corson really felt the threat engendered by the animal's escape, it was heading directly toward his hiding place, and halfway up the slope. The steer itself did not matter; but something else did.

Black Jack, being the rider nearest the animal as it passed the fire, whirled in pursuit; and Matt, vaulting into the saddle, joined in the chase. Black Jack was now on its heels, swinging his rope, but reluctant to use it, hoping that he could cut around in front and

head the steer off. Behind him rode his son, at a more
sedate pace, working off to his left to keep the fleeing
animal from breaking past in that direction.

The steer plunged on, straight for the mass of
boulders sheltering Corson, and now Black Jack was
even with it, forcing it a little out of its course; but
the sheriff could see that his hiding place soon would
be a hiding place no longer. To make matters worse,
Matt was now crossing over to take advantage of the
steer's change of course, and riding along the chord
of the arc. They both were due to pass his hiding
place within a score of paces. Well, why not? He was
armed only with Colts, while every man there had a
rifle slung to his saddle. He dared not face them all
at the ranges they could and would choose. Here was
a choice of the lesser of two evils, a chance to engage
two of them at his own range, and perhaps reduce
the odds by a third. After all, that was what he had
come for, that was what his job meant in a showdown;
and if this wasn't a showdown, he never had known
one. Why wait until he was discovered, with the odds
two to one? Surprise would be a valuable ally. The
two men were passing him at less than twenty paces,
when he suddenly stood up, hands resting on belts,
and called out to them.

"Hey!"

Black Jack's answering action was reflexive. He
pulled the horse up short as he turned in the saddle,
and then his hand dropped swiftly to walnut. Matt

replied to the hail by swinging his mount around and also reaching toward his holster.

The shots smashed out across the basin were played with by the towering upper ridge and sent crashing out over the range, multiplied until they sounded like a fusillade. Only three were fired. One of them spanged from a boulder just above Corson's head and screamed into silence. Matt was a fancy, gun-thumbing, gun-rolling shot, excelling in exhibitions; but he was cleanly killed by a man who thought only of plain, straight shooting. Black Jack's horse, suddenly freed of a hundred and thirty pounds, dashed away at better speed, Matt's piebald crowding it. Corson dropped down again and prepared to face a deadly rifle fire. He was in a tight corner, but he had been in tight corners many times before.

The riders down with the herd had whirled at the sound of the first shot, and now were gathered together, the cattle behind them and forgotten. Then Franchère yelled a warning, and the group spread out swiftly, each man racing for cover. The herd heaved, broke, and set off on a run down the arroyo, gathering speed as panic and momentum got hold of it. The thunder of its hoofs shook the plain.

Maurice Meadows crept from rock to rock, boulder to boulder, his eyes on the pile of rocks, his rifle at the ready. Franchère was a hundred yards to his left. They had hurriedly decided upon a plan of action, and now were putting it to the test.

Over on the other side, far to their right, Red and Slim were creeping through their own cover, intent upon gaining the high ground behind the rock pile. The four rustlers had worked it out pretty well, each pair for itself: there was but one man behind those rocks, one man who had seen too much. Perhaps he was the only man who knew what was going on up here. His identity was easily guessed. The long-deferred job that they had set for themselves was here, right at hand. This time there would be no bungling. Maurice glanced out over the basin and swore angrily as his gaze settled on the quiet figures huddled on the earth. He would soon pay up for that.

Franchère, being farthest from the rock pile, pressed on more rapidly. He had to gain his position before the sheriff could figure out a way to crawl back and shift his hiding place; not knowing that the sheriff already had done that to the distance of a dozen yards. Franchère peered cautiously at the rock pile and then estimated his next advance. It was a five-yard dash across open ground to the next tumbled patch of rocks. He turned his head and called out in a voice he hoped would only carry to his companion.

"I've got to make a dash. Cover me, Maurice."

"Go ahead!" came the answer, and Maurice fired at a gray hat which showed over the top of a distant rock.

Franchère arose with his feet gathered under him and leaped forward. From the innocent east side of the rock pile there came a burst of powder smoke, and the runner finished his dash in a headlong dive, killed instantly by a lucky snap shot over a range of forty yards. It was a lucky shot, but not for Franchère. Again Maurice threw down on the hat, but held his fire. Tricked! Fooled by a moth-eaten trick as old as hats themselves!

He squirmed with rage and chagrin, desperately resolved to get this sneaking dog of the law. He did not believe that the sheriff's shot had made a hit. He raised his voice.

"Work around more to yore left, Franchère! We can work th' crossfire then, an' drive th' —— —— out, or kill him."

He himself was working slowly but steadily in the other direction to make the crossfire even more effective. There was no reply to his words.

"Franchère!" he called, in a louder voice. "Franchère!"

"Franchère's in hell, waitin' for you," said the sheriff's voice. "How you like this little party? Hey! Yo're movin' th' wrong way! *I'm* over *here!*"

"He's waitin' for *you!*" shouted Maurice, reversing his direction and crawling swiftly back the way he had come. He'd fool the badge-toting skunk! He'd work quietly over to where Franchère had started his dash, and then lie still. And as he planned it, he brushed against a sagebush; and ten minutes later, as he settled down in his new cover, he brushed against another. The jiggling twigs flashed their messages.

Nueces jogged up the draw, saw his friend's horse, and drew rein. Corson's bootprints led straight to the bottom of the lower escarpment.

"Huh! Got restless," chuckled the horse-faced foreman. He dug out tobacco and papers and leisurely rolled himself a cigarette.

Around the great shoulder of the mesa, Jerry and his riders had searched the basin in vain. The little bunch of cattle had not returned to their favorite grazing ground on the Broken Jug. He looked up at a place where the escarpment had crumbled, and growled.

"They shore would never climb up there, with good grass down here. They must have worked south, to our open range."

"Yeah," said a companion. "They've been all choused up by th' round-up, an' scattered to hell an'—"

The shots sounded plainly above their heads, and each man instinctively ducked. Who was shooting, up there? What was there up there to shoot? Corson's forebodings came to Jerry's mind, and he acted on impulse. He slipped from the saddle, his rifle in his hand, and his companions followed on his heels toward the break in the great wall.

Nueces had the flaring match halfway to the cigarette when the shots made him freeze. In his case there was no doubt at all. He knew that his friend was up there, and shots meant shots, which was enough. Before the match had struck the earth his horse was running at top speed toward the end of the draw. Nueces climbed with the speed, but not the grace, of a frightened lizard; but for reasons known only to himself, he did not choose the place selected by the sheriff.

Corson's thoughts were not on Maurice, now in Franchère's old cover. There was a sterner threat than that. Somewhere up on the slope of the main ridge, two men were working persistently among the rocks and along the ledges, striving to get on the higher ground behind him. Their shooting would be done at ranges hopeless for accuracy with a Colt. He wriggled around on Maurice's side, keeping low and under cover of the rocks. It would be a joke on Maurice to seek safety almost under the muzzle of his gun. The thought was intriguing, and he tried to develop it. Perhaps it could be done. Perhaps he could get away from the prominent rock pile and lie low. And in doing this he would shift Maurice's range from rifle distance to that of Colt, and perhaps give that person the surprise of his life. And if the two men on the hill stalked the rock pile, they might give him a shot at a closer range. He was very careful to make no noise or to touch any growing thing.

There came a voice from the upper slope, nearly behind the pile of rocks, and perhaps four hundred yards away.

"Where is he?"

There was no answer. Franchère could not speak, and Maurice did not care to. The damn' fools! Let them do their own stalking! Here he was, all snug and ready for a big surprise, and they wanted him to answer them!

"Where is he?" came the query again, this time a little louder. Slim waited a moment for the answer. It did not come, and he grinned at his companion.

"Layin' chicky," he grunted.

"Yeah," grunted Red. "Don't blame 'em. That coyote has got a buffalo Sharps. We want to watch ourselves. He can shoot like th' hammers of hell."

"Then he ain't used it," countered Slim. "Them was pistol shots. *I* know th' sound of a Sharps buffalo gun."

"That's right," admitted Red, without any particular enthusiasm. "He ain't, yet; but he *will.*"

"Not on me," grunted Slim, crouching a little lower.

"He ain't got a chance to get outa this," commented Red with a deal of pleasure. "With them two layin' down there, we got him in a double crossfire; but we don't want to forget that Sharps."

"Lookit that damn' herd!" said Slim, swearing whole-heartedly. "Run to hell an' gone. We'll have to round 'em up all over ag'in."

"Hell with th' herd," retorted Red, who was thinking in terms of Sharps buffalo guns.

Maurice was becoming suspicious. He reacted to danger as keenly as a hound to scent. Something was wrong. If Red and Slim, now up on the hill, couldn't see the sheriff, and if *he* couldn't see him, then that doubly damned arm of the law had either turned into a tumblebug or had moved away from the rock pile: and Maurice did not believe in such miraculous metamorphoses as sheriffs turning into any kind of bugs. He inched backward, bearing to his left and away from the now suspicious rock pile. He made good progress, but he was still careless about bumping into weed stems and little waving things like that. He did not know any better, not being range-raised. Therefore it was with utter and panicky surprise that he heard three words in a strange but hearty voice behind him.

"Well, well, well!" said Nueces, grinning over the top of a rock.

Maurice's mouth popped open as his rifle slewed around, but it closed again almost instantly. It closed upon the passage of a hunk of lead that never touched a tooth.

"Chew on *that,*" growled the horse-faced foreman, and slipped back again into the shelter of the rocks, ready to hunt himself a brand-new job.

Red and Slim suddenly realized that they were all alone in a cold, cold world. Judging from the last shot, that coyote down below could spread himself over more territory than a scared jackrabbit. They almost expected to hear his cold voice behind them. Their loneliness was further emphasized when they saw three punchers riding around the distant herd, heading up the arroyo as fast as they could travel. The herd, having run itself out, was now getting back some of its breath. The feeling was still further emphasized when they heard voices above and behind them, and the significant sound of rolling pebbles clicking down the slopes. It was plain enough now: they were surrounded. While the damned sheriff had kept their thoughts on the doubly damned pile of rocks, his triply damned men had been moving according to plan.

"I'm through," said Slim, and he raised his voice. "Don't shoot!"

"Why not?" came the ironical reply, followed by a short laugh.

"My hands are up, an' empty!" shouted Slim, earnestly.

"Keep 'em that way," called out another voice. It sounded like that of the foreman of the BLR.

"Watch his pardner!" came a bellow from below, where the still invisible sheriff seemed to be keeping an eye on things.

"Watch yore gran'mother!" yelled Red, indignantly. *"My* hands are up, too! Think I'm a damn' fool!"

"Then step out where we can see you," ordered the Baylor foreman, not quite certain what it **was** all about; but there seemed to be no harm in keeping **a** man covered.

Slim and Red, weaponless now, obeyed, their hands reaching toward the heavens.

Jerry slid down the last ledge, gun in hand, and stopped before the two men. One by one his companions followed and joined him. Nueces popped into sight not far away, and the sheriff slowly gained his feet. The three riders were now close at hand and looked to be disappointed.

The prisoners and their escort worked down the slope and met the sheriff on the lower bench. Shorty, with Bludsoe and Burns, drew rein alongside.

"What's it all about?" asked Jerry, thirsting for details. He was soon told.

"Rope these boys an' take 'em in to Bentley," ordered Corson, turning to the three riders. "Nueces an' I have got to go round th' other way: our horses are down below, on th' Kiowa side."

He turned to the BLR foreman.

"Can you get yore hosses up here? Yeah? Then mebby you'd better ride herd on those cattle."

"All right," said Jerry. "We'll hold 'em an' send a man back to th' ranch for help. Accordin' to my way of thinkin', that damn' Association ain't got no claim to this bunch. They shore won't have, if they don't hear about 'em. No tellin' how many we've lost. These cattle were plumb stole from all of us."

"Suits me," growled the sheriff, revising his definition of mavericks. "I'll get word to th' other outfits, an' they can send over their reps. We'll divide 'em up th' best we can, an' throw a few cold hands for what's left." He looked at the figures on the earth and let his gaze slowly drift over the rocky cover where two more lay. "I'll send out for *them,* too," he said. Suddenly he turned to Nueces.

"When did Franchère cut his string?"

"That time you saw him in th' Cheyenne. He didn't come back. Why?"

"He's over there, among th' rocks. I made a lucky shot on him."

"Yeah? Well, he won't have to bust no wild ones now," drawled the JC foreman.

"All right, boys; get started. We'll see you in Bentley," said the sheriff, and he turned toward the distant rock pile. "See you as soon as I can, Jerry."

"Take yore time, Bob," said the BLR foreman, with a smile. He watched the sheriff and the long, lanky deputy walk toward the edge of the escarpment. Then he looked down the arroyo, where Shorty and his friends were on their way to town, their prisoners ahead of them. Then he looked soberly and long at the huddled figure nearest to him, out on the edge of the basin.

"*That's* th' time yore hole card was a deuce, Black Jack," he said.

CHAPTER XXI

THE two friends mounted and rode down the draw, Nueces' face wearing a look of extreme satisfaction. Various little puzzles had been cleared up, puzzles which had bothered him, and while he had had little to do in their solving, he had done his own job with neatness and dispatch. His friend ought to be very well pleased with his own part; but something seemed to be wrong.

"I knowed that just as soon as they begun to figger that you was loco, you'd clear it up," he said, glancing sidewise at his companion.

"Yeah," grunted Corson, moodily, his eyes fixed steadily on the ground ahead.

"How'd they keep them cattle up there, with Jerry's crew sweepin' th' ridge?" asked the deputy.

Corson told him, as briefly as possible.

"Huh!" mused Nueces, letting the play run through his mind. "An' so Franchère was in with 'em all th' time, huh? Only wish I'd knowed that before!"

The wagon road moved steadily toward them, and the sheriff urged the bay into a lope, his companion's sorrel keeping head to head with it.

"I'm turnin' in my badge an' resignin'," said Corson, abruptly, as the Shell Canyon road went past.

"Huh?" exclaimed Nueces, incredulously, doubting his ears.

"I'm quittin'. To hell with th' job!"

"Great land of cows!" marveled Nueces, turning sideways in his saddle. *"Quittin'!"*

"Yes."

"But you just won th' game, hands down!" protested the deputy.

"Yeah; an' lost a damn' sight more," growled his friend and boss.

"Yeah?" inquired Nueces, turning this surprising bit of information over in his active mind. Their friendship, oak-ribbed and copper-riveted, gave him certain rights. "How's that?"

"There's a Meadows girl," growled the sheriff. "I've just killed off her menfolks."

Nueces reflectively chewed on this chunk of information and after a few moments made adequate reply.

"I'll be eternally —— ——!"

The road to the Gap went swiftly past, neither of them giving it more than a glance, but the sheriff bitterly thought that it made no difference now how many shoes were worn by the bay. The Jackson Canyon road forked to the right, and was past. A mile and a half farther on they took the left-hand road leading up to Saddlehorn Pass. The trail up from David Canyon, leading to the same point, was steadily bearing toward them. As the two routes drew close together Nueces saw a horseman riding rapidly along the trail, heading in their direction. His big hand slid out toward the stock of the scabbarded rifle at his leg.

"Wonder who *that* is?" he suddenly asked, his eyes on the stranger.

"Huh?" demanded Corson, stirring out of his bitter reverie. He looked toward the trail, and grunted. "Marshal of Bentley. A friend."

"Oh," grunted Nueces, and drew his hand back to rest on the pommel.

The tired, stiff, and sleepy marshal, returning from the Turkey Track, urged his tired mount into a little swifter gait and reached the intersection of trail and road as the other two drew up. His old but keen eyes were on the sheriff, reading dejection, bitterness, rebellion.

"Lick you?" he asked, craftily.

Corson stiffened indignantly.

"Like hell!" he snapped. "Got 'em all. Th' two that are alive will be waitin' for you to open up th' jail."

"I ain't done so much ridin' in years," growled the marshal, trying to hide his satisfaction over the successful conclusion of several enterprises: "but I reckon I'll live long enough to open up th' jail. Who was they?"

Corson told him, briefly, sullenly.

"Huh! Then they *are* all gone," said the marshal, almost smacking his lips.

"All but Mort Meadows," grunted the sheriff. "Somebody else can get him. I'm turnin' in my badge by mail."

"Reckon that's all you can do," agreed the marshal, winking slyly at Nueces. "Nobody's got to get Mort. *I* got him, with his stepsister watchin' me do it. Th' skunk woulda killed her th' minute she stepped outa my door. He tried for me, instead, with a *de*fective cartridge, an' I blowed him to hell an' gone before he could try ag'in. Now she ain't got none of them coyotes to break her heart no more."

Corson was staring at the old man, the expression on his face undergoing bewildering changes. Had he heard aright: killed Mort Meadows, *with his stepsister looking on!*

"This is Sat'dy. There won't be no mails leavin' Carson till Monday mornin'," said the marshal, chuckling. "You'll have plenty of time to make up yore mind about turnin' in that badge. You comin' along with us, or are you figgerin' to set here all day?"

"Neither!" snapped Corson, wheeling the bay. "See you both in town before dark!"

"Hey! Not th' Gap!" shouted the marshal, in quick alarm. "She ain't there no more!"

Corson checked the bay and whirled again.

"What you say?" he asked, incredulously.

"She's cleared out. Cut plumb loose from th' JM an' everythin' belongin' to it. She rode down to town to tell me all about them coyotes, an' was worried near sick for fear they'd kill you."

"Where is she then—Bentley?"

"Bentley was too close to home," shouted the marshal. "She could smell th' stink of it from there."

"—— —— you!" yelled the sheriff, impolitely. "What have you done with her?"

"Took her where you said for her to go," shouted the marshal, nudging Nueces in the ribs. In a low voice he said to his bewildered companion: "Lookit him r'ar an' snort!"

"Where *I* said to go?" yelled Corson. "Where'n hell was that?"

"Turkey Track—she was hell-bent to go there, long ride or no long ride, because you once told her——"

"Great Gawd!" yelled the sheriff. "You let that woman ride sixty miles!"

"*Let* her!" shouted the marshal, indignantly. "She damn' near drug me all th' way! We changed hosses at th' Bar W an' yore own ranch. I'm near dead, right now, but she didn't look no tireder than if she'd just come from a dance."

The only reply to these remarks was a partial wheeling of the bay and a string of dust shooting along the David Canyon trail like a low-aimed rocket.

"There!" said the marshal, with smiling satisfaction. "We shore got rid of *him*. Now let's ride on, slow an' peaceful. You must be that Nueces feller.

I've heard a lot about you: how come yo're still alive?"

The Bar W foreman loafed to the door of the bunkhouse, wondering what was up. The sound of the hoofs bespoke the urgency of a horse race, but there was only one horse in sight, and it was coming down the wagon road as fast as its fanning legs could carry it. The horse slid to a stop with the sure facility of a trained cutting-out animal, and foam slipped down its heaving sides to drop to earth.

"Want a fresh horse," said the sheriff, crisply, as he reached toward the cinch buckle.

"Shore," replied the foreman. "Somethin' up?"

"Yes. Rustlin' is. It's all over, down in this part of the country. Th' gang's cleaned up."

"Good! Find any herd?" asked the foreman, somewhat derisively.

"We shore did. Take my pick?"

"Yeah; but that black's th' best in th' corral," replied the foreman. Then he scratched his head and grinned faintly. "Hope folks don't get th' idear that this ranch is a damn' relay station. Anybody else comin' along that wants to swap for a fresh hoss?"

"No," answered Corson over his shoulder, but without checking his stride.

In a moment he had the black cut out and outside the bars. Another moment saw the hackamore in place and the saddle on. His fingers were moving with the swiftness and sureness of instinctive motions. He swung up, wheeled the animal, and raised his hand.

"So-long, an' much obliged. I'll send one of th' boys to swap back."

"So-long," grunted the foreman. "You will if you don't kill th' black!"

At the JC bunkhouse the cook's choppy, bow-legged stride took him to the door to see what the trouble was. His hopes flared suddenly: that sounded like business. He patted the gun on his thigh and poked his head out of the door. Yes: it was Corson, riding as if the devil were after him. Whose black was that, and what had happened to the bay?

"Roan in th' corral?" shouted the sheriff as he slid to a stop near the corral gate.

"Naw; but that chestnut is damn' near as good," answered the cook. "What's up? Where you goin'?"

"Where's th' roan?" demanded Corson, impatiently, slipping off saddle and hackamore.

The cook shifted uneasily and tried his hand at evasion. He had felt that he should not lend that animal, felt it in his bones.

" 'Tain't here," he said. "Gimme that rope, an' I'll get you th' chestnut."

"Where's th' roan?" insistently demanded his boss, vaulting the corral gate, the rope in his hands.

"Loaned it to a lady. She was with th' marshal of Bentley. He said it was all right. Said you told him to swap here. Come bustin' in here after I was asleep, an' wouldn't take no other hoss. Said that hoss had made so much trouble that it oughta work it out. What th' hell he was talkin' about, I didn't know: but it was all right, wasn't it?"

"Yes. Get outa th' way!"

The cook sighed with relief and barely escaped the quick leap of the chestnut.

"Great Gawd!" he said, his mouth sagging open in wonderment. His boss didn't care whom he ran over.

Corson's hands were swiftly working with straps and buckles, and almost before the wondering cook knew it, his boss was pointing a little cloud of dust up the trail leading to Horsethief Pass.

Placidly grazing cattle, with the indignities of the round-up fresh in their minds, raised their heads and uneasily watched the chestnut comet streaking along the trail. Their fears were groundless, for the animal rocked steadily ahead.

The cook had been right, thought Corson: the chestnut was a mighty good horse, nearly as good as the roan. Mile after mile slid behind. The Alkali Holes were ahead, to the side, and then in the rear. At the fork of the road Corson swung to the left without drawing rein, and flashed down into the little hollows and up over the little hills on the last stretch of the run. He swung sharply around the last shoulder and raced along the creek which ran past the Turkey Track ranch buildings. Then the buildings themselves popped into sight, and he was shooting down the last long slope straight for the ranch-house door.

Owen French was just stepping out of the house, his wife telling him to be sure to fasten the chicken-house door or the coyotes would get every last one of them. Then they both looked up at the sound of drumming hoofbeats.

"Land sakes," she said, with a smile. "Ain't that th' sheriff?"

"Reckon so," grunted French. "He must want to kill that hoss!"

"Huh!" said his wife. "There was a time when you woulda killed a hoss! Let's clear out: them young folks won't want us to clutter up th' house. Hurry, Owen: you *are* so slow!"

Corson drew the chestnut to a swift stop, leaped to the ground, and then lost all urge for speed. He stepped slowly into the house and found no one in sight. There came a sound from the other room, and he moved toward the door.

She stood near a window, gravely, wistfully studying him. She quickly raised a hand, and he stopped, his hungry eyes full of fear, a fear that cut her like a knife.

"I knew you'd come, of course," she said, her voice low and strained. "But you should not have come, dear. It's very hard to have to pay for something that I've never done. Very hard. I just don't **know** what—I just don't know."

"Mebby it's still harder to pay for somethin' you *have* done," he answered, bitterly, and held out his hands, palms up. "To have to go to th' woman you love with th' blood of her———"

"Stop, Bob! You must not say that! I won't let you! It was your duty: you could do nothing else."

"But they're not clean, Alice, dear; not clean enough for you to touch."

"They never were and they never will be unclean to me!" she replied, swiftly. "It is I who am—who am———"

She was unprepared for it, but no amount of warning would have done any good. There was no use to struggle in those iron arms, so she did not struggle. And then, slowly her hands crept up his vest, passed his shoulders, and came to rest on his cheeks, his lean, tanned face tightly gripped between them. His head bent down.

Through the open window came the voice of Owen French's wife, although they two did not hear it.

"If you'd put hinges on th' gates of this ranch, instead of that eternal balin' wire . . ."

But the round-up was over, and this story with it.

THE END